A MATCH MADE IN HIGH SCHOOL

A Match Made in High School

Kristin Walker

First and foremost, I thank my husband, Sean, and our three sons for being so encouraging, patient, and ready with a hug whenever I need one.

I also thank my parents, Sue and Charles Ramberg, for their unwavering love and support (as well as for their sense of humor); Eric Ramberg and Anna Brunzell for always being there for me; Brenda Stanley and Steve Gerry for their tireless advocacy and enthusiasm; and Nancy Viau for her wisdom, friendship, and many laughs.

Sincere thanks also go to Ginger Clark for being fantastic and for taking a chance on me, and to Ben Schrank, Laura Schechter, and the stunningly wonderful people at Razorbill who worked so hard to make my dream real.

And finally, my deepest gratitude goes to you for picking up this book and opening it.

Thank you.

A Match Made in High School

RAZORBILL

Published by the Penguin Group
Penguin Young Readers Group
345 Hudson Street, New York, New York 10014, U.S.A.
Penguin Group (USA) Inc., 375 Hudson Street, New York, New York 10014, U.S.A.
Penguin Group (Canada), 90 Eglinton Avenue East, Suite 700, Toronto, Ontario,
Canada M4P 2Y3 (a division of Pearson Penguin Canada Inc.)
Penguin Books Ltd, 80 Strand, London WC2R 0RL, England
Penguin Ireland, 25 St Stephen's Green, Dublin 2, Ireland
(a division of Penguin Books Ltd)
Penguin Group (Australia), 250 Camberwell Road, Camberwell, Victoria 3124,
Australia (a division of Pearson Australia Group Pty Ltd)
Penguin Books India Pvt Ltd, 11 Community Centre,
Panchsheel Park, New Delhi – 110 017, India
Penguin Group (NZ), 67 Apollo Drive, Rosedale, North Shore 0632, New Zealand
(a division of Pearson New Zealand Ltd.)
Penguin Books (South Africa) (Pty) Ltd, 24 Sturdee Avenue,
Rosebank, Johannesburg 2196, South Africa
Penguin Books Ltd, Registered Offices: 80 Strand, London WC2R 0RL, England

10 9 8 7 6 5 4 3 2 1

Walker, Kristen
p.cm.
Summary: When the principal of her high school announces
that every senior must participate in a year-long marriage education
program, Fiona learns some unexpected lessons about people, friendship,
crushes, and cheerleading.

ISBN: 978-1-59514-257-3

1. High schools—Fiction. 2. Schools—Fiction. 3. Interpersonal relations—Fiction.
4. Dating (Social customs)—Fiction. 5. Friendship—Fiction.

PZ7.W15299 Mat 2009
[Fic] 22
2008039670

Printed in the United States of America

For all my boys. I lola.

CHAPTER 1

I SHOULD HAVE KNOWN.

I should have known the minute I went to get my favorite White Stripes peppermint tee and found it not in the drawer, but temporarily forgotten in the back of my closet, curled up in a crusty ball. Caked with two-week-old, nuked syrup that had shot out of the bottle, bounced off my waffle, and splattered me like a sweet paintball.

I should have known when I came downstairs and found my parents tasting each other's tonsils in front of the kitchen sink, and nearly barfed on my sneakers.

Or when my best friend, Marcie—actually she's my only friend, which is fine; you only need one—called to say she was running late and couldn't pick me up. So I had to ride my freaking *bike* to school for my first day as a senior.

I should have known right then that I was pedaling toward disaster.

But I just chalked all that crap up to my normal, everyday bad luck.

I jumped on my bike and rode the five blocks to school. I live in the actual village center of East Columbus, not in one of the vanilla developments that have sprung up over the past ten years, circling the town about a mile out into the cornfields. Lots of kids from East Columbus High School live in those. The wealthier kids. Not that my family is poor. We just like old houses with cool architecture, like the ones in town. Most people who live in the developments and subdivisions think new construction equals money equals social status. Fools.

Living in town is the best. I can walk or bike just about anywhere. Well, okay, maybe not to the Prairie View Mall. But the library, coffee shop, and music store are all just a few blocks from my house. Which really comes in handy when I want to get the hell away from my parents.

Plus, the streets in town are all lined with these gorgeous, massive oak and maple trees that have been growing for, like, a century. And since the sun that day was insanely hot for seven-thirty in the morning, I stayed on the shady side of the street as I rode to school. I got there, locked my bike, and was flapping the armpits of my shirt in a futile attempt to dry the sweat when Marcie pulled into the lot. She yanked the rearview mirror over to check her face, dabbed her bottom lip, and got out of the car.

"Mar!" I called. "What's with not picking me up?"

She half ran over to me as the bell rang. "Sorry, Fee. Ran out of time. Couldn't get my hair right."

Her hair was in a ponytail, just like we'd both worn all last year. Always either a ponytail or a braid. We'd called ourselves hair twins, even though her hair was a straight, silky dark brown, and mine was nearly black and had this strange wave and dull frizz. Then, just before school started this year, Mar chopped her hair to shoulder length and got highlights and lowlights. So even in a ponytail, her hair made the braid I wore today look like a long fuzzy turd. Not that I really cared. I only kept my hair long so I could pull it out of the way. I didn't have the patience for hairstyles. Or makeup. Mar kept trying to get me to wear lip gloss because she said I had "full, pouty lips." Personally, I thought my pouty lips had less to do with beauty and more to do with bad moods.

As we climbed the concrete steps to school, I almost asked Mar how long it could possibly take to do a ponytail. Instead I just said, "It looks fine." She gaped at me like I was deranged. Clearly, a ponytail was her last resort. But I let it slide. I knew how nuts she was about her looks and crap lately. She used to just slather lotion on her face, pull her hair back, and go. But this summer she'd worked as a camp counselor. When she came home, she was in full hair and makeup—eyes, cheeks, lips—the works. She even set up a standing appointment for the first and third Monday of every month at a salon in the Prairie View Mall to get her nails done (which I thought was ridiculous, but I'd promised to go with her sometimes to keep her company). I figured she must have had a backlash reaction to two and a half months of roughing it in the woods.

We dashed inside and headed to the auditorium. Customary first-day-of-school assembly. But just as we reached the double doors, somebody slammed into Marcie. She lurched forward and dropped her purse, spilling a pack of eyeliner pencils everywhere. Before I realized who it was, I turned and said, "Watch it! You idio— Oh! Hi Gabe!"

Gabe Webber—the secret love of my life since third grade when I'd twisted my ankle during field day and he'd put his arm around me and helped me all the way to the nurse's office. How could I not fall for a guy who rescued me? Strong and quiet. Brown hair and wounded eyes. Totally hot. Totally cool. Always said the right thing. Never acted like a dork. Basically, the complete opposite of me. The kind of guy you figured probably spent weekends campaigning for homeless orphans, or replanting rain forests, or something. At least, that's how my fantasies ran.

"Sorry, Marcie," Gabe said. He dropped to the floor and helped Marcie gather her stuff together. When every rogue eyeliner was found and squirreled away safely in Marcie's purse, Gabe stood up and offered her his hand. She took it, and Gabe pulled her to her feet. "I didn't mean to bump you," he said. "Somebody pushed me."

I blurted, "Don't worry about it! She's tough." And I slapped Marcie on the back just to prove it. She stumbled forward again and Gabe caught her arm. Oops. I expected Marcie to lay into me or at least glare, but she didn't. She must've been hiding it so I wouldn't look like a goon in front of Gabe. She knew how I felt about him. Of course, I'd sworn her to absolute secrecy. No one else knew. (Well, okay, I had told Samantha Pickler, the eleven-year-old I babysit for. But that was during Truth or Dare; I had no choice. It was either tell, or climb the dogwood tree in her front yard, moon cars that passed, and yell, "Fresh buns for sale!")

Now, I'll admit that years of unrequited love had tempered my obsession with Gabe a bit. It wasn't nearly as consuming now as it had been in eighth grade. That was the last year the school took class pictures, and he and I were in the same homeroom. I bought a locket with my babysitting money, cut out Gabe's little face and my little face from the photograph, and glued them inside the locket. I wore that necklace under my shirt every single day. But it got worse than that.

I also listened to every sappy love song on the radio, convinced they were singing about me. I even wrote down the lyrics to one that I planned to slip into Gabe's locker anonymously.

You look at me but never see the love I feel for you.
But in your eyes I see the skies,
The endlessness of time and blue,
Like waves that span the raging sea,
And break upon the sandbar of your heart.

Of course, he doesn't have blue eyes, his eyes are brown, but it didn't matter. The song perfectly expressed my feelings for him, and when he figured out who sent it, he'd surely be moved beyond words and fall desperately in love with me. Luckily, Marcie stopped me before I gave it to him and made an absolute ass of myself. I mean, *sandbar of your heart?* Holy crap. Thank God for Mar.

Gabe touched Marcie's arm. "You all right?"

"I'm okay now," she said to him. "Fine. Thanks."

He patted Mar's arm and looked at me. "How about you, Fiona?"

He looked even better than he had last spring. Tan. Lean. But with just the right amount of muscle in just the right places. The way his T-shirt clung a little bit across his shoulders and pecs . . . Yum. I didn't want to seem too psychotic stalker–like, so I said, "I'm good. Totally together."

Then Gabe said, "Totally together women are my favorite kind," and he turned and walked into the auditorium.

My eyes bugged. I grabbed Mar's hand and squeezed it. I was Gabe's favorite type of woman? What? I couldn't believe he'd just given me that compliment. The very first morning of school.

Seeing him—wow—rejolted my feelings. I had to find a way to get him to notice me. No, not just notice me. More. I had to get to a place where I could reach up and caress that tan jaw without having Gabe issue a restraining order against me or call a mental hospital to have me forcibly removed. This would be the year. Senior year. Now or never. As Mar and I worked our way into the stuffy auditorium and found a couple of seats toward the back, I made a vow. This would be the year I got to touch Gabe Webber. I'd find a way to connect with him. Somehow.

"Welcome, students," Principal Miller said into the microphone up onstage. "And a special welcome to our freshmen." She was wearing the same tired beige skirt suit she wore to every slightly special event at ECHS. Good thing she was African American. If she'd been white, she'd have looked nude in that pasty outfit.

I stuck my foot up on the green vinyl seat in front of me and tried to keep awake as Principal Miller droned on and on about what a fan-freaking-tastic school East Columbus High was. One of the top-ranked schools in Illinois. Blah. Blah. We were lucky to be here. Yawn. School rules. No cheating. No stealing. No lying. Blah, blah, blah. Snore. I scanned the auditorium and zeroed in on the back of Gabe's head, seven rows up and three seats over. Then I tried to figure out whether the gum I smelled was watermelon or green apple.

Principal Miller said, "This next bit of exciting news concerns the seniors." We all perked up a bit. Exciting news for seniors? What was it? A game system in the senior lounge? Elimination of gym class? Fridays off?

Oh no. Those were not meant to be.

"The school board and I have formulated a plan to address an escalating problem in our country." Principal Miller paused to check her notes. "The divorce rate has exceeded a staggering fifty percent. One out of every two married couples will divorce. The family unit will separate. The marriage will dissolve and you will be left alone." She looked at us. Scanned the room. Took a shallow breath. "All by yourself. With no one. In your forties . . . way past your prime." She steadied her trembling body against the podium.

We froze, afraid even to breathe in Principal Miller's direction. She froze too, and then slowly lifted her hand to pat down her hair. She smoothed her skirt, took a deep breath, cleared her throat, and started speaking again. "Obviously, with these statistics facing us, we, as educators, cannot ignore the pressing need for instruction in the area of marriage. So, as a new prerequisite for graduation, seniors must complete a yearlong course in marriage education."

We unfroze pretty quickly here. I mean, this was a new low for ECHS. I thought the cafeteria food that tasted like wet navel lint was plenty bad. Or the eye-watering stench of the third-floor girls' bathroom. Or the gym uniforms that looked like they were leftover from a 1970s porno flick. Weren't those humiliating enough? Apparently not. Our groans rolled through the auditorium like a thundercloud. But it wasn't until she said the next thing that the lightning hit.

"Each male and female senior will be paired up and 'married' for the duration of the year."

WHAT THE HOLY HELL?

Everyone pretty much lost it. Girls started screaming and crying. Guys jumped up and booed Principal Miller. People everywhere yelled and squirmed in their seats. Except for Gabe; he stayed perfectly charming and composed as usual. Mar and I didn't move either, but only because we were completely stunned. This was totally unfair. Why hadn't we been consulted on this terrible decision? What happened to democracy? What happened to the will of the people? Apparently Principal Miller was a descendant of Mussolini. Was it our fault her husband left her for their boobalicious twenty-one-year-old nanny? Hey, it's a small town. News here travels faster than the flu.

"Quiet. QUIET!" Principal Miller cawed into the microphone. Everyone stopped shouting their indignant protests and kept the noise to a low grumble. "You have no choice in the matter. If you wish to receive a diploma at the end of the year, you must complete this course. That's it. Now, here's how it's going to work, so pay attention."

No need to say that. We were riveted to our seats by iron bolts of sheer terror.

Principal Miller snapped her papers, adjusted her red-rimmed glasses, and began reading. “We have purchased a curriculum called *Trying the Knot*, the materials for which you will receive in homeroom. The registrar’s computer was programmed to randomly pair up the male and female seniors into couples. First period, Friday morning, there will be a mock wedding uniting you in marriage, with a dance following later that evening. Attendance is compulsory.

“Each term, either the husband or wife will choose a semester-long activity in which to participate. Together. You will be assigned a mock budget with mock expenses to cover using a monthly income derived from *real money* you must earn as a couple.”

A bunch of idiots started yelling, “What?” and “Hell, no!” and “No way!”

I yelled, “Bite me!”

“Now wait! Before you complain, listen up! The money everyone earns will be collected here at school. At the end of the year, the couple with the most successful marriage *will split half of the total money collected*.”

The idiots and I did some quick math in our heads and shut up fast. That could be a lot of coin.

“The other half of the money will be donated to a charity of the winning couple’s choice. Additionally, each month, the couple who earns the most real money for that month will be awarded a prize sponsored by a local business. Prizes include items such as mall gift cards, concert tickets, and a free limo to prom."

A bunch of ditzy cheerleaders squealed like guinea pigs at that.

"At random points throughout the year, you may be given a life issue to deal with, such as a surprise pregnancy or a job promotion, a debilitating injury or a lottery windfall. You will keep a journal of your private thoughts and feelings concerning the marriage. To aid you in this journey together, you will attend weekly sessions on marriage skills presented by our guidance counselor, Ms. Klein." Maggie Klein rose from her seat down front and gave one of those fake, twiddly-fingered waves to us. She sported her usual phony look of calculated disarray: a flowy yellow sundress accented with gold bracelets and gold dangly earrings, her hair tied back neatly with a white scarf. Definitely granola, but clean and put-together. She always reminded me of the women in douche and tampon commercials.

Principal Miller went on. "She and I are in full agreement that now is the perfect time for you to learn how . . ." She closed her eyes for a second. Opened them. "To maintain and sustain a possibly . . . challenging . . . relationship."

Principal Miller squared her shoulders, leaned into the podium, and scanned the room again. "I feel obliged to make it clear that we are not in any *way* condoning physical consummation of these marriages."

Well, everyone pretty much cracked up at that. Todd Harding started howling like a dog and pumped his fist in the air. What a jackass. He and his Porn Star Barbie girlfriend, Amanda Lowell, had been "consummating" like crazy for over a year and a half. It was common knowledge. Spread by Todd, of course.

While Todd hooted, Amanda leaned over and tickled him. He draped his arm around her and inhaled her face into his like a vacuum hose, or like a zombie sucking her brains out through her mouth. That'd be if Amanda actually had brains. Which was doubtful. The only time in history that she'd demonstrated the least bit of cleverness was in second grade when I wet my pants on a pony ride at Callie Brooks's seventh birthday party and Amanda started calling me Pee-ona instead of Fiona. Then she'd say, *Your last name should be Pony. Then you'd be Pee-ona Pony. Get it? Pee-on-a-pony?*

Yeah, I got it. Hi-freakin'-larious.

She still called me Pee-ona, too. In ten years she hadn't been able to think up anything more original. But whatev. At least now it was just her, and not the entire second-grade class.

I made a gag face at Todd and Amanda's vacuu-kiss and rolled my eyes at Marcie, but she didn't notice. She just sat, white as a sheet, with her eyes fixed on Principal Miller. She picked at her brand-new French manicure. I gave her an elbow. "Are you okay?" I whispered.

Marcie turned her bug eyes toward me, shook herself, and said, "Uh, yeah." She looked like she might puke. I wasn't feeling too well myself. The idea of marriage education had gotten my pits all sweaty again. Next, my stomach started churning.

Then, deep in my mind flickered the tiniest thought. Maybe, just maybe, I'd get paired with Gabe.

And that was the moment. Right then.

The moment I allowed myself to have the slightest bit of hope that I'd be lucky and things would work out for me. Right then I should have known.

Principal Miller raised her hands above her head and motioned for everyone to settle back down. Once we were relatively quiet, she said, "Mr. Evans has signaled to me that the list of paired couples and their respective homerooms has been posted on the bulletin board outside the auditorium. Seniors are now excused to—"

She probably said more, but there was such a spastic rush of people and noise, I couldn't hear another word. The seniors scrambled over their seats, spilled into the aisles, and crammed through the auditorium doors. Marcie and I got trapped behind Johnny Mercer, who was over six feet tall and the size of a small bulldozer. He couldn't move fast if a burrito's life depended on it. Plus, he was listening to his MP3 player like always, so I'm sure he couldn't hear the shrieks and screams coming from the hallway as everyone read the name of their . . . spouse.

Marcie and I finally made our way out the auditorium doors and over to the bulletin board. Marcie's forehead glistened with sweat, and she kept puffing these shallow breaths out of her half-open mouth. I skimmed the alphabetized list for the *S* names. There was mine: *Sheehan, Fiona*. I prayed that for once in my miserable life I'd be just a little bit lucky and then slid my eyes over to the name next to mine. *Harding, Todd.*

My legs nearly fell out from under me. "Son of a *bitch*."

Marcie grabbed my arm and yanked me sideways. I seriously thought it could not get any worse until my eyes passed over the *W*'s. I tugged myself out of Marcie's grip just long enough to read *Webber, Gabe—Lowell, Amanda.*

Un-freaking-believable.

CHAPTER 2

MARCIE PULLED ME AGAIN AND WE DUCKED INTO THE girls' bathroom. "Did you see that?" I cried.

"I'm sorry, Fee," Marcie said. "You cannot possibly complain to me."

"Todd Harding? How am I supposed to spend the year with that no-necked Neanderthal?" I leaned over the sink, willing it to suck me down the drain. The fluorescent light buzzed above us.

Marcie said, "He has a neck. And an ass and abs. Nice ones. And even if you haven't noticed them, pretty much every other girl has." She pulled out a tube of lip gloss and started applying it as she spoke. "Plus, in case you missed it, he is *not* three times your size, like the guy I got."

"Johnny Mercer is not three times your size," I shot back.
"Okay, maybe twice. But at least he's a nice person." Mar held the lip gloss out for me. I shook my head. She dropped the tube back in her purse.

"How would you know?" she cried. "He's gone to school with us for years. Have you ever had one conversation with him?"

I picked at the stringy hairs on the end of my braid for a

second, then gave up and just watched Mar primp. "No, but he keeps to himself. He's got his damn earphones on all the time. He might be nice."

"And he might be a serial killer," she said. She adjusted and readjusted her ponytail in the mirror and tucked a stray highlighted strand behind her ear.

I rolled my eyes at Mar and then checked under the five gray stalls to see if anyone was there. It was all clear, so I said, "Did you see that Amanda freaking Lowell got Gabe? That is *so* unfair! Do you think we're allowed to trade? She'd never trade anyway. Plus, I would never *ever* ask her, because then she'd know that I liked Gabe. Or, wait! I could just say I was being nice by giving her Todd. Oh, screw that. That would make her even more suspicious. I can't believe she got Gabe. So typical. She gets everything."

"Good Lord, Fiona. Take a breath," Marcie said. "It's not real life. Let it go."

"Hey, you're the one who's so choked about being matched with Johnny Mercer."

I took off my glasses to rinse them in the sink. I dried them on my shirt and slipped them back on. Several girls filed into the bathroom. Cheerleaders. Vomit. They set off on such a frenzy of giggling and makeup application that I didn't even notice in the mirror that Her Royal Cheerleading Highness, Amanda, had come up behind me.

"Listen, Pee-ona," she said. I turned around, but she looked past me at her reflection and fluffed her already perfect blond hair. "I guess you think you pulled the golden ring by getting Todd."

I shifted over to block her view of her reflection. "Before we begin, Amanda, please clear up your metaphor. Are you trying to say 'golden ticket' or 'brass ring'?"

She cocked her jaw. "What?"

"I just want to understand completely the complexities in your locution and lexicon."

She blinked at me as her mental gears (the two of them) ground together. God might not have made me pretty, but He made me smarter than Amanda Lowell, and that was enough for most days.

"Look, loser. Let me make it clear that if you think that just 'cause you got"—she did the quote thingy with her pale pink, pointy-nailed fingers—"'married' to Todd that he's going to be with you and not me, then you are wrong."

"See how much better you do when you stick to single syllables?" I said.

Amanda smirked. "Here's a single syllable for you." She stuck up her middle finger, then turned and swished out of the bathroom. The rest of the cheerleaders flocked and flapped after her.

"Why do you love goading her so much?" Marcie asked me through her reflection in the mirror. She licked her thumb and wiped off a speck of mascara below her eye.

"I'm just trying to even out the scales of the universe," I said. "Maintain homeostasis. Why should she be given a life of such utter perfection without the least amount of payback?"

"Why do you feel it's your responsibility to level the field?" Marcie fancied herself an amateur therapist at times. I was her favorite patient.

"I don't," I said. "It's just fun."

"Try to focus on the positive, Fee," Mar said. "At least we got the same homeroom. Let's go."

That was true; we'd both gotten Mr. Tambor, who was pretty decent, even if all his sentences went up at the end like everything was an emphatic question. It must have been Mar's good luck that did it, though, because it sure wasn't mine. My luck had resulted in Todd being in our homeroom as well. Mar and I saw him and Amanda outside Mr. Tambor's room, huddled against the lockers. She had her face nuzzled in Todd's neck as he stroked her hair. When we passed, both of them—right on cue—looked at me like I had pus-laced phlegm dripping out of every orifice in my body.

I opened my mouth to say something just as Mr. Tambor boomed, "Okay, *people*? Take your *seats*?"

Marcie grabbed my arm and yanked me inside, saying, "Leave it."

CHAPTER 3

WELCOME TO *TRYING THE KNOT*!

Congratulations! Your school has invited you to participate in a revolutionary course on marriage education. This folder contains all the materials you'll need. Below is a list of "rules" you must follow to gain optimum benefit from this course.

1. Shared Activities

Each semester, one member of the couple will select an activity in which both partners will participate (one person picks first semester; the other picks second semester). The activity should have a duration of at least three months, and should meet at least once a week. Of course, more is fine!

2. The Budget

Every month, each couple must earn real-world cash money by doing a job (or jobs!) together. In addition, by a random draw, they will receive an "Income Factor," which is the number by which all real-world cash earnings will be multiplied. The resulting figure will be the couple's income for the month. For example, if you select an Income Factor of 50, and you and your partner earn $20 that month washing cars together, then your total income for the month is 50 x $20. Or $1,000. That $1,000 is what you must use to create a budget from the "menu" choices below. (Remember, all expenses are per month!) So the more real-world cash you earn, the more you have to spend! At the end of each month, the couple must turn in a balanced budget using the enclosed budget sheets, as well as the earned cash, and written validation that the money was earned at a job. (No cheating with your own money!)

LIVING EXPENSES (choose one):

HOME A

A four-bedroom, two-and-a-half-bath house in a gated community. Excellent school district and no crime.

Mortgage and insurance: $2,000

Utilities: $500

HOME B

A three-bedroom, one-and-a-half-bath house in an established neighborhood. Decent school district and low crime level.

Mortgage and insurance: $1,500

Utilities: $400

HOME C

A two-bedroom, one-bath apartment in an apartment building. Marginal-quality school district and moderate crime level.

Rent: $1,000

Utilities: $300

EXTRAS (choose any or none):

Cable TV: $75

Cell phone: $50

Internet: $30

CAR PAYMENT (choose two):

Brand-new luxury hybrid: $400

Pre-owned midsize: $250

Used compact: $150

FOOD EXPENSES (choose one):

Gourmet, all organic; frequent takeout: $600

Average grocery; occasional takeout: $500

No name-brand grocery; infrequent takeout: $300

ENTERTAINMENT (choose one):

Country club membership, three movies a month, etc.: $350

One movie a month, video rental, etc.: $150

Video rental only, etc.: $50

BANK IT OR BLOW IT:

Any remaining income either can be spent on a luxury item or vacation, or can be listed under SAVINGS and be banked to the next month.

3. The Journal

Enclosed, you will find a journal in which to write your thoughts and feelings concerning the "marriage." You may evaluate the course, your spouse, or yourself! Try to make an entry at least once a week, or more if you feel like it!

4. Weekly Sessions

Each week, you and your partner will attend a brief counseling session with a school guidance counselor to address issues in marriage, such as the three C's: Communication, Compromise, and Commitment. But don't worry! Everything you say will be a fourth C: Confidential.

Sounds easy, right? Well, just to keep things interesting, you may or may not be given a life-altering issue (ranging from a sudden illness to a pregnancy with twins!) along with a new monthly cost or a lower Income Factor to address in your budget. Of course, you may get lottery winnings or a sudden inheritance, and you could buy that new house or car! It's up to you as a couple to decide how to handle these situations. Your school guidance counselor will offer assistance at your weekly counseling sessions.

Don't forget! Your school will keep a running tally of all real-world cash earned. Each month, the couple who earns the most may win a prize. Also, at the end of the course, the most successful marriage as determined by your guidance counselor (in terms of effective communication, successful budgeting, conflict resolution, and personal growth) WINS HALF OF THE TOTAL MONEY COLLECTED, TO BE SPLIT BETWEEN YOU!

Good luck and have fun *Trying the Knot*!

"Have fun?" I cried. "Does this really say, HAVE FUN? These people are sadists." I shoved the marriage ed packet into my backpack as Marcie and I headed to lunch. I hadn't been able to bear reading the damn thing until just then. Now I'd pretty much lost my appetite. The stench in the hallway outside the cafeteria didn't help either. There was no way to tell from it what they were serving. Could be spaghetti. Could be boiled baby diaper. Thank God they always had hot dogs.

"Have you talked to Todd yet?" Marcie asked.

"He bolts whenever I see him. What about you and Johnny Mercer?"

She didn't answer, because just then Johnny rounded the corner and shuffled toward us. He plucked out his left earphone. "Hey Marcie," he mumbled. He glanced for a split second at me. "Hey Fiona . . ." He tugged up the waistband of his oversized khaki cargo shorts and pulled at the side of his denim jacket. I didn't think they still made those. But then again, it didn't look too new.

"Hey Johnny. How's it going?" Marcie asked.

He was nearly a foot taller than me, so he kept his head down and kind of eyeballed Mar and me from there. "Uh, fine," he said. His voice was deep. "I, uh, wanted to let you know that we're supposed to meet at guidance Friday after the . . . uh . . . wedding ceremony thing. At ten-fifteen." He darted his eyes toward me from under a strand of sandy blond hair. "Everybody has a time. They're posted on the bulletin board." Eyes back to Mar. "I didn't know if you'd seen it yet. Thought I'd just . . . you know . . . let you know."

"Thanks," she said. "See ya there."

"Sure. See ya." Eyes to me one more time.

"'Bye," Marcie and I both said at once. He sidled between us and lumbered into the cafeteria.

"See? He *is* nice," I whispered.

"Maybe."

"I'm gonna go check out our time," I said to Mar. But I was really going to see what Gabe's time was. In case I could arrange to run into him in the hallway. "Save me a seat," I said.

"Sure." Mar went into the cafeteria, and I headed for the bulletin board. I got there just as a couple of girls skulked away from it, snickering. For a sec, I wondered what they were laughing at. Then I saw.

Right there was the paper with everyone's counseling times on it. Right next to 9:45 a.m. were Todd's name and my name. And right next to my name was an arrow pointing to a cartoon of a girl with glasses, sitting on a horse, with pee running down her legs and pooling on the ground. Underneath, it said: *Pee-ona Horse.*

Good old Amanda. Clearly this was her work. She'd forgotten it was Pony, though, not Horse. I reached out and ripped the picture off the rest of the sheet of paper. Unbelievable. The first day of school, and I was already a joke.

I marched down the hall to the cafeteria, thinking of a dozen different insults to launch at Amanda. I pulled open the door and found myself face-to-face with Gabe Webber as he was leaving.

"Oh! Hey Fiona," he said. "How's it going?"

I crumpled up the picture and crammed it into the back pocket of my jeans. "Great. Fine. How about you?"

His porcelain smile gleamed. "Better every day." He held the door open for me, and I slid by him. "See ya soon," he said.

"Okay, sure," I said. "See ya, Gabe." I loved saying his name out loud. I watched him stride down the hall until the door swung shut on my view. Then I turned and searched the lunchroom for Amanda. I looked the cafeteria over three times, but I didn't see her anywhere. I did, however, see Marcie sitting with a bunch of people, and she had apparently forgotten to save me a seat. Perfect. Whatev. I'd just sit by myself and read. I was no good at girl talk anyway, even if there had been room for me at that table. Designer clothes, bubblegum pop music, celebrity heartthrobs—I couldn't give a fat rat's hairy ass. Just give me my hotdog and Jane Austen, and I'm good.

I got in line for said hotdog and pulled out *Pride and Prejudice.* I pretended to read as I tried to calm down. I told myself the picture was just a joke. I could deal. Probably no one had seen it, anyway. And if they had, maybe they hadn't understood. Or didn't remember second grade. Of course, the shifty eyes Johnny Mercer had given me pretty much shot that theory to hell. He'd seen it for sure. But who cared what he thought, anyway? No biggie.

I had just convinced myself that the stupid picture was *so* beneath my contempt, when I noticed Todd Harding line up about five people behind me. I tucked my book in my backpack, took a "cleansing breath," as Mar would say, and decided I would say hello. Just to make sure he knew about the appointment on Friday and all. I pride myself on my maturity.

When I got to the entrée counter, I stood back, like I didn't know what I wanted. "Go ahead," I said to the girl next in line. And the next: "Go on, I'm still deciding. Go ahead." Right up until Todd was next to me. Then I stepped forward. "Pardon," I said smooth as cream. "Just need to grab a hot do— Oh, hi Todd." Like I hadn't even noticed him.

"Yeah. Uh, Fiona, right?"

I chuckled. "Uh-Fiona. Yep that's me. Uh-Fiona. So, I

guess we're married, huh?" I squeezed some ketchup on my hot dog. It splurted all over my tray.

Todd made that pus face again and said, "Look, nothing personal"—which of course always means something personal—"but I'm not spending my senior year hanging out with you. It's not happening."

"Um, it's not?"

"Nope. Sorry to ruin your wet dreams."

"Uhhh . . . 'scuse me?"

He smirked. "I mean, I'm sure you need the money and all." He cocked his head to the side and eyeballed my outfit. "For a pair of socks that match, maybe. Or a bra, once your tits start to grow. But I don't need it. I'm good."

I just stood there, limp and rigid at the same time. Like a rag doll with a broomstick stuck up its ass.

Todd's bonehead buddy sniggered next to him and nudged him along the line. As they pushed past me, Todd leaned over to his friend and whispered, "Poor horse."

Then he whinnied.

And that's when I knew. Todd had drawn the picture. That was why Pony had been wrong: because Todd thought it was a horse. Amanda hadn't done it. Todd had. Just to publicly humiliate me.

That asshole.

I picked up my hot dog and hurled it at the back of his pretty-boy white-blond head. SPLAT. Ketchup everywhere and a greasy wiener tumbling down his back. Bull's-eye.

"*What the* . . . ?" Todd spun around.

"That was for your little piece-of-crap artwork," I said.

Todd took two giant strides toward me, leaned in to my face, and growled, “You want to play, Princess Pisspants? Fine. We’ll play. See you Friday morning. Welcome to married hell.” Then he stalked away, leaving me standing there with one thought in my head.

Game on.

THAT NIGHT AT DINNER WHEN I TOLD MY PARENTS about marriage ed, my mom said, "That is absolutely ridiculous." She sliced through a piece of spicy Thai chicken.

"Why?" my dad asked.

"What can they possibly hope to gain by forcing these kids together when they barely even know each other? It's not like they got to choose their partners."

"So?"

Mom set her knife and fork down on the pottery plate she'd bought a set of at an art fair last year. "So how is it applicable to real life? How does it teach them about choosing a good mate when they didn't get to make the choice themselves?" she asked.

Dad leaned in. "How do you suggest the course should work?"

Now, let me take a moment to explain something about my father. He's a political science professor at Northern Illinois University, and he likes to teach using the Socratic method of basically just asking questions. That's it. Anything a student says, my dad simply turns around and puts it back on the poor sap in question form. He could teach an entire hour-long lecture using only the words, "Why?" "How?" "So?" and "What do you think?" Sometimes I wonder if he knows anything at all about political science. But he's one of the most popular professors on campus. Unfortunately, he tends to bring his teaching method home, which makes him not-so-popular with my mom and me at times.

"Don't talk to me like I'm one of your pupils," Mom said. "I can have my opinion without needing to defend it."

"Okay, if you want to have an unfounded opinion, go right ahead." He stabbed a bite of spinach salad and popped it in his mouth.

"My opinion is not unfounded; it's just none of your business," she said.

"You made it my business when you said it out loud," he mumbled through chewed green stuff.

"Are you kidding here?" Mom asked. "Because you're starting to actually piss me off."

Dad swallowed, smiled, and grabbed my mom's hand. "Of course I'm kidding. Don't get mad." He leaned across the table and kissed her. "I'm just playing with you."

That's what my parents call playing. It's twisted, but they seem to love it. Whatever steams your clams.

"Mom's got a point," I said. "These random matches are a disaster."

"Why?" Dad asked. "What happened; did you get a dud?"

I slowly spun my knife on the table. "Not a dud. The opposite. Extremely popular and a total jerk. There isn't one thing about this guy I find at all appealing."

"Hey now. Come on. Don't be mean. Popular guys have feelings too," he teased.

"Not this one. Unless you count feeling up his girlfriend in the hallway before class."

"Feeling up a girl always counts," he said.

Mom swacked him with her cloth napkin, "Ethan—"

"It's true. I've counted every single time." And I swear to God, he reached over and honked her boob right in front of me. "Six thousand, two hundred, eight."

I leaned back from my parents as far as possible. "*Ethan*," I cried, "this is the *dinner table*."

Dad toggled his head at me. "Pardon me, Your Ladyship."

My mother struggled to compose herself. "Fiona, Principal Miller really said you can't graduate if you don't take this course? And the school board okayed it?"

"That's what she said."

"I find that objectionable," Mom said.

"For once, we agree," I said. I flicked grains of jasmine rice around my plate with my fork. I lined them up into a little *T* for *Todd*, and then smooshed it with the back of the fork tines.

"Well, I'm not standing for it," Mom said. "I'm calling Principal Miller tomorrow. Then the school board. Maybe I'll even write a letter to the paper." She drained her wineglass. "Ridiculous."

"Uh-oh," Dad said. "Hide your daughters. Viv is on the warpath."

Mom swacked him with her napkin again.

"Yeah, that's all well and good, Mom, but it's not going to change anything. Meanwhile, I still have to deal with this jerk."

Mom picked up her plate and took it to the sink. "Fiona, I think this course is absurd. But for the time being, you're going to have to play along. Just try to find one thing about this boy that you like, or respect, or can at least stand. Just one thing. That's all you need. Focus on that one redeemable quality, that one thing you like, and you'll be surprised how long you can stand him for."

"Is that how you and Dad stay together?"

"What can I say? He makes a mean chocolate milk shake."

"And she can really sing," Dad said.

"I'm a terrible singer," said Mom.

"You are? Well, in that case, I guess we're through." He shrugged. "Hmmm . . . I wonder who I was thinking of who can sing."

"Your mother is a good singer. Perhaps you should go live with her."

Dad said, "At least *she* lets me feel her up."

I stood up. "That's it; I'm done. And I'm not even going to ask to be excused, because you two are sick and depraved and no longer hold any authority over me. I'll be in my room." I set my plate in the sink and left them giggling behind me.

Upstairs, I sprawled out on my bed and pulled out the marriage ed packet. I grabbed the journal and a pen. Figured I might as well record this horrific day.

Wednesday, September 4

I thought today would be the first day of a fantastic senior year. Instead, it sucked. Now I have to spend the whole year SHACKLED to a person (who shall remain nameless, but his initials are TODD HARDING) whom I despise. I have been advised to try to find one redeeming quality in him to focus on. So far, the only thing I can think of is that he is breathing. But even that is questionable, because he is very likely a zombie or some other form of the undead. I would seriously rather spend my entire life as a virgin spinster than spend it with Todd Harding. I'd be perfectly happy living as the crazy cat lady. I have an uncle (Tommy) who is totally the male version of the crazy cat lady, and he's happy enough. Actually, come to think of it, he's really not.

Like this one time about three years ago, we went up for my Nana's seventy-fifth b-day. We ate at this restaurant, and I got stuck sitting next to Uncle Tommy. I tried to make polite small talk, but he started snapping at me, saying that one of his two cats was sick. Some kidney problem or something. He asked me if I had any pets. I said no, and he said, "Good. They're heartache. I bought Sarsaparilla and Knee Hi this year for my fortieth birthday. They just remind me of how old I am. And now, Knee Hi's sick. I don't know what Sarsaparilla would do without her sister."

I said I was sorry to hear that, and he said, "Well, it's par for the course for my life. God forbid I have one small thing that isn't a disappointment."

Ooooohhhhkaaaay.

What the freak could I say to that? Luckily, the appetizers came out, and I could suddenly develop an all-consuming interest in the construction of shrimp puffs.

That was Uncle Tommy three years ago. I can only guess how bitter and frightening he is by now. I hope to hell the cat didn't die. I have no idea what any of that has to do with marriage education, but at least it took up a couple journal pages.

CHAPTER 5

FRIDAY MORNING. FIRST PERIOD. THE SENIORS WERE gathered in the auditorium. Up onstage stood this crappy white archway left over from last year's production of *Much Ado About Nothing* covered in fake pink flowers and lit up with a spotlight.

Principal Miller's fingers fluttered at her hair and neck as she walked to the podium next to the arch. "All right, seniors. Settle down, now. Let's get through this ceremony and you can go to class. I'd like the young women to line up on the right side of the auditorium according to the alphabetical order of your last names. Young men, you will line up on the left side of the auditorium across from your partner."

This took several minutes, as many of the senior girls had not yet mastered the intricacies of the English alphabet. Plus, none of us was in too much of a hurry to get to the actual wedding part. Principal Miller tried to help out as best she could.

"No, Maja, Bjorkman comes before Bloomberg. Catherine, is it McHenry or MacHenry? Okay, that means you're after Juliana. Rhiannon, I know you and Joscelin have the same last name. Line up according to first name, then. No, that means you're behind Joscelin, not in front. There you go. No, Elizabeth, you do not have to kiss. In fact, you should not. No kissing! Do you hear me, everyone? No kissing! Rashmi Kapoor, get back here! Well, too bad, you'll have to hold it."

There's a saying about herding cats. Like how impossible it is. But that would have been a piece of cake compared to this. Finally, we slid into place, and so did the guys. I looked across the expanse of green vinyl seats to the line of them huddled against the wall. They looked like game animals that had been shipped in for a controlled hunt. Some oblivious to their fate. Some bucking and kicking against the enclosure. Some resigned to their impending demise. But all trapped.

I scanned the line. Johnny Mercer was toward the front, leaning up against the wall with his arms folded above his stomach. He was completely motionless except for his right black boot, which kept tapping and tapping furiously on the floor.

Gabe stood about halfway down the line. His tangerine shirt made his skin look like burnished bronze. He chatted with the guy next to him and laughed casually, showing his perfect white teeth. It reminded me of how he'd tried to make me laugh on the way to the nurse's office in third grade so I wouldn't think about the pain in my ankle. His smile was still the same.

All of a sudden, Gabe turned and looked across the auditorium toward the girls. I could see his eyes passing down the line. In a second he'd be looking right at me. Should I let him see me watching him? Would it surprise him? Or should

I look away and appear coy and delicious? Should I wave? Try to hold his stare? Try to send him psychic messages?

I caved. I dropped down and pretended to tie my checkered Chuck Taylor sneakers. I didn't know what to do. What a wimp. And as a reward for my cowardice, when I stood up, my gaze fell on someone much less savory. Toady Todd. (I was trying out new nicknames for him. So far I'd rejected Todd the Clod, Hard-head Harding, and "TH" pronounced in the form of a raspberry. He wasn't smart enough to get that one.) Todd turned to his buddy and whispered something. At least, it looked like he was whispering. All bent over and shadylike. And then I watched with dread as he looked and pointed at me, and then started laughing. His buddy laughed too, and I felt all my blood drain into my feet. Todd was up to something.

He saw me watching him, shook his head, and smiled his sinister grin. I tried not to look scared, but what could I do? I couldn't say anything to him; he was way across the auditorium. I did the only thing I could think of. Gave him the finger.

Well, that just pleased Todd to no end. I'd egged him on. I'd accomplished the social equivalent of poking a bear with a sharp stick.

"Is everyone ready?" Principal Miller said, adjusting her glasses. "Everyone? Okay, let's begin. When I call your name, please come up onstage, meet your partner behind the arch, hold hands, and pass through the arch and down the risers in front of the stage. Then you may continue up the center aisle and exit to class. Does everyone understand? Yes? Fine." She waved to someone in the back of the auditorium. "Please bring in the underclassmen. Ah . . . and women."

Suddenly, the double doors flew open and a wave of students poured into the auditorium. Judging from the expressions on the seniors' faces, it was safe to assume that none of us had dreamed we'd have an audience for this. But there they were. Freshmen, sophomores, juniors—witnesses to the execution. Sophia Sheridan nudged me. "What are *they* here for?"

"I dunno," I said. "Maybe Principal Miller wants to scare them into switching schools so next year the faculty can retire to Buenos Aires."

She snorted. "I doubt it. I mean, who'd want to retire in Mexico?"

I blame the educational system; I do. It wasn't poor Sophia's fault that she'd never been taught the geography of North and South America. Or maybe she had, but the information had somehow gotten lost between the teacher's lips and her hair spray–fumed brain. Either way, I decided to let it go. She clearly had missed the point, anyhow.

Principal Miller flapped her hands above the podium. "Take your seats, please. Take your seats." When the room settled, she cleared her throat, tossed her head back, and gave a crooked smile. "We are gathered here today to join—" She stopped. Blinked a few times. Forced the smile wider. "To join these young men and these young women in—" She swallowed. Breathed. "Matrimony." Inhaled. Exhaled.

"A marriage is not something to be entered into lightly. It is a commitment made between two people. A commitment that is—" She tossed her head back and snorted. "Well, it's *supposed* to endure." Her voice wavered. She stopped again and dabbed at her eyes. Then she grabbed the podium. "You should stick with it through adversity. Not just run off at the first temptation like a kid who's just discovered candy. Sure, candy is sweet. But candy offers no sustenance. Meanwhile, the solid, nourishing potato that you married lies rotting in the cupboard. Make the choice before you make the commitment, ladies and gentlemen! Don't choose a potato if what you really want is candy. Do you understand?"

It was pretty clear that none of us did. Even though she studied our stony faces for an answer. A tear dribbled down her cheek. She swiped it away.

"So. Marriage. Yes. Marriage is a commitment between two people . . . a commitment that . . . that . . . Oh, you know the rules. Let's get on with it. When I call your name, come up on the stage, join hands with your partner, and I solemnly declare you united for the purpose of marriage education for the year. The end, goodbye. Mr. Evans? Music, please. Carla Adams and Peter Hauser."

Pachelbel's Canon in D started blaring over the sound system as Carla and Peter climbed the stage steps. They joined hands, walked under the arch, and stepped down the risers at the front of the stage. As they strolled up the aisle, the underclassmen started clapping and hooting.

Now I understood why they were there. It was a gauntlet of humiliation.

Two by two we climbed the gallows. Two by two we descended into hell. Okay, maybe I'm overdramatizing it a bit, but I can tell you this much: I used to like Canon in D. It used to sound like hope and beauty and purity and joy all rolled into one. But suddenly, and from that moment on, Canon in D sounded like a death march. A dirge. A slow, inevitable spiral toward the grave. Without a doubt, I would never, ever like Pachelbel again.

I watched Marcie and Johnny cross the stage toward each other. Marcie was wearing these wedge heels, so she walked kind of slowly. Johnny waited for her with his hand outstretched. She took it and they walked forward through the arch. When they stepped down onto the aluminum risers, the metal groaned under Johnny's weight a bit louder than usual. Some of the underclassmen laughed, but Johnny kept on going without missing a beat. I thought I saw Marcie give his hand a little squeeze, which was likely, because she's that type of person.

I inched forward in the line, trying to keep a sideways eye on Todd. I didn't know what he had planned, but it couldn't be good. When Gabe and Amanda got onstage, I looked back and forth between Gabe and Todd to see if Todd had any reaction to his girlfriend getting cozy with a totally smokin' hot guy. But Todd didn't seem to care. I was more jealous than he seemed to be. Even when Gabe offered not only his hand, but his muscled arm, which Amanda took, giggling. She was a pro at being coy; I'd give her that. She made flirting a religion, and right now she was worshipping at the altar of Gabe. But Todd didn't bat a lash.

I, on the other hand, was not so cool. In fact, I had started to sweat like a beauty queen at the last minute of a pregnancy test. I closed my eyes and tried to imagine ice cubes in my armpits, and cool water dripping down my neck and arms. I had almost gotten my heart rate slowed from frantic to merely anxious when Principal Miller called out, "Fiona Sheehan and Todd Harding."

Oh God. Up I went.

I climbed the steps and turned to face Todd. We walked toward one another, glaring into each other's eyes. I didn't want to trip, but I didn't want to break his stare, either. When we got within arm's reach, I held out my hand, trying to be dignified. But Todd broke my gaze and walked right past me to the curtain at the side of the stage. He reached into the velvet drape and pulled out . . . a doll. A blow-up doll. A blow-up sex doll with a black wig and brown glasses like mine, and a silver plastic tiara taped to its head with duct tape. The doll did have pants on—cargos, like I wear. Only, the crotch of the cargos was soaking wet. Dripping down the inside of the legs. As for the top—there was none. The boobs had been smashed in and taped over with duct tape so that the doll was flat-chested. But there were a pair of very attractive black Magic Marker nipples drawn on the duct tape. In the interest of maintaining anatomical correctness, I'm sure.

The auditorium exploded in hysterics. Todd grabbed the doll, straddled it, and galloped around the stage like it was a horse—whip action, and all. Then he ran through the arch to the front of the stage (dodging Principal Miller, who seemed shocked into immobility anyway). He held the doll as high as he could and yelled, "PRESENTING PRINCESS PISSPANTS!" A handful of underclassmen laughed. Then more joined in. Then Todd's bonehead buddy started chanting, "PRINCESS PISSPANTS, PRINCESS PISSPANTS," and soon everyone was either cracking up or chanting along.

Principal Miller said, "All right! Quiet down," but no one really did. Todd marched down the risers with the doll on his arm and paraded it up the aisle as everyone cheered. I stood alone on the stage. Well, me and the principal, who shuffled me to the edge and shooed me off. Evidently, she had become quite skilled at pretending not to notice things.

I toddled down the risers and stood frozen at the bottom. Everyone was chanting louder than ever. And laughing. And pointing. At me. I had no idea what to do or where to go. Suddenly, I saw Marcie striding toward me. She took my arm and walked me up the aisle. Johnny met us halfway and someone shouted, "Ooh, a threesome!" But I was beyond caring. All I wanted was to get out of there. Well, that—and to figure out a way to pay Todd back.

We got through the doors to the vestibule outside the auditorium, and Johnny asked, "Are you okay?"

"No, I'm not okay," I said. "That goddamn bastard." I looked around the vestibule for him, but he was nowhere to be seen. Sonofabitch coward.

"Todd Harding is a total prick," Marcie said. "I can*not* believe he did that."

"I can," Johnny and I both said at the same time. A little laugh popped out of me. "Jinx," I said. "You owe me a beer." Johnny blushed and ran his fingers through his thick, shaggy hair.

I stared at the bulletin board with the marriage ed lists on it. I pulled out one of the thumbtacks and stuck it right through Todd's name. "Listen Mar," I said, "I'm getting him back, and I'm gonna need your help. I'm thinking tonight, at the dance. Are you in?"

Marcie clucked her tongue at me. "Come on, Fee. Be the bigger person."

"Bigger person? What you mean is back down. No way. I'm not hiding from him. Then he wins."

"Yeah, but it's not a battle. You're supposed to be married."

"Screw that."

She crossed her ivory arms. Even after being outdoors all summer, she'd managed to avoid any sun damage. "Okay, but like it or not, that's the way it is if you want to graduate and get the hell out of high school."

"Marcie, are you going to help me or not?"

She sighed and dropped her arms. Her bracelets clinked together. "Yes, I'll help you. You know I will."

"Thank you."

"Uh . . . you know, I could . . . help too," Johnny said. "I mean . . . if you need it."

"For real?" I asked.

Johnny twitched his head. "Sure. I can't dance anyway. What else is there to do?"

I reached up and patted him once on his beefy shoulder. "Awesome, Johnny. Thanks."

I checked the clock above the auditorium doors: eight-forty-five. Exactly one hour for me to figure out what I was going to say to Todd at our counseling session. I couldn't wait for him to get reamed out by Maggie Klein. I'd never seen her go ballistic before, so it was going to be a treat.

And afterward, I'd have the rest of the day to plan my revenge.

CHAPTER 6

"PLEASE COME IN, FIONA. TODD IS ALREADY HERE."

Maggie Klein had been the guidance counselor at East Columbus ever since I was a freshman. She couldn't have been more than eight or nine years older than me, but she carried herself like a middle-aged ex-hippie. She insisted that everyone in school call her Maggie, and everything she said sounded like a meditation mantra. She always wore scarves and smelled like vanilla and roasted almonds. She'd never been married, so I wasn't sure what she thought she could teach us about marriage. But maybe she'd picked up some tips from the string of men she'd been seen with around town over the past few years.

"Take a seat, Fiona," Maggie Klein said. I did. But not before I sent a barrage of eye daggers through the back of Todd's skull. "Okay. Welcome, Fiona. Welcome, Todd. I think it's obvious that we need to begin this session by addressing what happened earlier at the mock wedding ceremony. Todd, would you like to start?"

"Ha! Why does *he* get to start?" I blurted.

Maggie Klein turned her head to me the exact way an owl does when it's scoping out its prey. "Because Todd was here first, Fiona." Her head swiveled back to Todd. "Now, tell me, Todd. Why did you think it was acceptable to bring that doll to the wedding?"

Why did he what? Acceptable? Um, hello? Where was the part where she yells at him and he gets in trouble?

"Well, Maggie," he cooed, "I noticed that some of my classmates were a bit . . . well, uptight about the marriage education course. So I took it upon myself to add some levity to what was surely a stressful moment for many of my fellow seniors."

Hold the phone. What was Todd up to? I sat up higher in my cushioned chair and watched him.

"Todd, I understand your desire to help your fellow students," Maggie Klein said, reaching over to adjust a vase of daisies on her pristine desk. "And although your motives may be honorable, you must understand that your actions were disturbing. Can you see that?"

I snorted. Loud.

"Fiona? You will get your turn to speak in a moment. Now, Todd. Do you understand how your actions in the auditorium could be taken as something other than funny?"

Todd furrowed his brow and nodded. "I do understand that. Believe me; I had a totally different objective."

Yeah, I bet you did, you jackhole. For a second I imagined grabbing the wooden Buddha off Maggie Klein's bookshelf and using it to give Todd's face a totally different objective. But of course, I didn't. I pride myself on restraint.

Maggie Klein continued. "And you realize that a doll like that represents the objectification of women in a most deprecating way?"

Aha. All right. Finally she was going to let loose. She must've been one of those roundabout hell givers. The kind who trick you into getting comfortable and thinking the noose is a necktie. Until they sneak up behind you and pull the lever.

Todd shook his head and leaned toward Maggie Klein. "Objectify women? Me? Come on, Maggie, do you really think I'm the kind of person to objectify women?" He flashed his phony smile at her.

Maggie Klein melted in front of me. "No, of course not," she said, returning his smile, and throwing a few girly giggles in on top. Todd had slipped out of the noose. "I'm glad we cleared that up." She clapped her hands together and said, "Okay! I think we can really start this session from a place of peace now."

Todd looked at me and beamed. His charming bullshit was getting him off scot-free, and he knew it.

Wow.

It seemed that I had grossly underestimated the No-necked Neanderthal.

I slammed my hands down on the arms of my chair and cried, "What the *hell*?"

Maggie Klein issued a condescending sigh and said, "Fiona, in my office, there is no yelling, and *no* cursing. All communication is done in a mature, constructive fashion. Do I make myself clear?" She gave me what I suppose was meant to be a stern face. Looked more like the side effects of severe constipation.

"No," I said, "you don't make yourself clear. Nothing

you've said makes any freaking sense at all. How is it that this jerk-face can humiliate me in front of the whole entire student body, and you don't bat an eye? But if I say the word *hell* in your office, *then* you get mad? *No*, Maggie Klein, that is not clear at all."

Maggie Klein blinked a few times and said, "Humiliate you? What makes you think Todd's little antics were directed at you?"

Todd leaned over the arm of his chair. "Yes, Fiona. Why on earth would you think that was about you? *Hmmmm*?"

I sat there with my yap open. Maggie Klein had never connected that the doll was me. And how could I explain that it was? By going over the soggy details of Callie Brooks's seventh birthday party? From ten years ago? And in front of Todd?

No freaking way. Nope. I was stuck. I was screwed.

I rubbed the soles of my sneakers together. "Well, I just . . . figured it . . . was," I mumbled.

Maggie Klein said, "Now, Todd. There's no mistaking that the doll was inappropriate. But you didn't intend for it to represent Fiona, did you? That would be extremely mean-spirited. Not to mention a clear case of sexual harassment."

I noticed Todd's grin slip when he heard that. He crossed his arms, looked down at the floor, and started bouncing one leg up and down.

Maggie Klein went on. "And I'm sure that was far beyond the scope of your intentions for your little caper. Am I correct?"

Todd shrugged. "Sure."

"Because that would be a serious offense requiring disciplinary action."

Todd nodded slowly but kept quiet. Maybe he wasn't in the noose, but Maggie Klein was definitely dangling it in front of him. I figured that was about as close to resolution as I was going to get. Revenge, however, would get much closer.

"Okay, let's push on. First, we need to figure out what your shared activity will be for the semester. Who's going to choose this time?"

Todd and I each belted out, "*I am.*"

"Well, you both can't pick. Let's try Rock Paper Scissors. Whoever wins picks this semester. The other person can select the real-world job."

Todd and I turned to face each other. It was a gunfight in the MK corral. I figured I had him pretty well sussed. He was macho. Pseudo-tough guy. He'd definitely go Rock. We balled our fists. Slapped them on our palms three times saying, "Rock, paper, scissors, *shoot.*" I threw out my hand as Paper.

Todd had thrown Scissors. Damn. I should have known. Scissors cut. Scissors could stab. Scissors were shiny and sharp, like Todd.

"What will it be, Todd?" Maggie Klein chirped.

"Well, Maggie, for our first-semester activity, Fiona and I will share the experience of cheerleading."

Let me just pause to give a brief history of Todd Harding and cheerleading. It's a legendary story at ECHS.

Freshman year, Todd moved to East Columbus and played football. He was some kind of prodigy or star or whatever. Anyway, halfway through the game with Lincoln High, Todd gets sacked and cracks four ribs. He's out for the season. Todd's mother goes mental and forbids him from playing football ever again.

Fast-forward to sophomore year. Todd and Amanda have been dating for a while. She's a cheerleader and convinces him to try out for the winter squad so they can spend more time together. Barf, I know. But he does, and, because he's strong, they can do these crazy mounts or stunts, and bigger pyramids and crap now. So the cheerleaders love him. But one day Brendan Jackson, who was the varsity quarterback, calls Todd queer because he's a cheerleader. And Todd says (and this is the really famous part), "Lemme get this straight, Brendan. I spend all afternoon with my hands between a hot cheerleader's thighs, looking up her skirt as I hold her above me. Meanwhile, you're bent over, sticking your fingers in some fat guy's butt crack again and again. But *I'm* the gay one?" That shut up Brendan and anyone else who ever thought of giving Todd a hard time. But it wasn't going to shut me up.

"No way. I'm not taking part in some costumed display of bouncing boobs that espouses phony school spirit and is disguised as a sport." That was my little way of hiding the fact that one, I have no boobs, and two, I couldn't do sports.

"Don't worry," Todd said, "you won't be doing any actual cheering." He bounced his head from side to side. "You can be the squad water girl." He slurped from an invisible water bottle.

I opened my mouth to object, loudly, but Maggie Klein cut me off. "It's settled, then! Cheerleading it is." She wrote it in the stupid marriage ed file. "Fiona, have you given any thought to what job you'd like to share with Todd to earn your real-world cash?

No, of course I hadn't. I had blocked this damn course from my mind as much as possible. "Yes," I lied. But only one job popped into my head—the one I already had. I said, "I babysit for an eleven-year-old girl. I'd have to check with her parents, but if they give the okay, then Todd and I can babysit together." The instant those words hit the air, I did a mental head-smack. I'd just forfeited my only source of spending money for the entire semester. *Ugh.* I hoped, hoped, hoped Todd would object. Then I could make up something else. Leaf raking, maybe. Leaf raking would've been perfect!

But Todd waved his hand in the air, saying, "Pshhh, no prob."

"Wait, I changed my mind," I said. "Leaf raking. We'll rake leaves."

"No, no," Todd said. "You said babysitting. We'll do babysitting." He grinned at me and blinked a few times. "It'll give us more quality together time."

"Oooh, nice observation, Todd!" Maggie Klein said.

I tried to object. "But—"

Maggie Klein scribbled on the sheet. "I've already written it down. Okay, you two are babysitters. Great."

Dammit.

"Now, let's move on to the budget." Maggie Klein held out a red velvet bag with a drawstring top. "Todd, I'd like you to reach in here and select a coin."

Todd stretched out his hand. I thought I saw his fingers graze hers as he reached inside. I was almost sure I saw his wrist brush against her thumbs as he playfully swirled his hand inside the bag. I definitely saw her blushing.

He pulled out a coin with the number 150 on it.

"Well done, Todd! One-fifty is the highest Income Factor available. There are only two of them in the bag. Okay, multiply any cash you earn by 150, and that's how much you have to spend on the monthly expenses outlined in your packet. You decide together what to spend it on, and turn it in to me at the end of each month." She leaned closer to Todd and made her voice all lilty. "I'll bet you can buy the nice house." I swear she fluttered her eyelashes at him.

He leaned in to her. "And the luxury hybrid car." They both laughed.

"One more thing," she said. "Even though you perform your job together, you must decide who in the marriage is theoretically the breadwinner. Is it just one of you? Do you both contribute to the household? It may come into play later on in the course, so decide carefully. Questions?"

I pride myself on my ability to keep my mouth shut, so I shook my head.

Todd said, "No, Maggie, you've explained it very well."

Maggie Klein blushed again. Todd was some kind of charisma savant. A sexy hypnotist for lonely, aging women. Total cougar crack.

"Okay, then. Remember to write in your journals. And note on your schedules that we have a regular fifteen-minute counseling session every . . ." She snatched up a sheet of paper. ". . . Tuesday at eleven o'clock. So I'll see the two of you then, okay?" She really liked to make sure things were okay.

"Looking forward to it," Todd said, reaching out his hand. She clasped it gently and they shook. How is it that pretty boys can get away with so much crap?

THE ART OF PULLING PRANKS IS SOMETHING I'VE never mastered. In fact, I can't even tell jokes. I always mix up the words, or laugh too hard at myself, or get to the punch line only to realize I'd forgotten a key piece of information. ("Wait, wait, did I mention he was wearing a wet suit? I forgot to say he was wearing a wet suit. Pretend I said that.") So it was a good thing I had Mar and Johnny to help strategize a plan for revenge on Todd. By the time we got everything together and got to the gym that night, the dance had already started. We stopped in the lobby outside the gym doors to do a double check. Music thumped inside.

"Okay, so everyone knows what they're doing?" I asked.

Mar and Johnny nodded.

Johnny shifted his weight and hitched up his jeans. "You got it all ready?" he asked me.

I patted the pouch pocket of my Connells hoodie. "Locked and loaded."

"It's not too late to walk away, Fee," Marcie said.

"No chance." I tightened my ponytail. "All right, let's go in, split up, and make a recon sweep around the room. We'll meet back up by the entrance. Sound good?"

They both said yup, so we went inside.

The gym walls and ceiling were strewn with silver and white streamers, silver balloons, and white tissue-paper wedding bells. It looked like a giant wedding cake had exploded in there. The lights were dimmed except for these colored dance lights and some kind of strobe-effect fixture. I peeled off to the right while Johnny and Mar went left.

I'd told them that we were looking for Todd. What I hadn't told them was that I was also looking for Gabe. I hadn't been to many dances (shocker, I know), so the anticipation of seeing Gabe at one was a major distraction. It was the main reason I hadn't been able to focus on planning a prank. Luckily, Johnny had come up with a rather twisted and hilarious idea to get back at Todd. But first, we had to find him.

Once my eyes adjusted to the low light inside the gym, I caught sight of Todd and Amanda over by the bleachers. She dropped her purse down on the lowest bench, and he covered it with his jacket, presumably so no one would steal her stash of lip gloss, breath mints, and birth control pills. I knew she was on the Pill because she'd made a big deal of telling everyone about it one day in gym class, sophomore year. Her periods were irregular, she'd said. Her mother's doctor *made* her go on the pill. Yeah, right. I guess it was only a coincidence that she'd started dating Todd a few weeks before. As for the lip gloss and breath mints, well, those were pure speculation. Her lips always looked like she'd been frenching a tub of margarine. And I hoped for her sake that she had some breath mints. She needed them.

Todd turned my way, and I jumped back around the side of the bleachers so he wouldn't see me. Just as I peeked to see if the coast was clear, whose hotness passed right in front of me? You guessed it. Gabe. I made a mental note: black shirt, blue jeans. How did he get those brown curls to fall so perfectly? He started walking down the length of the bleachers, so I did the only logical thing—I ducked underneath the bleachers to follow him from there. I could just see slivers of him through the slats in the stands as he walked. Then he stopped. He was talking to someone, but I couldn't see who. He sat on the bottom row. I had no choice but to get on my hands and knees and crawl closer to him.

Now, I don't know if you've ever been under the bleachers in a high school gym, but let me tell you, it's no carousel ride. In our gym, there's only so far the mops can reach under the bleachers. So even though it was the first week of school, the floor under the lower levels was revolting. Coated with sticky, dried soda, and encrusted with dust and dead bugs, candy wrappers, every variety of crumb and hair, and probably some unmentionable body fluids. But I didn't flinch. I was a girl on a mission. I gagged as debris stuck to my palms, but I kept on. Finally, I got within earshot.

"But I need to see you," he said.

Then a girl spoke one word. "Gabe . . ."

He wasn't just talking to anyone; he was talking to a girl. Needing to see her. I tried to swallow, but my throat closed. I craned my neck to see through the cracks between the bleacher seats, but I only got a glimpse of Gabe's ass. Not a bad view, really.

"You said we'd be together tonight," he said. "I want to be with you."

I strained to hear more, but suddenly, some superloud music started playing. I couldn't hear a thing. But I'd heard enough. After a few more seconds, Gabe stood up and walked away. I never saw the girl. But I'd be damned if I wasn't going to find out who she was.

First, I had a job to do, though. I crawled out, brushed my hands off, and met up with Johnny and Mar at the gym entrance. I pulled Mar to me and whispered, "I have to tell you something. Later."

"Uh, Fiona?" Johnny said. "My buddy Noah is running the sound. He said that at eight-thirty, he's supposed to stop the music. They're going to bring up the lights so Principal Miller can make a speech or something. Might be a good time to do it. With the lights on. So people can see."

"Ooooh, I like how you think, Johnny Mercer," I said. I also realized that if we waited a bit, I'd have a chance to tell Mar about Gabe. I figured I should probably wash the hepatitis C off my hands, anyway, so I said, "I'm gonna run to the ladies'. Wanna come, Mar?" I didn't really give her a choice, of course; I dragged her off by her elbow. We got to the bathroom and I checked around to see if anyone I gave a crap about was in there. Nobody was, so I said, "So guess what? Gabe is seeing someone."

Marcie fluffed her hair in the mirror. "He is? How do you know?"

I got some soap and started washing my hands. In the fluorescent light of the bathroom, I could see they were pretty nasty. So were the knees of my cargos. I kinda turned my back to Mar, but I think she might've noticed anyway. "I heard him talking to her," I said.

"Who was it?" She pulled a lip gloss out of her pocket and started applying.

"I couldn't quite see."

Marcie raised her eyebrows at me in the mirror. "What do you mean, you couldn't quite see?"

"I was sort of hiding." I left out where.

Marcie turned and glared at me. "You were eavesdropping."

"Yeah, so?"

She slapped the sink and looked at the ceiling. "Fiona. Dignity. Come on." I could read the pity in her face. She was so above these sorts of machinations. She always had been. Proper, well-bred. But stable and comforting. Actually, those were some of the reasons I liked her. Probably because I was none of those things.

"You don't have any idea who it is, do you?" I asked.

Marcie turned back to the mirror. "What makes you think I know?"

"I bet Amanda knows. I wonder if it's one of the cheerleaders. Do you think it could be Tessa Hathaway?"

"Tessa Hathaway? Her boyfriend started college this year. Do you really think she's gonna drop him to go back to high school guys?"

"Maybe she's lonely."

"Let it go."

"I've *got* to find out."

Marcie sighed. "Look, let's get back out there. Johnny's waiting for us." She straightened the little black stones on her necklace. Checked her amethyst earrings.

"Yeah, okay." I dried my hands and we left.

We found Johnny sitting on the bleachers across the gym. Mar and I sat on either side of him. His shoulders sloped as he scooted forward to the edge of the seat and looked at his watch. He said, "Twenty-seven minutes until the speech."

"We've got some time to kill," I said.

Marcie stood back up and adjusted the strap on her lavender tank top. "I'm going to get something to drink. You guys want anything?"

I shook my head. Johnny said, "No, thanks."

"Okay. I'll be back." She walked off toward the corner of the gym where the snacks were.

"Don't be late," I called, kidding. But not.

Marcie fake-smiled over her shoulder. "I wouldn't miss it for the world." Then she disappeared into the crowd of dancers gyrating around the gym floor.

"She doesn't seem too excited about this whole thing, does she?"

Johnny shrugged. "Not much."

I took off my glasses and pulled my hand into my sleeve so I could wipe the lenses with it. "It's not her fault. Pranks aren't her thing. She comes from a totally different social echelon. Her mother's family has old money. Made it from one of the original Chicago stockyards. I don't know how much is left, but Mrs. Beaufort still taught Marcie to sit up straight, use the right fork, write thank-you notes. Manners. You know."

"Oh," he said, squinting up at one of the multicolored light units hanging from the basketball net.

I slipped my glasses back on. "Not that I don't have manners. I do. But my parents aren't nuts about them like Marcie's mom. When I'm at her house, you know, I have to be *so* careful not to drink out of the toilet." Johnny laughed. I said, "Her mom is nice, but she can be pretty snobby. This one time, Marcie's parents took us into Chicago for dinner at Alinea, this molecular gastronomy restaurant."

Johnny looked at me and scrunched up his face. "Is that food? It sounds gross."

"Oh no, it's a crazy-good restaurant. Won all these awards. And it's nice—I mean linen napkins, real art on the walls, the whole nine yards. And men have to wear a jacket, right? So this one guy walks in, and not only does he not have a jacket, he's wearing a baseball cap. When Marcie's mom sees him over at the door, she gets all huffy and whispers, 'NOCD,' to Mar."

"What's NOCD?"

"Not Our Class, Dear. Marcie explained later. Anyone NOCD is clearly below the Beaufort family social station, according to her mom. She said her mom uses NOCD as a kind of code. Like a secret snob spy or something."

Johnny scratched his sideburn and ran his fingers through his hair. He tried to get a cowlick over his right eye to stay back, but it kept falling forward. "I don't get it," he said. "If the guy can't hear her, why use a code?"

I leaned back on the bench behind us and stretched my

feet out in front of me. "According to Marcie's mom, only people with no class actually use the word *class*. If you have it, then you never talk about it."

"Oh." Johnny nodded slowly. "Just like herpes."

I cracked up. I mean I really cracked up. I laughed so hard I got a cramp in my side and had to roll over. Then I sat up and smacked Johnny's arm with the back of my hand. "I've *gotta* remember that one."

Johnny smiled at the floor. He tapped the toes of his black boots up and down.

"Are those Doc Martens?" I asked.

"Yup." He reached down to retie the right one.

I nodded. "Nice."

We sat without talking while a seemingly endless techno dance song pulsed through the gym. I picked at a fingernail. Johnny crossed and uncrossed his arms. Tapped his foot some more to the beat.

He said, "So . . . do you like music?"

It was a pretty stupid question. I mean, who doesn't like music? Okay, maybe some puritanical zealot out in Hicksville. But really. It was kind of like asking, "Do you like food?" "Isn't oxygen great?" "Have you got skin? I do." I knew what he meant, though.

"Yeah. But this kind . . . not so much," I said. "You like it?"

"Nah," he said. Then tipped his head back and forth. "It's okay. Some people like it."

"I guess your friend Noah does."

Johnny shook his head. "Oh, he doesn't pick the music. He just operates the equipment."

"Huh," I said. I tried to blink my eyes fast enough to counter the strobe light. "Makes you wonder who picks the music."

"Well, actually . . ." Johnny straightened up and cleared his throat, "since you mentioned it—it's me. I do it."

I gaped at Johnny. "What? *No* way!"

"Yeah, I've been putting the playlists together for every dance since freshman year." He hitched his chin toward my hoodie. "You like The Connells?"

I shoved his shoulder. "Oh my God, you know The Connells? I *love* them."

"Know them?" Johnny said. "Personally, I think they're one of the most overlooked indie jangle pop bands of the post-punk movement."

I blinked. "Wow. Uh . . . yeah, I totally agree." I pulled my sweatshirt out straight to read it even though it was upside down and stuffed with prank ammo. "I don't get why they're not bigger."

"'74–'75 did pretty well in Europe." Johnny raised his eyebrows. "Who else do you listen to?"

I turned and put my knee up on the bench. "I'm a mad, psycho fan of the White Stripes."

"Totally understandable. They're beyond innovative. Jack White is a brilliant musician."

"No kidding. And the Raconteurs?"

Johnny swiveled to face me. "Oh my God, his work with them is insane. 'Salute Your Solution' is coming up later in the mix."

"Awesome."

We grinned and nodded at each other.

The Velvet Underground & Nico's "I'll Be Your Mirror" started playing, and I said, "Wow, nice choice. God, if I'd known you were putting together the playlists all these years, I might have come to more dances." Johnny opened his mouth like he was going to say something, but when the lyrics started, he just spun forward and hunched over his knees.

"You okay?" I asked.

"Super." He shot me an okay sign without looking up. "No problem."

I searched the dance floor for Gabe. Didn't see him anywhere. But I did see Todd and Amanda plastered together, bobbing to the music. She dragged her claws up and down the back of his polo shirt as they danced.

Johnny lifted his head and watched the crowd too. One guy wrapped a silver streamer around his girlfriend and held the ends as she slow-danced in front of him.

"Do you like dancing?" Johnny asked.

Oh God. This was awkward. Was he asking me to dance? My mouth hung open while I pondered the deeper meaning of his question. He must have sensed my apprehension, because he blurted out, "I hate dancing. I mean, I don't hate it. I just—I'm terrible. I'm totally into music, but I *really* can't dance."

Phew. Relief. "Yeah, you said that this morning. Neither can I." I hitched my thumb at the couples on the dance floor. "Not that I'd call that dancing."

"Heh. Yeah."

"Sometimes I wish I lived back when people had balls."

Oh God. That did *not* come out right.

I said, "I mean back when they had elaborate parties and dances and everyone dressed up and knew all the formal dances and everything."

"Heh. Yeah."

We sat not talking for several songs. There were one or two predictable crowd-pleasers, but also some obscure gems. A little Chairlift. There was a little bit of The Killers. Some Plain White T's (gotta play the hometown boys). And even this other local band I love called Kicked Off Edison. It was enough to show that Johnny Mercer's taste in music basically rocked.

I drummed my fingers on the bleachers. "How much time?"

Johnny looked at his watch. "Eight minutes."

I stretched my arms above my head and arched my back. "Where'd Mar get to?"

"Dunno."

"Maybe I should go look for her." As I stood up, though, the music suddenly stopped and Principal Miller blew into the microphone. Her watch must have been running fast. Maybe that was how she caught her cheating husband. The lights brightened, and I saw Mar wave and give me a thumbs-up from across the gym. It was nearly showtime.

Principal Miller said, "Seniors! Seniors! *Señoritas* and *señors*!" She paused to laugh at her own lame joke. "Let me interrupt you for one moment. Well, we're here to kick off the year with style! Yes! And to celebrate learning about marriage and partnerships! To start things right, I'd like each of you to dance the next dance with your marriage education partner. After that, have *fun*! And enjoy the evening!"

Nobody moved.

Except for Johnny, Mar, and me. I signaled to Mar and she made a beeline for Amanda. Johnny and I headed for Todd. We knew we only had seconds before the lights went back out. Mar got to Amanda first and started pointing to her face—distracting her with makeup talk, I assumed. Next, Johnny strode just in front of me. He circled to the right, turned, and "accidentally" ran into Todd from behind. Todd fell forward. Johnny caught him but continued to bump and fumble, apologizing profusely. As Todd was bent over, I casually walked up to him, pulled our secret weapon from the plastic bag in my hoodie pocket, and slapped it on the ass of his khakis. With all Johnny's bumping and fumbling, Todd hadn't felt it. Only when he stood up and Amanda shrieked did Todd realize he was wearing an adult diaper filled with chocolate pudding, axle grease, and taco meat. The sticky-tabs helped, but the axle grease really made it stick.

"WHAT THE HELL?" he yelled. He wheeled around and saw me.

I crossed my arms and smiled. "Oh, poor baby," I said. "Did Mommy forget to change your diaper?"

Todd peeled the diaper off his butt and made the fatal mistake of holding it up. Callie Brooks screamed like it was the severed head of her deity, Martha Stewart. Everyone around us turned and stared. Amanda heaved, covered her mouth, and went running off in the direction of the bathroom.

"Holy . . . What the . . . ? Oh, you are *so* dead, PRINCESS PISSPANTS," Todd said. Loudly. So everyone would hear the name.

Except I had a name for him, too. I'd gotten the idea from Principal Miller, in fact. I took a deep breath and said, "So glad you like it, SEÑOR SHITSLACKS."

A few people started laughing. A couple more joined in. Then someone yelled, "*Hola*, Señor Shitslacks!" and everyone burst into hysterics.

Then Todd Harding looked at me with an expression on his face that totally threw me. I'd thought he'd be scowling. Furious. But he wasn't. He was smiling. And there was something in his eyes. At first, I thought it must be malice. It had to be hate, right? But I swear to God, as he held my stare, I realized.

It was admiration. He'd thought it was cool.

My mind zoomed. Was he yanking my chain? Trying to lure me in with his phony charm, only to set me up again? I stood there like a robot with an electrical short. I think I actually twitched. Suddenly Principal Miller—who either had missed the whole prank or had decided not to notice it—was on the microphone again.

"Come on, turn those lights off! Find your partners and hit the dance floor! GET DOWN AND PAR-TAY!"

Todd glanced at Principal Miller and mumbled, "She's totally loaded." And I—I'm sorry, but I couldn't help myself—I laughed.

Todd said, "I'm not dancing with you, Princess Pisspants."

I said, "I'm not dancing with you, Señor Shitslacks. Your ass stinks like chocolate tacos."

Todd looked at me, looked at Johnny, shook his head, and walked bowlegged toward the bathrooms, holding the diaper away from himself. When he passed Callie Brooks, he thrust it at her face and she screamed again. What a wuss.

The lights went down and the music came back on.

Johnny clapped three times. "That was awesome!"

Marcie came over. "Well, Fee, feel better now? You know, you've got a seriously evil streak, girl."

Evil streak? Me? I'd never considered myself evil before. Was an evil streak something I should be proud of? I should have been proud that I'd humiliated Todd just like he humiliated me. I should've been proud that we'd executed the plan without a hitch. I should've been thrilled that everyone saw that I was the one responsible.

But weirdly enough, I was something less than ecstatic. "Yeah, it was cool. You guys were great. Thanks for helping me out." I high-fived both of them.

"That's what we're here for, Fee," Mar said.

"Yup. Nothing says friendship like, sweet, sweet revenge," Johnny said.

I tried to laugh at Johnny's joke, but truth be told, Todd's whole admiration reaction had totally messed with my head. And the idea of Gabe sneaking off with some girl just wrung me out like a dirty dishrag. "You know what, Mar? Whaddya say we blow out of here?"

Marcie's satin forehead creased. "Already?"

"Yeah, I just—I dunno. I don't really have any desire to stay. We did what we came to do, you know? I'm just done."

Marcie gave me the head-wag-with-one-hand-on-the-hip routine. "Well, I'm your ride, and I don't want to leave."

"*Mar*-cie," I said. As in, *Uh are you my best friend or what?*

But Marcie either didn't get it or didn't care. "Fiona. I helped you. Why can't you stay for me?"

"Come on, please? I just need to curl up and veg," I said.

"I—I could take you," Johnny said, and then to Mar: "I could take her and come back."

I didn't speak a word to Mar, but my eyes said, *You are not seriously going to make me go home with Johnny Mercer, are you?*

Mar didn't blink.

"Thanks anyway, Johnny, but you know what?" I waved my hand in front of him and Mar. "Forget it. I can walk." I turned and strode toward the door. I got five steps before Mar said, "All right, wait up, Fee. I'll take you." She caught up with me and we headed out together. I glanced over my shoulder, gave Johnny a wave of thanks, and we left.

CHAPTER 8

THAT NIGHT, I COULDN'T SLEEP. MY ANTIQUE BRASS bed creaked as I flopped around, trying to get comfortable. I kept playing the prank scene over and over in my head, trying to figure out why it hadn't been as satisfying as I'd imagined. I didn't get it. Sometime around two-thirty, I grabbed my iPod, pulled up *White Blood Cells*, and listened to music until I finally fell asleep.

I woke up Saturday morning feeling like I'd been dragged behind a bus driving through a minefield. I hoped I hadn't caught something like typhoid or Ebola under those bleachers. Besides not wanting to have a deadly contagious disease, I also didn't want to cancel babysitting for Sam that night. I had to ask her parents about Todd coming along, too. Marvelous. Couldn't wait for that.

I rolled over to face the window beside my bed. Outside, the sun had the translucent, washed-out look that was the sign of a humid day. I closed my eyes and tried to fall back asleep. When that didn't work, I decided I needed caffeine, stat. I threw off my covers and trudged down the narrow back stairs to the kitchen.

My mother and several other women sat huddled around

the kitchen table, conspiring over their coffee mugs. One of the women was Marcie's mom. As she caught sight of my torn nightshirt and moose-covered pj pants, a flicker of horror lit across her face. I said, "Hi Mrs. Beaufort. Uh, Mom?"

Mom startled. "Oh, Fiona, we were just talking about you. Your marriage course, that is. This is the executive committee of the PTA. Ladies, this is my daughter, Fiona."

They nodded to me, and I waved without making direct eye contact with anyone. They looked like a bunch of mobsters planning a hit. I inched over to the coffeemaker, which was empty, of course, so I started making a new pot. Normally, I would've just grabbed a Coke, but one, I needed megadoses of caffeine, and two, I wanted to eavesdrop.

"Vivian, did Principal Miller say exactly when she got school board approval?" asked a woman who had a curly mass of jet-black hair with a two-inch band of gray roots at her part. It looked like an electrocuted skunk had died on her head.

"All she said," my mother answered, "was that she appealed to them over the summer, and they called an emergency vote just prior to school starting."

"And we all know how conservative that school board is," Electrocuted Skunk said. "But there's conservative, and then there's crazy. No offense, Michelle."

Mrs. Beaufort composed a smile and raised a hand to mean, *None taken.*

"Appealed to them?" said a woman with gold earrings way too big and gaudy for 10:23 a.m. "More like cried on their shoulders. I grew up with Barbara Miller. So did half the board. It wouldn't shock me to hear that Barbara told them some sob story about trying to raise two kids and work full time while her dirtbag husband flits around the world, burning up her savings account with some young, sexed-up tramp."

Mrs. Beaufort bristled. "Well, however she might have phrased it, it's obvious that her divorce is coloring her judgment. Marriage is a sacrament, not a college prerequisite."

Mom got up and brought a plate of coffee cake to the table. "I feel terrible for what she's going through, but to hold our kids' diplomas over their heads—it's too much."

Electrocuted Skunk twirled her finger in her mug handle. "And what about kids who aren't even straight? It's cruel, if you ask me."

"And I'm sorry," Big Earrings said, "but how is some course going to teach them how marriage works? I've been married three times, and I haven't figured it out yet." She snorted. "I figured out how to call a lawyer, though." She held up her hand, and Electrocuted Skunk high-fived her.

A woman in a cream-colored jumpsuit who had been silent up till now set her mug down hard. "As president of the PTA, I move that we pledge our help to Vivian in her opposition to the marriage education course." Mrs. Beaufort seconded the motion. "All those in favor?"

Four hands shot into the air.

Mom beamed. She'd successfully allied herself with the most powerful group of women in our little town. Housewives with anger issues, plenty of disposable income, and way too much free time. Mom was set. "Thank you, Cybil. Thank you, committee. I think we should start with a petition," she said.

I grabbed a cup of coffee and crept upstairs. I fished my marriage ed journal out from under my bed to make an entry. Over the years, I'd learned that under the bed was the best place to keep anything I didn't want found, because there was so much crap—papers, magazines, dirty socks, grocery bags—that no one would ever suspect that anything of value was under there. Sort of like hiding in plain sight.

Not that I thought the journal had any value whatsoever.

Saturday, September 7

The dance last night was . . . well, let's just say memorable. Not that I stayed for long. I went, spent some "quality time" with Todd (now aka Señor Shitslacks), and left. Poor Mar—I dragged her out of there. But I was just fried. The planning beforehand, plus the stress of waiting, and then the deed itself. (Although Johnny Mercer kept me company, which was actually okay. Either he's really dopey or he has a wicked sense of humor. I suspect it's the latter. For example, when he and Mar and I were at the store before the dance, I told them about how I have to get the cheerleaders their precious water, as if they even break a sweat. And Johnny said, "Hey, look on the bright side. You could always spit in it." Isn't that hilarious?)

But re the prank. I have to say, I really expected to end up energized and juiced-up by the whole thing. Don't get me wrong; it was hysterical while it was happening. But once it was done, and everybody went back to what they were doing . . . I dunno. The coolness didn't last very long. I realized that I had absolutely no desire to stay. Bizarre. I had totally pictured myself spending the rest of the dance in full-on gloat mode. Which, okay, doesn't say much for my character, but then again, in the end, I just left. So maybe I'm not a complete jerk.

Oh, and one more thing. This journal may soon become recycling, because my mother has got this marriage ed course in her crosshairs. One of the things that can make my mom a huge pain in the ass sometimes is that when she sinks her teeth into a new project (like this, or say . . . forcing me to get a terrible haircut when I was twelve), she pretty much hangs on until the victim quivers in defeat. If you don't think it's true, then check out my seventh-grade yearbook picture. The yearbook company changed my name to Frank Sheehan because they were sure the kid with the buzz cut in the photo couldn't possibly be a girl. That's what they said when Mom called about it, anyway. She never nagged me about my hair again.

CHAPTER 9

I'D BEEN WATCHING SAMANTHA PICKLER EVER SINCE her family moved into Arborview Estates four years earlier. I'd seen Sam change from a nonstop-jabbering kid into a bright, sassy eleven-year-old. She was funny, beautiful, and way, way cooler than me. I never felt unlucky when I was around her. Plus, she made me laugh.

"Come on in, Fiona," Mr. Pickler said when I got there.

I stepped into their spotless foyer. Normally, I don't like houses in developments, but Mrs. Pickler had pretty decent taste, décorwise, even if she was a neat freak. The paint in the foyer was this organic copper color, set off by black accessories, caramel wood floors, and a giant glass vase filled with deep green eucalyptus branches. The whole place had that spicy, clean eucalyptus smell.

"Thanks," I said. "Actually, Mr. Pickler, I have a question to ask. We're doing this project in school"—I couldn't bring myself to say it was a marriage education course. I was humiliated enough just to say this much—"and my partner and I have to earn some money together."

"Oh, is it an economics project?"

"Uh, kinda. Anyway, I was wondering if it would be okay with you to have him come here to babysit with me."

Mr. Pickler drew himself up. "Wait a minute—your partner is male?"

"Uh, yeah. Is that a problem?"

"You know Sam's mother and I have a strict no-boyfriends policy, Fiona."

I literally felt myself gag. "Oh, *no way*, Mr. Pickler. Todd Harding is *not* my boyfriend. Please. Nooo."

"Todd Harding? Got hurt playing football a few years back? Is he your project partner?"

Uh-oh. "Do you know him?"

"He lives down the street. Moved in about the same time we did."

"Oh, great," I said without sounding like it was great at all. What can I say? I'm a rotten liar.

"I've got no problem with Todd coming to help babysit Sam." He turned sideways and pointed at me. "I'm not paying double, though!" He laughed at himself. I laughed too, because I had to—he was the guy who paid me.

"In fact, since it's warm out," he said, "you and Sam could take a walk down there so she can meet him, if he's home."

"What a terrific idea, Mr. Pickler!" I said with totally sarcastic cheer. He couldn't tell the difference, though. "We'll do that."

"His house number is . . ." He tapped his fingers together as he counted the houses. "319, it must be. To the right, down the street, fifth house on the right."

"Great! Thanks!"

Sam came galloping down the stairs. "Fiona! You're finally here. I've been waiting *forever*." She jumped to hug me and a strand of her strawberry blond hair got caught in my glasses. "Ow!" she cried. I took off my glasses and gingerly pulled the hair from the frame. The strand stuck out from her head, but it wasn't terribly noticeable, since the rest of her hair was kind of a mess too. Sam hated having anyone brush her hair, but she forgot to do it herself most of the time. It drove her mother nuts. But what really bugged her mother were Sam's fashion choices, which were not unlike mine. Our motto was: If it's clean and it fits, we wear it. Actually, clean is sometimes optional. Today must've been one of the optional days, because Sam had a red dribble stain down the front of her peach-colored shirt. A cherry Popsicle was my guess.

Sam's dad started tugging on the cuffs of his shirt and straightening his tie. "Sam's mom and I should be back around eleven." He called up the stairs, "Victoria! Time!" He kissed Sam on the head. "Don't get Fiona in too much trouble, Monkey-child."

"Sure thing, Ape-man," Sam said. "Not too much. Just a little bit. Got it."

"Guess what? Fiona's going to introduce you to a friend of hers. Won't that be nice?"

"Oooh! Who? Who, Fiona?"

Before I could answer, Mrs. Pickler strolled down the stairs in a cocktail dress, singing, "'Byyye Sammy. Lovvvve you." She ran her hands over Sam's hair to flatten it and then kissed her on the forehead, leaving behind a big old set of burgundy lip prints. She waved at me as she and Sam's dad walked out the door. "Hi Fiona. 'Bye Fiona."

"Have a nice"—she shut the door—"night. Okay. Whatev." I wiped the lip prints off Sam's head with my thumb.

She swatted my hand away. "Who am I meeting?" she demanded.

"You'll see. Get your shoes on."

"Why?"

"We're taking a little walk."

"Walk? You've never taken me on a walk in your whole life," she said. She pulled open the coat closet door and fished around for shoes. "That's exercise. You hate exercise."

"True," I said. "We'd better go really slowly then. Lumber, even."

"We could plod." She sat on the bottom stair and pulled on her purple canvas sneakers without untying them.

"Plod, yes. Nicely done! We shall go for a plod."

She jumped up. "It is a lovely evening for a plod."

"Shall we?" I offered my elbow to her.

"We shall." She slipped her arm into mine.

It was still light out, but the sun was getting ready to set. It was the time of day when the sunlight shines sideways, so everything looks like it has its own special spotlight. That time of day is always hushed. I like to think of it as the planet's big yawn before going to sleep for the night.

"Where are we plodding to?" Sam asked.

"Not far," I said. If I was lucky, Todd would be out ravaging Amanda somewhere, and not home. But then again, luck was not my thing.

I put my hand on Sam's shoulders and steered her in a zigzag down the sidewalk. "So what's our plan for later?"

Sam spun around to face me and walked backward with one hand on her hip and one hand flitting through the air between us. "Well, I couldn't decide between a scary movie and a romantic movie, so I got my tarot cards and laid them out. But I don't know how to read them, so I said, 'Forget it,' and threw them on the floor. And guess what? One with a heart on it landed on top of everything else, so I said, 'That's it!' And so romantic movie it is. *Sixteen Candles*. Our favorite. Is that okay with you?"

"Of course."

I'd give her anything. I don't have any brothers or sisters, so I guess I think of Sam as one. Besides, when she gets mad, she's like a wet cat. I've only seen her temper a few times, but never directed at me. I just like to make her happy.

She chattered on. "Should we do our nails too? My mom got a new color. Passion Plum. It's sort of purple, and you *know* how I love purple. But it's not really purple, just sort of dark purple, you know?"

"Sure." Despite her tomboy look, Sam loved pretending to get dressed up. She was forever trying to glamorize me. One time she'd insisted on giving me a complete makeover with bright red nail polish, matching red lipstick, black eyeliner, and black mascara. She thought I looked gorgeous. I thought I looked like an overzealous vampire after a feeding.

"Can I stay up till midnight?" she asked.

"Nine."

"How about eleven?"

"Ten."

"Okay, deal." We made these negotiations every time, even though I always let her stay up as late as she wanted. She usually fell asleep on the couch by nine-thirty or so anyway. "Just don't tell your parents."

"*Never*!" She laughed.

"Pinky-swear?"

"Pinky-swear!" She hooked her pinky through mine and squeezed.

We turned up Todd's driveway. "This is the place," I said. Sam shot ahead of me and rang the doorbell. I wasn't fast enough to stop her. My plan had been to knock lightly and tiptoe away. But Sam hammered the doorbell at least half a dozen times.

When no one answered, I thought I was off the hook. We started back down the driveway just as a silver minivan pulled in. Señor Shitslacks was at the wheel. I could tell by the look on his face that he was one, trying to piece together the puzzle of why I was there, and two, figure out if I had possibly set some explosives on his front porch. He slowly opened his door and got out. Never took his eyes off me for a second.

"Smooth ride," I said as he came around the front of the van.

"Beats walking, townie."

"How did you know I was a townie?" I said, all smart-ass like.

Todd chuckled. "You just told me."

Pshhh. I waved him off. I'd gotten the "townie" thing my

whole life, but it never bugged me. Kids who came to my house would always shut up when they saw our hidden back staircase, or took a ride in our dumbwaiter.

"At least I'm not polluting the universe, like you," I said.

"Nah, you're too busy hugging trees. Or rather, making out with them. I'm telling you, you really should stick to mating within your species, whatever that is."

"I would," I said, "but unfortunately, there are no gorgeous, all-powerful, all-knowing gods around here. I'd even settle for a demigod. It's a step down, I know. But alas, there are nothing but low-brained mortals here. And half-brains, like you."

Todd snorted. He nodded toward Sam. "Who's this?"

Sam marched forward, positioned herself between Todd and me, and pinned her fists on her bony hips. "My name is Samantha Louise Pickler, not that it's any of your business, because you are a rude, ugly fart-face."

Even though Sam had her back to me, I covered my huge grin with my hand. I knew I was supposed to correct her, but I couldn't. She was too freaking adorable.

Todd was grinning too. He put his fists on his hips just like her. "Well, I think it's rude to *call* someone a rude, ugly fart-face."

"Well, I don't care what you think."

"Really? You should."

"WHY?"

Todd licked his lips and crossed his arms. "Because I have a feeling you and I are going to get to know each other." He looked at me. "That right, Princess? Is this the kid?"

I said, "*Sí*, Señor."

I walked up to Sam and wrapped my arms around her shoulders from behind. She didn't move an inch from her warrior stance. I pointed to Todd. "That, Sam, is Todd Harding. We have to do this lame school project together where we earn money. We don't like it. But for now we have to do it. So Todd is going to help me babysit for you. Your parents okayed it. Todd, Sam. Sam, Todd."

Sam tilted her head toward mine. She kept her eyes drilled on Todd and whispered softly, "He shouldn't say such mean things to you, Fiona. It is truly tacky."

I whispered back, "Believe me, I know. But I need you to hang here, okay? As a favor to me?"

Todd kept slightly rotating his head left and right, trying to hear us.

"Please?" I whispered. "I'm gonna need all the help I can get in this situation."

I felt Sam's posture soften beneath my embrace. "Fine." She dropped her arms, shrugged herself out of my hold, and marched up to Todd. "Hello. My name is Samantha Louise Pickler." She stuck out her right hand and tossed her head. "You may call me Sam."

Todd shook her hand. "Nice to meet you, Sam. My name is Todd. You may call me Todd." Sam looked back at me and rolled her eyes. I shooed her on.

"Pleasure to meet you, Todd." She dropped his hand, swiveled on her heel, and strode back to me.

I mouthed, *Thank you.*

"So, you were planning to work without me tonight,

huh?" Todd said. "Funny you forgot to mention it. Trying to skim a little off the top for yourself?"

"No," I said. "I just hadn't had a chance to ask them about you yet."

"You just said they okayed it."

"Yes, Todd, they did—fifteen minutes ago. I asked them fifteen minutes ago, and they said yes. I'm sorry I didn't send you a Bat Signal or something."

Todd clapped his hands once and motioned up the street. "Great. Then let's go."

"Uhhh . . . 'scuse me?" I said. Holy crap, Todd was going to come over and babysit right *now*. Must stop. Code Red. "Go? Nononono. Aren't you busy? Don't you have to take Amanda out for . . . something?"

"Nope. Nope."

"Don't have plans? Out with your friends? Big guys' night?"

"Nope. Nothing. My schedule is *wiiiide* open. I've got the whole night free to spend with you two charming ladies."

He said "charming ladies" sarcastically, but I let it go. I pride myself on self-control. And I could tell that he wasn't going to give in. "Fine. Whatever," I muttered. "Let's go."

WE WALKED BACK UP THE STREET TOWARD SAM'S house. Todd lagged behind to call his parents to say where he was going. I held hands with Sam and jumped over the sidewalk cracks. A bullfrog started croaking somewhere, and the sun dipped below the horizon and winked out. The sky turned salmon, and the air had that damp coolness that comes with late-summer evenings.

"What's your project about?" Sam asked.

"It's a long story," I said.

"Tell me."

I never could keep a secret from Sam. "We're supposed to pretend we're married. Do stuff together. Figure out money, how to earn it and spend it. It's stupid."

"Why did you marry *him*? Why didn't you marry that guy you like, what's his name? Oh, Gabe! Why didn't you marry Gabe?"

Sam twisted around as I tried to clamp my hand over her mouth. "*Shhhhh*," I hissed. "Please don't say anything about that in front of Todd," I whispered.

"Okay. Sorry, Fiona," Sam said. "Do you think he heard?"

I glanced back to see if Todd showed any signs that he'd been listening. He wasn't on his phone anymore, but he wasn't that close, either. "I hope not," I said.

Todd called out, "Where is this place?" kind of loudly, so I thought maybe he was too far back to have heard us.

"It's right here," Sam said, running out of my reach and up to the door. When we got inside, she raced to the kitchen. Todd and I followed her. I walked over to the pantry and grabbed a jar of popcorn. "Where are we going tonight?" I asked.

"Going? What d'you mean?" Todd asked.

I explained to Todd that every time Sam and I watched a movie (which was every time I babysat), we made popcorn flavored with some international spice or seasoning. International Corn, we called it. Sometimes we hit a winner, like the time we'd popped the corn in sesame and peanut oil and seasoned it with Chinese five-spice powder. But other times we had to dump the bowl. Like when we'd wanted to visit Germany, so we'd popped the corn in sausage fat and tossed it with drained sauerkraut. Über-vomit.

"I was thinking Italy," Sam said, spinning the lazy Susan in the corner cupboard where her mother kept the spices. "We've got a packet of dry Italian dressing in here somewhere. Here it is."

"Mmmm," I said, "you know what would go great with that? Mini pizzas. We can use bread for crust. Do you have any cheese?"

Sam opened the fridge and checked the deli drawer. "Nope. Wait, there's cottage cheese."

I shrugged. "We could try it. How about pizza sauce?"

Sam rifled through the pantry. "Nope. No pizza sauce."

"Spaghetti sauce?" Todd suggested.

"Nope."

"Tomato paste?" I asked.

Sam pulled the fridge open again. "We have ketchup."

I paused a moment to consider the palatability of bread topped with ketchup and cottage cheese. Questionable. "We'll dump on lots of garlic salt and oregano. You do the pizzas. I'll get the popcorn going." I pulled out the soup pot and poured olive oil in the bottom. I added a layer of popcorn kernels, slipped on the lid, and set the pot over medium-high heat. Todd leaned on the counter and watched. How typical that he wouldn't help cook. "Hey Sam, how'd your first few days of school go?" I asked.

"Well. First of all, Ginny and I are *not* friends anymore."

"*What*?" Ginny Genovese was Sam's best friend. Her one true friend. Ginny was Sam's Marcie. "What happened?"

Sam slapped three slices of white bread onto the toaster oven baking sheet. She squeezed ketchup on them and began spreading it with a spoon. "Well. There's this new girl, Olivia Purdy. And she has a really big house with a pool and a big-screen TV and everything. She's really rich or something, I guess. So Ginny decides that she wants to be this girl's best friend so she can use her pool and all. So she goes to Olivia and says that the other girls, me included, are all jerks. And she will show Olivia around and stuff. And not to be friends with anyone else and neither would she. They'd be best friends."

"How did you hear all that?" Todd asked. As if he cared.

She glared at Todd and finally answered him. "Ginny told me." She sprinkled garlic salt and oregano over the ketchup.

"She told you?" I cried. "She told you that she said all the other girls were jerks?"

"Well, no. That part I heard from Dominick Mancuso. He heard it on the bus from Olivia's older sister. But Ginny told me about the part where she and Olivia were going to be best friends and everything." Sam swiped at her eyes with the back of her hand and then stood at the counter with her arms crossed. She was crying. I left the pot and wrapped my body around her. "I am so sorry, sweetie," I said.

I heard the popcorn oil sizzling and the first kernels pop. Before I could get back to the stove, Todd stepped in and started sliding the pot back and forth. The popping reached a fierce crescendo, and when it finally subsided, he moved the pot to a cool burner and shut off the hot one.

I kissed Sam on the back of her head and went over to the stove. I crossed my arms and tapped my foot on the floor until Todd moved out of the way. I opened the pot and sprinkled the dry Italian dressing over the hot popcorn. I put the lid back on, shook the pot, and said, "I can*not* believe Ginny would do that to you."

Sam straightened up and dug a spoon into the container of cottage cheese. "It was truly tacky." She dolloped the cheese onto the pizzas and slipped them into the toaster oven to broil.

"It was truly tacky," I said. "And anyone who would do

that is not worthy of Samantha Pickler's friendship." She shrugged.

"Hey, you know what you should do?" Todd said. "You should put a curse on her."

I rolled my eyes, but Sam turned to Todd and smiled. "Really?"

"Sure," he said. "Send her some bad mojo."

Sam's face lit up. "Yeah, voodoo style. Do you know how to do it? Or do you, Fiona?"

I shrugged. Then gave Todd the stink-eye. I didn't trust him for a second.

Todd said, "We can wing it. Have you got anything that belongs to her?"

"No," Sam said. "Wait, yes! I borrowed a bracelet from her a couple of weeks ago. Will that work?"

"Might as well try," Todd said.

Sam tripped upstairs for the bracelet.

"Have any candles?" Todd asked.

I wheeled around on him. "Why are you being so nice?"

"I'm not being nice," he said. "I'm just bored, Princess."

I stuck my finger right in Todd's face. "Listen, Señor Shitslacks. If you do anything to upset that kid, I am personally going to castrate you."

"Quit talking about my balls. You're turning me on."

"You are disgusting."

He smacked my finger away. "Just get a candle," he said. "Is there paper anywhere? And a marker or something?"

I pointed to the junk drawer but kept my eyes on him. "In there." I glowered at him on my way to the dining room to rummage around in the hutch for candles. The only one I could find was a cinnamon-and-cranberry-scented one called "Heartful Home." Not exactly voodoo material. Oh well. We weren't exactly voodoo priests and priestesses either. Or witches. Or hex putters. Or whatever.

Todd found a piece of paper and a black marker and drew a large circle with a pentagram inside it. Sam came barreling into the kitchen. "Here." She handed the bracelet to Todd. A silver chain with little purple stones dangling like charms.

"That's pretty," I said.

"Well, I'm *not* keeping it. Let's put a curse on her and a curse on the bracelet and then I'll give it back to her and she'll get a double dose of evil."

"I like the way you think," Todd said.

I lit the candle and Sam turned out the lights. The three of us sat on the floor with the pentagram between us. I set the candle in the middle of the star. I had no clue what I was doing, but it looked spooky enough.

Todd held out the bracelet. "Everybody grab hold," he said. We held it above the flame. "Now bow your head." Then he let loose with the bull. "Attention, spirits of the otherworld! We call upon you in this time of need. Young Samantha has been wronged by another, the owner of this worldly possession." We lifted the bracelet higher.

Sam chimed in. "Hail, gods of friendship and loyalty!"

"Yes, gods!" Todd called. "We humbly request that you wield your devastating power upon—what was her name?"

"Ginny Genovese," I whispered between clenched teeth.

"Upon Ginny Genovese! And bring her to her knees!"

"Give it to her! Give it to her good!" Sam cried.

We stretched our arms as high as we could, suspending the bracelet above our heads. Todd started to lower it, and Sam and I followed. I decided to jump in. "Unleash your powers, oh, great ones," I said. "Bring unto Ginny Genovese the pain she brought to our dear sister Samantha. Use this bracelet as a vehicle to carry your curse and all of your wrath. Deliver it to Ginny as we deliver this trinket to her."

"No mercy!" Sam cried.

Todd said, "By the powers of everything good, loyal, and true, we hereby declare this bracelet and its owner, Ginny Genovese, cursed for all time."

"Or until we decide to let her off the hook," Sam added. We set the bracelet on the pentagram and blew out the candle together.

"It is done," I said.

"What do you think will happen to her?" Sam asked.

I cackled and rubbed my palms together. "Time will tell."

The toaster oven dinged. The pizzas were done. Sam sighed and smiled. "Let's watch the movie."

But halfway into the movie, we heard a key click in the front door lock. Mrs. Pickler bolted up the stairs. Soon after, Mr. Pickler strolled in, peeling bills from his wallet. "Sorry, Fiona. Oh, hi there. Todd, right?" Todd stood up and shook his hand. "Jake Pickler. Listen, Sam's mom has a migraine. We won't be needing you anymore tonight." He held the bills just out of my reach, so I had to stand up to get them. Slight hint to get lost. "There's a little extra here for your trouble."

"But Dad, we're watching a movie," Sam whined.

"Not tonight, Sam. Head up to bed."

"But—"

"*Sam*," he barked. "*Bed*."

Sam trudged toward the stairs. I followed her as I headed for the door. "'Bye Sister-witch," I whispered as she turned and climbed the first step. But it didn't seem to cheer her any.

"See ya," she muttered and skulked up. "'Bye Todd."

"See ya, Squirt," Todd said as we walked outside. As soon as the front door closed behind us, Todd held out his open palm. "Hand over the cash, Princess."

"What? No! Why should you get to have it?"

"Because the man earns the money, that's why."

"Ha! Screw that," I said, stalking over to my bike. "I'm going to be the one with the job. This *was* my real job to begin with."

Todd followed me. "Real job, maybe. But *theoretically*, I'm the breadwinner. *Theoretically*, you're fat and lazy and stay home watching TV all day, getting fatter and lazier."

I spun around. "*Theoretically*, you are a butt-head caveman—oh, I'm sorry, did I say theoretically? I meant really."

He put on an exaggerated hillbilly accent. "No woman—or whatever you are—in my household is gonna earn cash money."

I gaped. "You are not seriously that chauvinistic?"

"Hmmm . . ." He stroked his chin dramatically. "Maybe not in real life." Hillbilly again: "But as your fake husband . . . yes, I think I am."

I eyed him up and down. "I need to call the *Guinness Book*

of World Records or *Gray's Anatomy* or something, because I am standing here looking at the single largest asshole ever known to man."

He snapped his fingers and held out his hand again. "Just give me the money, honey."

Honey? Had he actually just called me *honey*? I was about to lay into him again when I realized I truly didn't give a rat's ass whether or not I earned any fake money in a fake marriage to a jerk I hated in real life. Let the poor bastard have it. "Fine." I slapped the cash into his hand. Hard. "But it'd better all be there when you hand it in on Tuesday."

Todd counted the bills. "Twenty-five times 150—damn, we already have $3,750."

"Tell me you just did that in your head."

"What? Easy. Divide 150 by four, then multiply by a hundred: 3,750. Duh." Todd laughed. "Poor Amanda. She and Gabe pulled a 50. They'll be lucky if they make all month what we made tonight."

"Oh, what a shame," I said. I grabbed my handlebars and booted up my kickstand. "Guess dating her means that you're slumming now, huh?"

Todd pocketed the money. "Should I tell Gabe you said that?"

I froze with one foot on my pedal. Holy crap. He *had* heard. I felt hot blood pulsing up my neck and into my face. I tried to laugh lightly, but it came out sounding like a high-pitched machine gun. "What? Why? I don't care."

Todd tapped his fingertips together. "Oh, don't you?"

"*No*," I insisted way too forcefully.

"Okay." He winked. "Whatever you say. I'm outta here. See ya, Princess Pisspants." He strode off down the driveway.

As I stood there on one foot, my whole body buzzed like someone had scooped out my insides and filled my empty skin with bees. I couldn't move. I couldn't even respond to the name-calling. Not that it really mattered. Because one thing was for sure: being called Princess Pisspants was nothing compared to Todd Harding knowing about Gabe.

TUESDAY MORNING I STOOD OUTSIDE MAGGIE KLEIN'S office, waiting to go in for our counseling session. No sign of Todd yet. Just as well. I took out *Pride and Prejudice* to read until Señor Shitslacks got there. I must've been pretty into the book, because I nearly hit the ceiling when Johnny Mercer tapped me on the shoulder. "Holy crap, Johnny!"

He twitched his head and blushed. "Sorry. Didn't mean to scare you. I just wanted to know if you were feeling better."

I shut my book. "Yeah, thanks. How was the rest of the dance?"

"Boring. Oh, except when Principal Miller started dirty-dancing with Mr. Evans."

Mr. Evans was the janitor. Old-school style. He wouldn't let you call him anything but janitor, not some wussy title like sanitation engineer or custodian. Rumor was, he'd worked at the high school ever since the day he graduated from it thirty years ago. He was one of those guys who looked like he'd been born with a crew cut, muscles, and a lit Marlboro hanging out of his mouth. But he'd do anything for a student, especially if it meant putting one over on the administration.

So to picture him grinding with Principal Miller was, well . . . a stretch of the imagination, to say the least.

"Mr. Evans?" I asked.

Johnny scratched at one of his long sideburns. "Well, it was only one dance. Part of one dance, actually. She kind of grabbed him and started dancing and he went along with it. Pretty funny."

"Maybe I should've stayed."

"Next time," Johnny said.

Suddenly, Maggie Klein's office door clicked open. "Oh, Fiona. I thought I heard voices."

I waved to Johnny. He gave me a nod, popped in his earphones, and took off.

Maggie Klein said, "Come on in. Todd's inside already. He and I have been having a little chat about your. . . . interactions last week."

Interactions? Right. Try war games. And what was he doing here early? Soaping up Maggie Klein, no doubt.

"Now, I understand that you two have been . . . shall we say, at loggerheads? I think we need to address the situation." She looked at me for some response. "Fiona? Would you like to begin this time?"

Argh. I rolled my eyes. I shrugged my shoulders. I gave her all the little cues that said I didn't want to talk, but she just stared at me with an expression of utter compassion and persistence. Fine.

"He started it," I said.

"I did not."

I gaped at Todd. "The mock wedding?"

"You threw a hot dog at me first."

"After your little drawing on the bulletin board."

"That was just a joke."

I snorted. "Yeah, well, I missed the punch line."

"What about what you did at the dance?"

"You deserved it."

Maggie Klein clapped twice. "Todd, Fiona, this is serious. I understand that there is some resistance to this course. However, I believe strongly in its merits, and so does the school board. And until they say otherwise, this course will continue. You two must find some common ground. Like it or not, you're marriage partners. Now, I want you to look at each other. Really look. And then I'd like you each to say something positive about the other person." Todd and I both sighed and shifted in our seats. I looked past Maggie Klein and watched a squirrel with an acorn in its mouth climbing the tree outside her window. "Come on," she said. "Turn and face each other. Now Todd, you go first."

Todd eyeballed me up and down. "She appears to have all her teeth."

"Ooh, good one, Todd," I cooed. I turned to Maggie Klein and smiled sweetly. "And Todd smells very little like a pile of goat crap."

Maggie Klein shook her head. "Kids—"

"Fiona has enough self-esteem to not care about the condition of her wardrobe."

"And Todd is kind enough to volunteer his time with mentally deficient students. Like his girlfriend, Amanda."

"Leave her out of this."

"How can I? She's practically surgically attached to your groin."

"*Kids.*"

"At least I *have* a girlfriend. Oh, wait. I forgot about your lesbian lover, Marcie."

"In your dreams."

"You mean nightmares."

"TODD! FIONA! ENOUGH!" Maggie Klein rubbed her face and sighed. "Right. Look." She laced her fingers together like she was praying for us to stop. "I know neither of you is happy about this situation. But this course is important. Finding, choosing, and maintaining a life partner isn't easy, you know. Believe me; it can be scary out there. Some people . . ." She drifted off and shook her head. "What I mean is, this is a skill that can be learned and should be learned, for your own good. Do you see?"

We responded with dead silence.

She threw her hands in the air. "Okay, look at it this way," she said. "If you want to graduate and get into college and get as far away from each other as possible, you need to finish this course, got it?" She looked at us each in turn as we sulked like a couple of three-year-olds. "Okay. Now, what's the status on your budget and your shared activity? Are you on the same page?"

Todd dug into his back pocket and pulled out the cash from Saturday night. He handed it to Maggie Klein. "Here ya go. Twenty-five big ones we made this weekend."

She looked at the money like it was about to burst into flames in her hands. "You've already started the babysitting job?" Todd and I nodded. "How did it go?" She looked back and forth between us like a Labrador retriever at an egg-toss. I figured Todd would take this opportunity to suck up, and he didn't disappoint.

"It went very well, Maggie," he crooned. "She's a sweetie."

"Fiona is?"

Todd snorted and bent double like it was so funny it hurt. "*No.* The *kid.* The kid is a sweetie."

I opened my mouth to say something back, but Maggie Klein cut me off. "Okay, well, still quite encouraging." She plucked out one of the identical pens she kept in a clean terra-cotta flowerpot on her desk, and scribbled in our file. "I've made a note that you're the first couple to turn in some income. Well done. Just don't forget to get a note from the parents validating your payment. You can turn that in with the budget at the end of the month. And how is the theoretical earning of the income divided? Do you both work? One of you?"

"I'm the one with the job," Todd said. Maggie Klein gazed at him like a teenage groupie after her first beer. "Oh, Todd, I figured as much," she lilted.

I pretended to cough.

Todd scooted up in his seat. "Yeah, I like to take care of my woman. Keep her at home. Barefoot in the kitchen, where she belongs. I'd say barefoot and pregnant, but unfortunately, my wife is frigid and infertile."

I kicked Todd in the shin. "You are such a jackass."

"Fiona!" Maggie Klein exclaimed.

"Me?" I cried. "Aren't you going to yell at him?"

She tilted her head at Todd and giggled. "Well, we know he's kidding."

"Oh, *do* we?" I said.

Maggie Klein sighed. "Fiona, you must get in touch with your partner's personality. His quirks and foibles."

Todd muttered, "Yeah, Princess, you should touch my quirk."

I gagged loudly, but Maggie Klein ignored Todd's lewd innuendo. "Now, what about the shared activity? Any news on that front?"

"We haven't started it yet," I said, glaring sideways at Todd.

He put his finger in the air, "Actually, Maggie," he said, "cheerleading tryouts start today after school."

I swiveled. "Tryouts? Why do I have to go to tryouts?"

Todd mocked sipping through a straw again. "We might get thirsty, Water Girl."

"Don't call me Water Girl."

"You're right. Your name is Princess P—"

"*Shut up.*"

Maggie Klein shot up out of her seat and yanked open her office door. "Okay, it looks like our time's up. You may return to class. Don't forget to write in your journals and work on your budget. 'Bye now."

We stood up and filed out of her office. I peeled off

without a word, but Todd called after me, "Don't forget. Football field. Three o'clock. See you there, Princess." I gave him an over-the-shoulder-finger. He chuckled and walked away.

My only consolation was that this was going to make one hell of a college application essay. "How I Learned About Diplomacy from Señor Shitslacks, the No-Necked Neanderthal."

CHAPTER 12

AFTER SCHOOL I CALLED MY MOM TO LET HER KNOW I'd be late, and then I headed down to the football field for the cheerleading tryouts. The official cheer coach was this ancient history teacher named Mrs. O'Toole. And I don't mean the history was ancient; Mrs. O'Toole was. She started coaching cheerleading at ECHS in the late 1950s when cheerleaders wore those bowling-style shoes and said things like "peachy-keen." But as the decades passed, she couldn't get on board with all the new mounts and skills that evolved, so her coaching became less and less hands-on. Now, she mostly just sat somewhere and snoozed through tryouts or practices. I guess the administration didn't have the heart to fire her after so many years. Or maybe she hadn't thought to ask for a raise in half a century, so her "coaching" was insanely cheap. At any rate, for tryouts Mrs. O'Toole did nothing more than sit at the end of the football stands with an umbrella over her face for shade. Whether she was awake or asleep was anyone's guess. Hell, she could have been dead and no one would have noticed until the flies started swarming.

I sank down onto one of the bleachers and opened my copy of *P&P*. I was just at the part where Mr. Darcy first recognizes his feelings for Elizabeth. I didn't get very far, though. I couldn't help daydreaming that I was Elizabeth and Gabe was Mr. Darcy, fighting against his blossoming feelings for me. Discovering that his passion was beyond his control and finding me more and more desirable each time we met. I, of course, was coy and witty and said all the right things at all the right times and filled out the top of my empire-style dress quite nicely. I played the pianoforte as he listened and watched me with sultry eyes. It was a love that would grow despite the denial of both parties. Despite the opposition of others. It was simply irrefutable. But we would have to wait for it. Wait. Because you can't hurry love. You just have to wait. Love don't come easy. It's a game of give and take.

Oh, dammit. Now I had a song from one of my father's crappy old vinyl records stuck in my head.

I set my book down and watched Todd, Amanda, and a whole gaggle of girls squawk around. There were even a couple of guys waiting to try out, too. I guess Todd had degeeked cheerleading enough for them. Or maybe the whole "looking up girls' skirts" thing had finally caught on. Jamar Douglass was there. And Oskar Leahy. And who was the guy on the opposite bleachers? Was it . . . ? Hold the phone.

I jumped up and "casually" strolled a bit closer. I blinked my eyes in the sun. It couldn't be, could it? But it was.

Gabe.

Why was he here? He couldn't be trying out. He was just sitting there. Watching. With sultry eyes like Darcy's. And suddenly it hit me. The girls. One of the girls was the one he was dating. Had to be. Then Amanda went over and sat next to him, and I did a mental head-smack. Of course. He was only there because they were fake-married. That was it. Right? But there was a girl, somewhere, who he was seeing. Maybe she was here. Wait a minute; did he just smile at Sonja Pressman?

"You know, if you're going to stalk someone, you should be less obvious."

I wheeled around. It was Todd. He'd snuck up on me.

He said, "For starters, try not standing in the middle of a field, gawking at your prey," he said.

I kicked at a dusty clump of grass. "Gawking? I . . . I'm . . . not gawking. I was just watching your girlfriend putting the moves on someone else. Jealous?"

"Of Gabe Webber?" Todd laughed. "Uh . . . *no.*"

I shielded my eyes from the sun. "Why? What's wrong with Gabe Webber?"

"Nothing. As in, there's nothing there. He has the personality of dry toast."

How dare he insult my Gabe? "Oh yes. I forgot. You prefer the company of assholes and jerks. As they say, 'Birds of a feather . . .'"

"That must be why you hang around."

I opened my mouth to come back with a zinger, but I couldn't think of anything to say. Blank. I just stood there with my yap hanging wide open.

Todd smiled and shook his head. "Ya got nothing?"

I did the only thing I could. I shut my mouth, shrugged my shoulders and said, "Nope. Nothing."

Todd laughed again. A real laugh, though. Not an evil one or a suspicious one. A real, hearty-type chortle with his face all loose and bright. "Give it time. You'll think of something," he said. He started walking back to the crowd, but said over his shoulder, "I'll wait."

I stood rock-still in the field as tryouts began. The sun scorched the top of my forehead, but I didn't budge. I needed every ounce of energy in my body to figure something out. Something was familiar. Something about the way Todd looked at me and spoke to me reminded me of . . . what?

Then it clicked.

My parents. The verbal sparring. That's what they did. They liked it, but why?

Because it was exciting. And Todd probably liked it for the same reason. That was why he hadn't really freaked out at the dance. And why he'd come over to Sam's. It was fun for him. He liked fighting. But what was worse was that he seemed to like fighting with me. Oh, barf. I slunk back to the bleachers and sat with my head between my knees. I felt a light tap on my shoulder, and looked up. "Mar! Johnny? What are you guys doing here?"

"We have an hour to kill before dance class," Mar said. (Mar had gotten to pick their shared activity. Ballroom dance lessons. All I could say was, poor Johnny.)

"We came down here to give you some moral support," Johnny said. "Or extra spit in their water. Whichever."

A light breeze blew down the football field. "Thanks," I said. I scooted to my right and pulled Mar over for a bit of privacy. "I need to talk to you," I whispered. Johnny must've gotten the hint, because he sat down a few feet away, pulled out his MP3 player, and popped in the earphones.

Mar sat. "What's up?"

I took a deep breath. "I have a problem. I think Todd actually enjoys my company."

Mar reached out and fiddled with a curl at my hairline. "And that's a problem because . . . ?"

"Because all this marriage has to go on is our hate for each other. That's our one thing we have in common. Unwavering mutual disdain."

She set her hands neatly in her lap. "But you just said he liked you."

"No, I said he enjoys my company. That is, he enjoys hating me. Or pretending to hate me. I don't know which. But I'm finding it difficult to completely dislike someone who gets pleasure from having me around." The breeze died down and I felt sweat collecting under the nosepiece of my glasses. A dribble of it also ran down my cleavage. I dug in my backpack and got my clip-on sunglasses and a tissue. I snapped the sunglasses on my glasses and shoved the tissue down my shirt. Mar made a face, of course. But I didn't care; I'd rather be comfortable.

"So he likes being mean to you," she said. "And you like that he likes being mean to you."

"And I like being mean to him, too, don't forget."

"Of course not. Pleasure from meanness. There's a name for it: sadomasochism."

"Thanks a lot," I said, pressing my stomach in with both hands. "That's just what I need. A mental picture of Todd Harding laced up in a black leather bodysuit with a whip in one hand and his wang in the other."

"I hope he's hitting you with the *whip*."

I smacked her thigh. "I'm serious, Mar. I don't know how to act around him now. I can't be nice, because he'll hate that. But I can't be mean just to be nice."

"You really need medication."

"I'm in a quandary. A catch-22. I'm screwed. Help me, Mar, please."

Marcie lifted her hair off the back of her neck for a few seconds and then let it fall. "Okay, you like fighting with him too—you said so yourself. So keep fighting with him."

I shook my fists at her. "How?"

"Look, you don't love the guy. There are plenty of reasons to hate Todd Harding. Pick one."

"Yes. *Yes*," I said. "I just have to find one thing. One thing about him that I hate and focus on that. But what?"

Marcie glanced at the cheerleading tryouts. "How about his taste in women?"

I looked over to where Amanda was hooked onto Todd's middle with her arms wrapped around his waist so tight that he actually crimped over sideways. "Brilliant, Mar," I said. "I'll funnel all my dislike for Amanda into Todd. You're a genius. It's refreshing to see you using your psychology skills for evil as well as for good. It adds character." I stood up. "Wait here. I'll be back."

I waltzed over to Todd and Amanda. Without releasing her death grip on Todd's waist, Amanda sneered at me and said, "Hello, Water Girl. Or should I say, Water Bitch?"

I completely ignored her. Instead I addressed Todd, but tipped my head to indicate Amanda. "You know, you really should see a doctor and have that thing removed. It's getting pretty nasty-looking."

Todd's eyes narrowed. His lip curled up and he said, "And you should get that ugly thing cut off your head, too. Oh, wait, it's your face."

Amanda snorted and guffawed. But I noticed Todd subtly remove her arms from his torso and step away from her just an inch.

Bingo.

I strolled back to the bleachers, looking forward to bragging to Mar, but she was gone. I reached over and plucked out one of Johnny's earphones. "Where'd Mar go?" I asked.

Johnny rubbed the back of his neck where it was pink from the sun. "She had to run inside for something," he said. He scrunched up his face. "Uh . . . some kind of brilliant gloss or something? Said she'd be right out." He pulled out the other earphone and set the MP3 player in his lap.

I sat next to him. "Oh God, she forgot her Joico Brilliantine Spray Gloss? How can she possibly survive without it?"

"What is it?"

"This hair product she's addicted to. Makes her hair shiny or polished or some such garbage. She keeps trying to get me to use it. She paid, like, sixteen dollars for one bottle. I told her I'd rather keep the sixteen bucks and spit on my own hair for free."

"You can spit on your own hair?" Johnny asked. I almost wasn't sure if he was joking at first. But then he said, "Wow, you're talented. Maybe you could join a carnival sideshow or something with that."

I laughed. We didn't seem to have anything else to say, so Johnny went back to his MP3 player, and I went back to my book. It was hard to focus on reading, though, with all the yelling and clapping coming from the cheery hopefuls bouncing around in the grass. They were kind of mesmerizing, really. I watched for a minute and then spotted Mar weaving her way back through the tryouts. Todd stopped her for a second before she came over.

"Todd wants to see you," she said.

I slapped my book shut. "What for?"

"I dunno."

I blew a raspberry, got up, and trudged back to the tryout area. Todd was standing next to this decrepit yellow water cooler the size of a small child. He patted it with his hand. "Here's your big jug, Princess." He stroked his chin. "Unless you brought one with you already. Have you got any big jugs of your own?"

I sighed at his tone. "No."

"No," he said, staring directly at my chest, "I see that you don't." He laughed at himself. I ignored him in a dignified manner.

"Well, don't worry," he went on. "It's not as big on the inside as it is outside. Here, check it out."

I should have known better than to do anything Señor Shitslacks said. And any other time, I would have. But I was thrown off by the eureka moment I'd just had when I realized that he might actually like me in a twisted, hate-filled way. So I stepped over to the cooler and lifted the lid.

Inside was a wriggling mound of wet, green things. Frogs. Dozens of them. Big ones, leaping all over the place. I shrieked and jumped about five feet backward. Todd burst into hysterics. So did Amanda and the rest of the cheerleader wannabes, along with Todd's bonehead buddy from the cafeteria (who, judging from the mud on his legs was the dickweed frognapper).

Crap, what about Gabe? Had he seen? He wasn't on the bleachers anymore. Mrs. O'Toole sure hadn't noticed anything. Maybe Gabe had missed it too. But no, there he was, walking on the sidelines less than thirty feet away. Laughing. Oh God, no. But then . . .

Gabe winked at me and gave me a little wave. I swear I didn't imagine it. Gabe Webber winked at me.

Todd yelled, "What's the matter? I thought princesses liked frogs!"

In fact, I hate frogs. I hate everything about them. Their bulgy eyes, the way they move. They're like giant, live, jumping boogers. There was no way Todd could've known that, but I threw the lid hard at his stomach anyway. He caught it, pretending it knocked the wind out of him. He kept laughing. And after a sec I realized that, despite Gabe seeing it, the prank was kind of good. Pretty funny. So I started chuckling too.

Now, if everything had ended there, with all of us laughing, then things would've been just fine. But as soon as Amanda saw that I was laughing along with Todd, she decided to change the game. She waltzed over to the cooler, hoisted it up, drew back, and heaved the contents directly at me. I only had a second to duck and drop and scream again before a mass of slimy bellies and webbed feet slapped and pelted my body.

"*Amanda*!" In a heartbeat, Todd grabbed the cooler from her. "What the hell are you doing?"

Moments later, someone was next to me, gently lifting me out of my cowering squat. For one sweet second, I thought it was Gabe. But it wasn't. It was just Johnny Mercer. "Are you okay?" he asked. As he lifted me to my feet, his face was so close that I could see how long the lashes were on his deep-set eyes. I shivered at the frogs hopping every which way around me, but I nodded that I was all right. Johnny said, "Stay there." He took the cooler from Todd, set it on the ground, and started scooping up the runaway frogs with his broad hands and putting them inside. "I'll take them back down to the stream," he said.

I didn't move. I couldn't. But I did listen. To Todd reaming out Amanda. And she didn't like it one bit. She referred to me as a few choice synonyms for the female genitalia and then stormed off the field. Todd went after her.

Marcie came up behind me, tiptoeing over the few remaining frogs Johnny was chasing. She went to wipe some slime off my cheek but couldn't quite bring herself to touch it. "I can't believe she did that. That was *so* not cool."

"That's Amanda," I rasped.

"Are you going to be okay?" she asked.

I rubbed at a frog stain on my T-shirt, but it just smeared more. "I would have preferred it if Gabe Webber hadn't just seen me get slimed, but other than that . . ." I sighed. "I'm fab." A bigger sigh. "Hey, at least he winked at me. How about that? I got a wink 'n' wave from Gabe."

"Yeah? Great." Mar yelped and jumped out of the way as a frog hopped toward her strappy hot pink sandals. "Um . . . are you . . . gonna stay here? Like that?" she asked.

I figured I had no reason to stick around, since one, I was covered in amphibi-goo, and two, Todd and Amanda had left. Tryouts couldn't happen without them—they'd been last year's varsity co-captains, so they were guaranteed a spot, and they also judged tryouts. And I wasn't about to hang out until they made up.

"Actually, Mar, do you think you and Johnny could drop me home on your way to dance class?" I asked.

Mar managed to pick one wet blade of swamp grass off my shoulder. "Sure, Fee. No problem."

Good ol' Mar. I knew I could count on her.

Wednesday, September 25

I haven't written in a couple of weeks, so I guess I'd better make this a good one. Todd and I have come to some kind of twisted truce wherein we hate each other but don't. I'm not really sure how it works, but basically, we get done what we need to get done, but in a totally hostile way, which actually isn't hostile at all. (I just reread that and it makes no sense whatsoever. Oh well.)

Here's an example. Last week we played against Fallbrook. It was an away game and I, as water girl, had to fill up the ginormous cooler/thermos thingy (a new orange one—not the frog pot). Except, the only place to fill it was from a spigot on the side of their lame-ass school about a mile around the corner from the football field.

So I'm hauling this thing, which now weighs a ton since it's filled with water. And I can't carry it that far. It's too heavy. All the cheerleaders see me and start laughing because I'm having such a hard time. So I, of course, give them the finger. Then Todd says, "Come on! Lift! Use those pecs! Maybe they'll grow!" And then he pulls out the front of his uniform to make boobs. The girls laugh and go skipping over to the football field. But Todd comes over to me, picks up the cooler, and carries it the whole way to the bleachers for me. Doesn't say another word. Weird, I know. But what was weirder was that the minute I saw him watching me struggle with the cooler, I knew he was going to help me with it.

I don't think this is what they call a healthy relationship. Not that anyone really knows what one is. And yet, people still find each other. It's a freaking miracle, when you think about it.

Take my uncle Tommy. We saw him last weekend when we drove up to visit Nana for dinner. During the appetizers she always serves—celery sticks and Little Smokies (Little Smokies, if you don't know, are mini hot dogs in a pool of barbecuelike sauce. They look like a bowlful of little severed penises)—Nana announced that Uncle Tommy would be joining us, and that he was bringing a friend. A good friend. She told us that Uncle Tommy had gotten his real estate license and moved into a new apartment, so maybe this woman would be the next step.

Anyway, the doorbell rang, and when Dad opened it, I did a total cartoon-style double take. It was Uncle Tommy, for sure, but he looked different. He looked *great*. His hair was combed. His face was shaved. He wore a dress shirt and khakis. But it was more than just improved grooming. He was like . . . shimmering.

Nana asked, "Where's your friend?"

Uncle Tommy says, "Just outside. But first, I want to announce that we're more than just friends. We're together. We're in love."

Nana flipped out in a good way. "Oh, Tommy! A girlfriend! I'm so happy for you," etc.

But Uncle Tommy got really quiet. Then he said, "And this person's name is Alan." He stepped aside, and this absolutely gorgeous, dark-haired man walked through the door. I swear to God his eyes were the exact color of this jade pendant my mom has. *Swoon.*

So Nana says, "Is this another friend? Where's Ellen?"

Gorgeous Guy totally stifled a grin.

Uncle Tommy said, "No, Ma. Not Ellen. *Alan*. Ma, I'm gay."

Nana ran off crying but came back about five minutes later and eyeballed Alan from head to foot. She said, "Well, you're no Ellen. Have you got a job?"

Alan: "Yes, ma'am. I'm an architect."

Nana: "Got any of those diseases?"

Alan: "No, ma'am. Totally clean."

Nana: "Let's get two things straight, Mr. Totally Clean Architect. If you ever hurt my boy—body or soul—I'll break your kneecaps. And second, nobody calls me ma'am. It makes me feel like an old lady. You may call me Agnes."

Alan: "Thank you, Agnes."

Nana said, "Go on and help yourself to a Little Smokie, there, Ellen."

Dad burst out laughing. Alan laughed too, but said, "No, thank you," because he's a vegetarian.

"Vegetarian?" Nana cried. "Now that's too much!" She turned to Uncle Tommy. "You're not a vegetarian are you?"

"No, Ma," he said. "I eat meat."

Dad muttered, "I bet you do," and Mom socked him in the arm.

Uncle Tommy said, "Ma, I'm sorry if I hurt you."

"Hurt me?" she said. "For forty-three years I've watched you live a life of misery. And I suffered along with you. That was hurt. Now, after all that time . . . I'm finally not hurt, Thomas Daniel Sheehan. Not hurt. No. I'm relieved. I only wish it hadn't taken you forty-three years." She hugged Uncle Tommy and whispered, "My baby boy. My baby boy."

It would have been a perfect—albeit twisted—Hallmark moment if Dad hadn't blurted out, "Wait a minute. Are you saying you knew all *along* he was gay?"

She said, "A mother knows her son."

Uncle Tommy kissed her cheek. "Thank you, Ma."

Dad said, "I need a drink." He helped himself to a large glass of whiskey and slumped on the couch. Mom sat next to him, took his drink, swilled a mouthful of it, and then handed it back. He put his arm around her and pulled her closer. It was like they'd had a conversation without saying a single word. Like Dad had said, I don't know how to handle this. Then Mom said, I know. This is a tough one. But I'm here for you. And then Dad said, Thanks. I love you for that.

Bizarre.

But wait! It gets better. Several fat whiskeys later, Dad and I were alone at the table. He was absolutely soused. He turns to me and says, "You're not gay, are you, Fiona?"

I said, "*What*?"

Drunk Dad: "I mean, you've never had a boyfriend. And you're not exactly . . . girly."

Me: "Uh, thanks a lot there, Dad."

DD: "Nononono. I don't think there's anything wrong with the way you are."

Me: "Ohhhkay . . ."

DD: "I wouldn't want you to think you couldn't be who you really are and that we wouldn't love you for whatever or whoever you are and so you had to be somebody you didn't want to be just for us, 'cause it's not what we want for you. Ya know?"

Nope. I did not, in any sense of the word, know. "Dad, what the hell are you talking about?"

He gulped some more whiskey. "I juss don't want you to be unhappy for forty-three years. Thass all."

"Dad. *Dad.*" I thumped the table so he'd look at me. "I'm not gay, Dad. I'm just unpopular."

Dad wheezed, "Thanggod. I'sso happy to hear that." Then he passed out on his dinner plate.

Needless to say, Mom drove home.

I guess what I'm trying to say is, you just can't tell who you're going to end up with. You might spend your whole life dreaming about one type of person, only to find happiness with somebody completely different. Someone you figured you had nothing in common with just might turn out to be your dream guy. And you know he's your dream guy because you become a better person. He brings out all these great things in you that you never knew or believed were there. And if you're really lucky, you do the same for him.

It makes it even more incredible that people find each other, considering most of them are looking in the wrong places to begin with.

CHAPTER 13

BY THE TIME HALLOWEEN CAME AROUND, TODD AND I had already earned a total of forty bucks, giving us a budget of six grand for October, on top of the twenty dollars we'd banked from September's budget. Six thousand twenty was way more than our September costs had been, so I volunteered to take Sam out trick-or-treating and babysit afterward for free, just to get some time with her without Señor Shitslacks there. Marcie said she wanted to come too, so we decided to make it a "ghouls' night out." Get it? Okay, that was bad. Actually, we decided to be zombie princesses. Mar and I went crazy buying makeup and tiaras and glow-in-the-dark jewelry and crap. We got so into it. Probably because it'd been a while since either of us had dressed up for Halloween.

When we got to the Picklers' house, we could hear them from the driveway. The yelling coming from the master bedroom window was probably traveling through the whole neighborhood. She screamed that he didn't have any respect for her. He bellowed that she overreacted to everything and never gave him a moment's peace. Mar and I weren't sure what to do. The yelling stopped the instant I rang the doorbell.

Half a minute later, the door opened. "Oh, Fiona," Mrs. Pickler faltered. Her eyes darted behind me. "Come on in. Sam's in the family room." We followed her inside. "Sam? Fiona and Marcie are here."

Sam sat curled up in a corner of the couch, reading. She didn't even look up. She had dark circles under her eyes and her hair was even messier than usual. I noticed she'd chewed the nail polish off her fingers. Mrs. Pickler went back upstairs, so Mar and I sat next to Sam. "Are you okay?" I asked.

Sam stayed quiet and shrugged. Then she muttered, "I guess."

"What are you reading?" I asked.

"*Island of the Blue Dolphins*."

"Oh, I love that one," I said.

"What's it about?" Marcie asked.

Sam inhaled shakily. "A girl whose parents leave her behind on an island and she lives there by herself and has a great time. Just her and her dog." Sam wouldn't look up from her book. I saw a dark spot appear on the page. A tear.

I scooted close to her and put my arm around her shoulder. "Hey Sister-witch, don't be upset. It'll be okay. People fight sometimes."

"They fight all the time."

"Well, maybe sometimes people fight all the time, but it doesn't mean they don't like each other. Deep down."

"They don't," she muttered.

"How do you know?"

Sam turned her puffy-eyed face to me. "Because they say, 'I hate you,' and, 'I hate you too.' I've heard them." Tears spilled down her perfect cheeks. I couldn't take it. I wrapped my arms around her and squeezed.

Marcie said, "People say all kinds of things they don't mean. Especially when they're fighting."

Sam seemed to soften a bit. "They do?"

"Absolutely," Marcie said.

I lifted Sam's face. "Listen, dry your eyes. If they see you crying, they might not go out and we won't be able to have our awesome night together. Now, let's talk about something else until they're gone. Deal?"

She wiped her cheeks and forced a smile. "Deal. Can I stay up until midnight?"

"Nine."

"Eleven-thirty?"

"Ten."

"Deal."

Sam's parents finally left, and we started getting into our costumes. I pulled Sam's shredded lace gown over her. I drew even darker circles under her eyes with some eyeliner, and pinned a bloody rhinestone tiara on her head. "You make a gorgeous princess of the undead," I said.

"Thanks," she said.

"All you need is a prince," Marcie said.

Sam's face turned bright pink. She stooped down to adjust her torn white stockings, even though they looked fine.

"Are you blushing?" I teased. "Why are you hiding?" She started giggling and shaking her head no. "*Samantha Louise Pickler*! *Spill*! *Now*!" I started tickling her ribs. She wriggled and laughed, and finally said, "*Okay*!" so I let her go.

"What's his name?" I demanded.

Sam grinned. "Logan Clarke. He's in my math and science classes."

"I knew it!" I cried. "So what's he like? Does he like you back?"

Sam shrugged coyly. "I dunno. Maybe. He's nice. Super cute."

Marcie and I both squealed like we used to in middle school whenever we saw our favorite boy-band on TV. We pulled Sam to the floor between us and peppered her with questions. How long had she liked him? (Only a few weeks.) Did she ever talk to him? (Sometimes.) Did he ever talk to *her* first? (Sometimes.) Did she know that if he talked to her first, that it meant he probably liked her? (It did? Omigod.) Did he ever seem nervous around her? (No, but she was nervous around him.) Did he ever mention doing anything together? (Actually, he did say maybe they could do some homework together sometime.)

"Omigod, he totally digs you!" I said.

"Do you think?" Sam said.

"Totally!" Mar said.

All three of us squealed this time. We were so hyper. Sam grabbed her trick-or-treat bag and we spilled out of the house laughing and jumping around like total dorks. It was awesome.

We were in such good moods, we even decided to hit Todd's house for candy. Sam rang the doorbell, and when it opened, this hideous, rubber monster face roared at us. Sam screamed. Todd started laughing and took off the mask. I yelled, "Put it back on! Put it back on! Your hideousness is terrifying!"

Todd did a fake yuk-yuk-yuk at my joke. "What are you guys supposed to be? Is it Prom Night Massacre or something?"

Sam sighed at Todd's obvious stupidity. "We're zombie princesses, Todd. Can't you tell?" She stuck her arms straight out in front of her and said, "BRAINS! BRAINS!"

I patted Sam on the head and said, "Sorry, Sam. You're wasting your time with this one."

Todd rolled his eyes at me. "Zombie princesses, huh?" He looked us up and down. "I see. Nice job, Squirt. Hey Marcie."

"Hi Todd."

He gave my lower half an extralong stare. "Hey, hold on. Well, look at you, Princess. You stayed dry! Congratulations!" He reached into his candy bowl, and while he dropped a handful in Sam's bag, I positioned myself directly behind her and gave Todd the finger so she wouldn't see it.

"Why do you keep flashing your IQ like that?" Todd said.

I gave him the same yuk-yuk-yuk back.

"By the way, Princess," Todd said, "our budget is due tomorrow. Did you do it?"

"*Me*? No. Did you?"

"Nope."

"Crap."

"How long are you guys going to be out?" he asked.

"I dunno. An hour?"

"I'll stop by Sam's and we'll hammer it out. That okay with you, Squirt?"

"Fine with me," she said, examining the contents of her bag.

Todd put in an extra handful of candy. "See ya then."

Sam grinned at Todd. "*Gracias*, Señor," she said. "Sayonara."

Todd raised an eyebrow but said, "Have fun trick-or-treating, Squirt. Make sure Fiona takes lots of potty breaks." He waved and shut the door before I had a chance to fire back.

"What did he mean by that?" Sam asked.

"Nevermind," Marcie and I said together. We hooked our arms into Sam's and set off.

"Todd isn't that bad," Sam said.

"You're not fake-married to him," I said.

"Do you have to really be boyfriend or girlfriend with the person you fake-marry?" She kicked an orange, decapitated chrysanthemum blossom down the street.

"God, no," I said. "Don't make me puke."

"Besides," Marcie said, "some people already have boyfriends or girlfriends, but they didn't get matched together."

"You guys don't have boyfriends, right?"

"Nope," I said.

"Todd has a girlfriend, though," Marcie said.

"Is she fake-married to someone else too?" Sam asked.

"You'll never guess who," I said.

"Don't make me guess, then," Sam said. "Just tell me."

I whispered, "Gabe Webber."

"*Gabe*?" Sam said. I shushed her. She dropped her voice to a whisper. "Doesn't Marcie know about him?" She waved to some other trick-or-treaters we passed—a dinosaur, a skeleton, and a mermaid.

"Yes, I know about Gabe," Marcie said with a sigh. I guess after nine years, she was getting sick of the subject. Oh well. Too bad.

Sam said, "Wouldn't it be great if you could trade?"

"That's what I said!" I cried. "But we're not allowed."

"Well, look on the bright side," Sam said. "Maybe Gabe's not that great after all."

"Oh yes, he is," I said. "He's perfect. Right, Mar? Tell her."

Marcie kicked at some soggy yellow leaves and nodded. "Yes, Gabe is all right. In fact—"

"All right?" I cut her off. "He's more than all right. He's gorgeous, for one. Totally sweet, for two. Don't you remember when he picked you up after he accidentally knocked you down, Mar?"

"How could I forget? You keep talking about it," she said.

"Hey, I can't help it if I have a major weak spot for blatant gallantry. Talk about a dream guy. And he, like, oozes cool. He's so confident about everything. Never freaks out. That I've seen, anyway. I've never once seen him with a bad temper. Have you, Mar?" Marcie shrugged.

"He sounds *per*-fect," Sam said.

"He is," I agreed.

Marcie sighed really loud this time. "Fiona. Please. I can't take it anymore."

I elbowed her. "All right, I know, I know. I'm sorry. I go on and on about him to you. I'm sure you're so over the subject. Okay, okay, I won't mention him again . . . tonight." I giggled. Sam giggled with me.

"Let's try this house," Marcie said.

By the time we finished trick-or-treating, Sam's bag was almost too heavy for her. She carried it over her shoulder and told everyone that it had a couple of spare heads in it in case she wanted a snack. Too cute.

We got back to her house, and she dumped the loot into a huge pile on the family room carpet. We decided to watch *Sixteen Candles* again, since we hadn't gotten through it before. Marcie and I made Mexican-flavored International Corn (taco seasoning and corn oil), and Sam alternated between handfuls of popcorn and fistfuls of candy.

Halfway through the movie, the doorbell rang. Todd. Budget. Damn. I was never going to get to finish watching this movie. Then again, I'd seen it so many times that I knew every line by heart. I hopped up to get the door.

"TRICK-OR-TREAT," TODD SAID.

"I wish it was a trick, because seeing you is no treat," I said.

Todd handed me a plastic grocery bag. "Our leftover candy," he said. "For Sam. Not you."

"You know, even when you do something nice you manage to be a jackass," I said. "It's remarkable, really. If only there were a way to harness this talent."

He pushed past me into the house. We set up in the dining room. We sat on either side of the table with Todd's *Trying the Knot* packet spread out between us. "I saw your mother's article in the *Daily Ledger*," he said.

"What? When was she in the paper?"

"This morning. Didn't you see it? Oh, right, sorry. I forgot you're illiterate."

"Very funny, Señor Shitslacks. What'd it say?"

"It talked about her campaign against the marriage ed course, and how the school board insists that we keep the course going, even while they're debating it, yada yada."

Between going to school, buying Halloween stuff, and being at Sam's, I hadn't been home all day. But that didn't really make me feel like less of an ass for not knowing about Mom's article. I'd have to check it out as soon as I got home.

"All right, Princess, let's get this over with," Todd said, pulling out the budget sheet. "We earned forty dollars of real cash, so we have six thousand bucks. Plus the twenty we banked from September. Damn, this month we're rich."

"You do the math; I'll fill in the sheet," I said. "Start with living expenses."

"We already had the big house last month, so we're not changing that."

"Fine with me." I wrote it down. "Home A. Mortgage two thousand. Utilities five hundred."

"That leaves $3,520," Todd said. "Let's get all the extras this time. Cell phone, Internet, *and* cable. I hated not having cable."

"Whatev." I filled in the sheet. I heard Mar and Sam crack up at something in the other room. Probably Long Duk Dong. "How much is left?" I asked.

Todd subtracted in his head. "That'd be 3,365."

"Really?" I said. "Right on."

"Cars next. A luxury hybrid for me, and nothing for you."

"Why don't I get a car?" I cried.

"You're a townie. You ride your bike."

"Screw that," I said. "We're rich. I want a luxury hybrid too." I wrote down two hybrids. "Now how much?"

"Twenty-five sixty-five."

"We still have that much?"

He double-checked the math. "Apparently."

I looked at what was left to budget for. "I don't think we can possibly spend all of it. Even if we go for top-of-the-line food and entertainment—should we?"

"Of course."

"Then we still have over sixteen hundred left."

He spoke into an invisible microphone. "What will our contestants choose? Bank it or blow it?" The dork.

"We should bank it," I said.

"I think blow it."

"On what?" I asked.

"Forty-two-inch plasma TV, baby."

"What do we need that for?"

He leaned back and laced his fingers behind his head. "The sweet cable package we have now. All the sports channels. I'm not watching the games on some nineteen-inch piece of crap."

"You're a lunatic. This is *fake*. Okay. You take half and spend it on whatever you want," I said.

"Hookers?"

"Something we could *both* use."

"Hookers?"

"For the *house*. Ugh! Why are you making this so difficult?"

"Why not?"

I ignored him and did the division myself. "We'll put $807.50 toward a new TV, and the same into savings. Done. Hardly worth the effort."

Todd gathered together everything but the budget sheet and walked back around the table. "I'm outta here," he said.

"So you'll turn in the budget, right?" He patted me on the head. "Thanks, little woman. What a good little wife."

I smacked his hand away. "Kiss my ass."

"Wouldn't you love it."

"Only if I were a dog, like you."

"You're not too far off," he said, and strolled out.

When I got back to the family room, Sam was asleep on the couch with a half-eaten piece of red licorice clutched in her fist. "She crashed," Mar said. "I think she was literally high on sugar."

"Seriously," I said. "I thought she was going to start free-basing Pixy Stix."

"Todd gone? You guys get done?"

"Yup. He's such a dickhead. I don't understand why he makes the extra effort to be a prick. Otherwise, he might be a decent guy."

"Speaking of decent guys, remember at the dance last month when you, me, and Johnny pulled that prank?"

"Oh yeah, Johnny. I know, he's actually an okay guy. He's kind of a riot, too, sometimes. Did you notice that?"

"I know, but Fiona—"

"Guess what he said to me that night? He said that people with class are like people with herpes."

"Listen Fio—wait, he said what?"

"Hold on—no, that wasn't it. That couldn't have been it. What was it he said? It was hysterical."

"Tell me later. Listen, Fiona, I need to talk to you about something."

"Oh! I remember what it was! If you have class, then you

don't talk about it, just like if you have herpes. That was it. Omigod . . ." I clapped my hands together. "I just got the best idea to prank Todd! Oh, this is priceless. But I need a speaker set for my iPod. You don't have one, do you? It needs to have some kind of alarm function. And I'll probably have to download some software."

Marcie slammed the couch with her fists. "Dammit, Fiona! I'm trying to tell you something, but you just won't shut up for five seconds so I can say it! I'm so sick of listening to you blab on and on about Todd, and pranking him, and how miserable your life is, and everything. I can't take it! Other people have lives and problems too. But you never notice because you're always too wound up in your own drama. You're totally self-absorbed and inconsiderate lately. I'm sorry, Fiona, but I can't handle it. I need a break from you for a while. I gotta get home."

She grabbed her stuff and was out the door before her words stopped echoing in my brain. Once they did, I felt the full blow of the realization that my best friend—my only friend—had just screamed at me and walked out. Never in my life had I thought Mar could be so mean. She'd never blown up at me like that before. So I had no idea what to do about it. I just stood there dazed, hoping that she'd cool down sometime soon.

Thursday, October 31

I have a few things to say about marriage, as I see it. First of all, what is the point? Is there any reason to put yourself through torture—or to torture those around you—just to say you're married? Where's the payoff? And second, if you get married just to have kids, forget it. They'll know it and it will screw them up royally. So again, what's the point?

Sex can't be the reason, because if you ask me, you have much better odds of getting laid if you have the entire population of the Earth available to you, rather than just ONE person. And by the way, how unbelievably boring would it be to have sex with the same person for fifty years? To me, marriage seems to be an archaic institution left over from the age when survival of the species was important, and people didn't live past thirty-five years old.

It's time for marriage to go the way of the dodo: fondly remembered, but utterly extinct.

CHAPTER 15

GIVING MAR SOME SPACE WASN'T TOO HARD, OTHER than having to ride my bike to school the next day. And sit by myself in homeroom. I just hid in the back and read *P&P*. At the end of the day, Principal Miller came over the PA to make the Friday announcements.

"Good afternoon, students," she said. "First, I want to wish the chess team good luck in their tournament. Here's hoping you make some king-size moves. Second, I'd like to announce that the senior marriage ed couple who earned the most real-world money for the month of October is Todd Harding and Fiona Sheehan. You two have won five complimentary pounds of sausage from Steuben's Sausage Shop, located at the corner of Main Street and Dover. 'Steuben's Sausage Shop. When only a hot, meaty sausage will satisfy . . . come in for a pound at Steuben's.' What? Oh, good Chri—" The PA squealed as she switched off the mic so we wouldn't hear her swearing. Not that we could've; we were laughing too loud.

After a few seconds and some more PA feedback, she came back on and announced that next week we wouldn't have counseling sessions. (Yay!) Instead, seniors were to report to the gym first period Monday morning for marriage ed trust games. (What the *freak*?) Rumor had it the trust games were Maggie Klein's bright idea. It seemed a lot of couples were failing to bond. So she wanted us to do some lame team-building crap to get couples to like each other. Yeah, good luck with that.

I figured Mar would have cooled off by then for sure, so maybe we could make a big joke about it. Plus, I decided the trust games were a gift from heaven, because all the seniors would be in one spot, giving me the perfect opportunity to pull my latest excellent prank on Señor Shitslacks.

But Monday came, and Mar didn't pick me up for school again. She must've still been pissed off. So I rode my bike, which wasn't easy with a new iPod speaker/alarm set in my backpack. I sat alone again in homeroom. Then first period came, and all the seniors filed into the gym.

Mr. Evans was running the dry mop around the perimeter, and grumbled when we walked over where he'd just cleaned. I dropped my stuff next to the plug under the clock and PA speaker. I plugged in my speakers, popped in my iPod, and set the alarm to go off in about forty-five minutes. I covered it with my stretched-out gray hoodie, and looked around for Mar. She was already across the gym. She must've walked right by me but never said a word.

Maggie Klein darted and yipped around like a hopped-up Chihuahua. She was giving it her all and then some; I'll say that much for her.

"All right, we're going to start with the trust fall," she yelled once our mumbled complaints dwindled down.

"Everyone get into a circle with your partner next to you. In this exercise, one partner will fall backward. The other partner will catch. The idea is to trust your partner not to let you fall."

Now, Maggie Klein was smart enough to realize that many of the guys, like Johnny Mercer for one, were quite a bit larger than their fake wives. So she instructed only the girls to fall, and the guys catch. Which would have been fine. Except for Zoë Kovac, who, in addition to her Eastern European name, had also inherited an Eastern European weightlifter's build. She'd already been offered full rides to three colleges for playing field hockey. Her partner, Izzy McCully, on the other hand, looked like he hadn't had a real meal in a decade. This guy was skin on a stick. And about six inches shorter than his fake wife.

"Okay, let's go around the room, one couple at a time," Maggie Klein shouted.

One by one, the girls fell back and their partners caught them under the armpits.

"Very nice! Well done!" she called. She made us clap for each pair.

Right before our turn, I whispered to Todd, "You'd better not try to cop a feel when I fall."

"Ha," he said. "Cop a feel of what?"

"Just don't drop me."

"I can't promise anything."

When he caught me, I looked at Mar to see if she was applauding. Not only was she not clapping, she wasn't even looking. She was staring at the wall. It had to be deliberate.

Johnny was clapping like a windup monkey, though. What was his problem?

When it got to be Mar and Johnny's turn, I didn't watch, either. Or clap. Two could play, as they say. I did peek just a bit to see if she saw me not watching. I don't know if she did. I think Johnny might have, though, so maybe he'd tell her.

I definitely watched Gabe catching Amanda with his gorgeous guns. And I swear I saw him cup her boobs. From the look on Todd's face, he saw the same thing.

Then it was Zoë Kovac's turn.

I could tell Maggie Klein realized the problem at the last second, because she made this squeaky inhalation. But it was too late. Zoë fell backward into the trembling arms of Izzy McCully, and continued falling with him beneath her. They thudded to the floor, and all that could be seen of Izzy were his spindly arms and legs flailing from Zoë's sides, making her look like a Hindu goddess on her back.

Todd's bonehead buddies just lost it laughing. Zoë rolled off poor Izzy, got up, and kicked him in the side. Mr. Evans rushed over and pulled Izzy to his feet. Izzy couldn't quite catch his breath, plus his head hurt, so Maggie Klein sent him to the nurse.

"Okay, okay, let's try something else," she called over the hysterics. "I have twenty-foot ropes here for each of you. Each couple. Each couple should come get a rope and then line up with the rope stretched between you."

Todd and I went up to get a rope at the exact same time as Amanda and Gabe. I thought, *perfect*, because Amanda would probably talk to Todd, and maybe Gabe would talk to me. So I started inventing blindingly witty things to say to him about the lame-ass trust games. But then Amanda fastened herself to Todd, and Gabe glared at me like it was my fault that Todd was drooling on Gabe's fake wife.

I decided to suck it up and ask, "Something wrong?"

Gabe looked away from me and answered, "I dunno. Something wrong with you?"

I was standing there like a moron, trying to figure out what the hell he'd meant by that remark, when I realized that Todd and Gabe had grabbed either end of the same rope. Now they were locked in this death stare to see who got the damn thing.

"I have this one," Todd said.

"I don't think so," Gabe said.

"Let go of it, Webber," Todd said.

"I had it first."

"Like hell you did."

Meanwhile, Johnny Mercer came up and tried to say hi to me, but I wasn't paying any attention because I wanted to see if Todd and Gabe were going to throw down. Finally, Amanda stepped in, picked up a whole different rope, and thrust it at Gabe's chest for him to carry. Gabe tossed his end and walked away with Amanda trailing behind him. Johnny mumbled something I couldn't understand. Todd gave me the end of the rope Gabe had dropped and dragged me back to the middle of the gym. He positioned himself right next to Amanda. Which meant . . . ? Yup, I was standing next to Gabe. Sophia Sheridan lined up on the other side of him with Mar and Johnny next to her. Then Sophia said, "I'm totally excited to do this!"

And Gabe—get this—said, "A totally excited woman is my favorite kind."

What?

I thought a "totally together" woman (i.e., *me*) was his favorite kind! But oh no. I had been a complete and utter dope. Gabe didn't have a favorite kind. Gabe had a favorite line . . . to feed girls. What an idiot I was. I turned my back to him and gave an aggravated yank on my rope. Todd laughed and yanked the rope harder. I yanked it back. Then he yanked again. Then I did. We tried to pull each other off balance.

Well, Gabe must've been intent on pissing off Todd, because he pulled on their rope so hard that it popped out of Amanda's hand and nearly clipped her in the face. She leered at Gabe and sauntered forward, plucked the end of the rope from the ground, and tugged it as hard as she could. Gabe lost his balance and nearly fell, and Sophia Sheridan cracked up. Then she started pulling on her own rope. Pretty soon, other couples were doing the same thing, and before we knew it, we were in a tug-of-war marathon.

It was at this choice moment that Principal Miller popped in to check on things. Maggie Klein hadn't seemed to notice, because she was shouting rather unprofessionally, "*Stop it.* Just hold the rope! Pick up a rope, line up, and *stand still.* How hard is that? *Hold the ends. Stop it!*"

"How is everything going?" Principal Miller called above the chaos.

Maggie Klein wheeled around. "Oh! Great! I mean, fine!"

"Was the student whom I just passed in the hallway a casualty?"

"Yes. Well, it was accidental. I'm sure Iggy will be okay."

"Izzy," Principal Miller corrected her.

"Is he what? Is he okay? I'm sure he is," Maggie Klein stammered.

"No. The young man's name is Izzy. Not Iggy."

Maggie Klein shook herself. "Of course. Of course. I meant that. I knew that." Her eyes narrowed the slightest bit and her face lit up. She said, "Would you care to join us?" so loudly that Principal Miller had no choice but to accept.

The principal almost got out of it when none of the guys offered to partner with her, but then Mr. Evans dropped his mop and strode over. He took one of the twenty-foot ropes and offered one end to Principal Miller with a slight bow. She let out a mini giggle, took it, and curtsied back.

"The object of this game," Maggie Klein yelled way too cheerfully, "is to create a knot and then work together as partners and as a group to untie it. So without letting go of your rope, everyone start moving around the space; step over the other ropes or go under them. Whichever. Just do *not* let go."

Again, Maggie Klein hadn't anticipated what seventy-some pairs of seniors could do. Amanda twirled herself around Todd, which unfortunately drew Gabe even closer to them. I did my best to knot myself into Mar's vicinity so that she'd talk to me, but she kept twisting away. Instead, Johnny got pulled right in my face.

Within thirty seconds, we had made a knot, sure. But Gabe and Todd were in an almost fistfight (only almost, because they were tied up), Amanda was standing there looking bored, Callie Brooks was crying, I was trying to squeeze by Johnny to get to Mar, and Mr. Evans was tied inextricably to Principal Miller with his face smashed into her boobs.

"Ms. Klein?" Principal Miller—still knotted—shouted over the sobs, screams, shouts, and shrieks of laughter, "I believe I have reached the end of my *rope*."

Everyone laughed at that one, and only then did I realize that Principal Miller would be there for my prank on Todd. Not good. I tried desperately to get out of the damn knot so I could run and turn off my iPod, but I was stuck. And it was too late.

A deafening honk came from the direction of the PA speaker. It was my speaker set blaring my downloaded attempt to mimic the PA bell. I briefly hoped no one heard it and that they'd keep talking and screaming. But it was so loud, everyone shut up. I froze. My electronically garbled voice boomed from the speakers. "Attention, Todd Harding. The doctor's office called to say that your herpes test has come back positive. Please report to the nurse's office immediately. Again, Todd Harding report to the nurse's office. You have herpes. Thank you."

A bunch of people started laughing, but not for long, because Principal Miller blew a gasket. "*Who did that?*" she yelled. I swiveled as best I could to see Todd. I knew he was going to throw me under the bus. If not him, then Amanda for sure. But not only did Todd say nothing, I saw him nudge and shush Amanda when she opened her mouth to turn me in. And she obeyed. How random. They must've figured Todd would get dragged into the whole pranking mess, so they kept quiet.

"No one leaves until I find out who was responsible for this disturbance." Principal Miller started wriggling out of her pseudo-bondage position with the janitor. Everyone dropped their ropes and started untying themselves. Todd and Amanda stepped out of the tangled rope like it wasn't even there. I shimmied out of the mess, looking back and forth between my speaker set and where Gabe was holding on to Mar's arms to keep her balanced while Johnny undid a huge knot around her knee. After a few minutes, we all were finally loose. Principal Miller stalked over to my stuff and found the speaker set.

"Whose things are these?" she demanded.

It was pretty obvious that she could identify me by my backpack, so I raised my hand. "Mine," I said.

"Fiona Sheehan. Is this your electronic equipment?"

I started to answer, but Johnny Mercer yelled, "No! That's mine."

Principal Miller glared at him. "Jonathan Mercer?" She checked the label in the hoodie. "Am I to believe that this woman's sweatshirt belongs to *you*?"

I tried to claim it, but Johnny stepped between me and Principal Miller and said, "It's my equipment, but someone else's stuff. Don't know whose. I just used it to cover my speakers." He loped up to Principal Miller with his hands in his pockets. "I was just pranking Todd. Trying to be funny."

"You think it's funny to spread salacious lies about someone's personal life and health?"

Johnny stopped dead still. "No ma'am. I guess not."

"No, it isn't. I will confiscate this electronic equipment until such time as I think your behavior warrants its return."

"Um . . . okay," Johnny said. "Sorry."

"The person to whom you should apologize is Todd Harding. Go on."

Johnny took his hands out of his pockets and hammered his fists on his thighs. He turned and shuffled up to Todd. "Sorry, Todd," he said.

Todd nodded. "No problem, Mercer." They shook hands. It was all so convincing, I wasn't sure whether Todd knew it had really been me or not. But as soon as he let go of Johnny's hand, he glanced at me and winked. He knew. Judging from the scowl on Amanda's face, so did she.

Principal Miller declared the trust games over, instructed Maggie Klein to clean up the gym, and ordered us back to class. I grabbed my stuff. I wanted to get Johnny alone to thank him, but Principal Miller was still reaming him out, so I left it for later. As I turned to leave, Amanda was suddenly in my face. "Why do you always have to be such a bitch?" she asked.

I leaned into her. "I dunno. When it comes to bitches, you're the expert, so you tell me."

Amanda drew herself up and tossed her fake yellow hair. "Just leave Todd the hell alone, Princess Pisspants."

"Tell him to leave *me* alone," I cried. "He started all this. Which is amazing, considering how deep your claws are in him. I'm surprised he can take a dump without your say-so." I shouldered past her and left the gym. Out in the hallway, Mar was waiting for me. Thank God. Finally. "Mar," I said, "I feel terrible about Johnny."

"Good," she barked. "You should feel terrible. Now do you see how other people have to pay for your selfishness, Fiona? Are you finally getting it?" Before I could answer, she spun around and stormed off.

I was pretty sure the questions were rhetorical anyway.

CHAPTER 16

AFTER SCHOOL, I LOOKED ALL OVER FOR JOHNNY Mercer so I could apologize. I finally found him outside the administration offices talking to his friend Noah.

"Johnny!" I called as I jogged to catch up to them. Noah waved, said, "See ya," and headed off. "Look," I said, "I'm really sorry about this morning. You didn't have to take the blame like that."

Johnny shrugged his wide shoulders and rocked back and forth on his heels. "I never get in trouble," he said, "so I figured I might as well say it was me, because she'd probably let me slide."

"Did she?" I asked.

He waved me off. "Everything's fine. No problem." He seemed to develop a sudden fascination with the blue and white linoleum floor.

"Oh, phew."

He reached out to one of the lockers next to us and spun the lock. "And I'll get your equipment back for you, too. Don't worry."

"Wow, okay. Great. Thanks." I gave him a friendly punch in the arm.

"If there's anything else you need, let me know," he said. He looked right in my eyes. "Anything," he said.

That loaded "anything" hung in the air long enough for several possible anythings to zip through my mind. Get a coffee. See a movie. Cry. Make out. "I gotta go," I blurted. I started walking backward. "I'm really late for practice. There might be a water emergency by now. But thanks again."

He took a step toward me. "Give 'em some spit for me."

I fake-laughed and waved. "Sure thing. Sorry again. See ya."

He waved back. "See ya, Fiona."

I spun around, and half ran for the gym.

I stopped at the locker room to fill the water cooler, and then dragged it out to the basketball court. But instead of the usual pep-o-rific cheer routines, there was total silence in the gym. The squad had bunched together and were watching something on the floor mats. Even old Mrs. O'Toole had gotten out of her usual napping chair to take charge. I got closer and saw one of the cheerleaders, Judith Norton, flat on her back, with a pair of EMTs crouched over her. They put one of those big plastic collars around her neck and a plastic splint on her leg. Then they slowly rolled her onto a backboard. They lifted the board onto a gurney and rolled her out.

"What happened?" I asked Simone Dawson.

"Jamar tossed her but missed the catch. They say she broke her ankle. But she has to get her spine checked too."

"Oh my God," I said. "Is anyone else hurt?"

"No. Jamar's pretty upset, though."

"I bet." After a few beats, I said, "So I guess practice is canceled then?" I wasn't being selfish. It just popped into my head. I swear.

"No way," Simone said, straightening up. "Next Friday is homecoming. We've got the pep rally at the bonfire before. We're supposed to showcase Catch the Fever. You've seen it. You know, the one with the mount at the end? That big pyramid stunt? Well, there was a pyramid. Not anymore, I guess. We'll have to figure something out."

"Bummer," I said. "But I'm sure you guys will fix it." I tipped the cooler onto its edge, rolled it over to the bleachers, hoisted it up onto the bench, and sat next to it. There was no need for cups. The cheerleaders just refilled their water bottles.

Once the ambulance left, Mrs. O'Toole muttered something about the damn dangerous modern mounts these days and hobbled off to call Judith's parents and Principal Miller. Everyone else started darting around the basketball court, squawking and gobbling about what to do about the homecoming pep rally. They needed all twelve bodies to pull off the stunt at the end of Catch the Fever. It had taken them all season to get it right.

Takisha King said, "What about pulling someone up from JV?"

"We can't," Amanda said. "Junior varsity's got an away game that night."

Todd stepped toward the middle of the group and waved them in for a huddle. They all flocked around him. I could see Todd talking, but couldn't hear him. Whatever he said must have been pretty funny, though, because everyone suddenly burst into hysterics. Ponytails and boobs bouncing all over the place; bawks and even a few whinnies echoing through the gym. Then Todd said something else that had the same effect as a bucket of liquid nitrogen thrown at them. The girls got as still as ice and gave Todd these bewildered looks. Then, one by one, they turned and looked at me.

Holy crap. What were they up to?

Amanda became visibly upset. Well, horrified and revolted would be more accurate. She stomped her feet and shook her head back and forth. Todd whispered something else in her perky pink ear and she calmed down slightly. She threw her hands up like she was surrendering to alien invaders and stalked off to the locker room.

Todd came toward me with the squad trailing behind him like a street gang of angry thugs with breasts. He stood in front of me and put his hands on his hips. As if on cue, and in perfect synchrony, the other cheerleaders put their hands on their hips too. Bunch of animatronic robot turkeys. I would have laughed, but something about the scene suddenly turned the air in my lungs to glue.

"Welcome to the squad, Fiona," Takisha said.

"Huh?" I squeaked. My mind raced forward, and the awful truth of what she meant filtered out of all the possible interpretations. "No."

"Yes," Todd said. "You're Judith's replacement."

"No, I'm not."

"You are."

This was a joke. Some kind of setup. Surely, this had to

be an elaborate prank Todd was pulling. One that involved Judith Norton breaking her ankle. He'd have gone that far just to get at me, right? Right?

Wrong.

"You've been watching all season," Takisha said. "You know the cheers."

It was true. I did. In fact, I often had trouble falling asleep at night because monstrous things like *We! We've got it! The fire inside is Eagle pride! Yes, we! We've got it! You other punks should step aside!* kept repeating and repeating in my head until I prayed for death. But knowing the cheers and actually performing them were two different balls of wax. Well, one was a ball of wax. The other one was a live hand grenade that had just landed at my feet.

I jumped up and started waving my hands, mostly to hide the fact that they were trembling. "*Forget it.*"

Todd said, "Come on, Princess, you won't have to do any climbing. You can be a spotter or even a base and Takisha will take Judith's place. All we really need is a warm body. But yours will have to do." Some of the robot turkeys giggled.

"*Ha-HA*," I yelled at him with the most sarcasm two syllables could carry. Todd took a step closer to me. The robot turkeys followed in unison again and I swear to God, I thought they were about to start clapping and chanting, *One of us. One of us. Eagles never make a fuss*, and then surround me and tear into my flesh with their perfectly straight, chemically bleached fangs.

Todd turned on the charm usually reserved for Maggie Klein and warbled, "Please, Fiona."

I scanned the makeup-spackled faces whose beady eyes looked everywhere except at me. I figured I had one way out. "I'll only do it," I said, already mentally congratulating myself on my brilliant escape, "if Amanda asks me. Nicely." There. I knew there was no way in hell that Amanda could muster the civility to ask me to help her. I was free.

"Come on—" Todd began to object. But I cut him off. "No, Todd. It's a deal-breaker. She's the co-captain and where is she? She couldn't even stand to be here to ask me." Then I decided to take it one step further, which, in retrospect, was probably too far. I leaned in and said, "How do I know that bitch isn't going to try to break *my* ankle? Or my neck?"

A wave of rage washed over Todd's face the likes of which I hadn't seen since the hot dog incident. He yanked my arm and pulled me toward the swinging doorway leading to the rest of the school. I had visions of him booting me out like I was being tossed from a bar for being drunk and disorderly. But he didn't. He just pulled me out into the hallway and stood me up against the wall.

What happened next, I can't fully explain. Maybe I was overwhelmed by the robot turkey assault. Maybe I was scared that Todd was about to kill me.

All I know is, without any warning, I started to cry.

"What the hell?" Todd said, clearly caught off guard by my burst of waterworks. He pushed back from me. "What the *hell*?"

"Oh, please," I said, smearing the tears off my cheeks with my palms. "Don't tell me you've never seen a girl cry before. You're dating the queen of melodrama."

The mention of Amanda snapped Todd back. "What the hell is it with you and her, anyway?"

I sniffled and wiped my drippy nose on my sweatshirt sleeve. "She's always attacking me. I just defend myself."

"Oh, bullshit. You give as much as you get. Besides, don't you ever think there might be a reason she feels compelled to attack you?"

"Well, I have considered the possibility that she has rabies," I said.

Todd rolled his eyes. "Your sympathy is overwhelming."

"Your sarcasm is overrated."

"Come on. Forget Amanda. I need you to do this for me. Help out the squad. Please."

"Why should I?" I asked, totally milking my pouty state.

"Because, Princess," he said. "Because I'm asking you to."

And that was it. Here was Señor Shitslacks, the No-necked Neanderthal, standing in front of me asking me for a favor on no greater basis than the fact that we were united in fake marriage.

And here I was saying yes.

"Fine," I mumbled. "I'll do it. But you have to make Amanda be nice to me. Decent, anyway."

Todd closed his blue eyes and opened them again. "Done. Thank you."

I fished a half-used tissue out of my pocket and blew my nose. I said, "Let's be clear that I'm not hauling around that damn orange water cooler anymore, either."

"No problem."

"And listen, I don't want to just be standing there looking

like some goon in a uniform. I want you to teach me the steps or moves or whatever it is you call them in cheerleaderese."

"Do you think you can handle it?"

I flashed back to the five years of ballet lessons I'd had as a kid. I was no Anna Pavlova. I shrugged. "I have no idea."

Todd held open the swinging door into the gym. "Well, let's go find out."

I shoved my soggy tissue back into my pocket. "What a day," I said. "I didn't think it could get much worse than this morning. God, I feel like such an ass for getting Johnny in trouble."

"Mercer's a big boy," Todd said. "He can handle himself."

"I still feel like a jerk."

"Well, get used to it," he said, "because practice is about to start."

"Perfect," I said.

"And anyway, that announcement prank you pulled?"

"Yeah?"

"Nice one."

We walked back into the gym together.

After practice, I barely made it home on my bike. Every muscle, ligament, and tendon in my body burned. As did my throat. As did my brain. Basic human decency and self-preservation prevent me from revealing any more details of that first cheer practice. The robot turkeys had made it look so easy. After all, cheerleading must be a no-brainer if they could do it.

Well, it wasn't. And that's all I'm going to say about that day.

A WEEK LATER, I WAS STILL SORE BEYOND BELIEF. I'D had no idea how out of shape I was. I knew I didn't exercise beyond riding my bike. Still, I'd expected to have a little more resilience than, say, my arthritic Nana. The first thing I did every morning when I got to school was dig my bottle of ibuprofen out of the bottom of my locker and pop a few. It took a while for them to kick in, though. On Tuesday it wasn't until my counseling session with Maggie Klein that I could actually sit in a chair without feeling like someone had punched me in the ass with a fistful of knives.

"Welcome, Todd. Welcome, Fiona. Okay. How are things going?" Maggie Klein crossed her legs, tilted her head to the right, and clasped her hands in her lap. Classic counselor pose. Todd and I both shrugged. I didn't bother with eye contact. Frankly, I was distracted by the empty candy wrappers scattered near the trash can. And the piles of papers everywhere, which looked to be photocopies of the same thing.

"Are those the kind of shrugs that mean everything's going fine? Or shrugs that mean things are too bad to even talk about?" Her head tilted even further. For a second I pictured it snapping off and rolling across the floor, picking up sticky candy wrappers on its way.

I was pretty sure Maggie Klein expected us to say that things sucked, because when Todd said, "Everything's fine," her eyebrows shot up toward the ceiling. "Really?" she asked. I gave the single-shoulder shrug and nodded once.

"Well!" Maggie Klein clapped her hands in front of her face and pulled her head upright, finally. My neck had been aching just watching her. She was clearly pleased by the thought that she had somehow brought peace to two warring factions. Of course, she had absolutely nothing to do with anything. "That *is* good news." She waited for us to say something. Thank you, I guess. We didn't.

Maggie Klein reeled herself down from her counseling-induced high. "So. First, I want to congratulate you on winning the monthly prize for October. Here is your voucher for Steuben's." She held it out, but neither Todd nor I took it.

Finally, Todd snatched the voucher, saying, "I may as well take this. I know Fiona doesn't go for sausage."

I came right back with, "Todd, though—once he wraps his hands around a long, thick sausage, he can't get it in his mouth fast enough."

"*Okaylet'smoveon*," Maggie Klein said. As she pulled herself higher in her chair, she accidentally leaned on her pink scarf and semi-strangled herself. She grabbed the scarf, unwound it from her neck in a fury, and threw it on her desk. She took a cleansing breath, in and out. "Okay. Second item of business is to let you know that the real-world cash collected over the past two months totals $2,464. Remember, the winning couple would split half the amount, with the other half going to charity. So as of right now, each of you would get $616. Not too bad, huh?"

Todd and I answered with shrugs again. But I couldn't help thinking of all the ways I could spend that money. Poor Todd would probably have to turn the whole wad over to Amanda to cover her hair dye and fake tan.

"Right, then. Since we didn't get to complete all the trust games last week . . ." Maggie Klein's voice faltered. She cleared her throat. "We'll try to make up for it today with a visualization exercise. Just a little trick to help a couple build trust and bond subconsciously."

Todd said, "Sorry, Maggie, but I'm not into bondage. Even the subconscious kind."

I snort-laughed.

Maggie Klein sighed. "Just close your eyes and picture a place the two of you could enjoy as a couple. *Just do it.*"

We shut our eyes, but someone pounded on the door, so I opened mine. Todd's eyes were still closed, and he was slumped down in his soft chair. I was pretty sure he planned to fall asleep.

"Who is it?" Maggie Klein demanded of the door.

It opened a crack, and a nose poked in. "Maggie, I need to talk to you! I don't know what to do. Aaron told me he's leaving me and he's taking all the money and the twins. He can't do that, can he, Maggie? There's no divorcing, is there? Of course, he says he's not divorcing me, we're still married, he's just leaving. He says I nag him too much and I'm a control freak. Is that true? I'm not, am I? Oh, I'm sorry, are you in the middle of something? I could come back. Or should I wait? How about I just wait?"

"Sophia," Maggie Klein said through her hands clasped over her face, "I appreciate your . . . enthusiasm . . . regarding this course, but as I said yesterday in counseling, it is *not real.* Please just fill out your budget, write in your journal, and *live your life.*"

Sophia Sheridan stuck her whole head in the door. "But Aaron says—"

Maggie Klein threw her head back. "*Sophia.*" Sophia stopped. Maggie Klein sighed. "Wait outside. We'll be done here soon. Then you and I can . . . talk."

"Okay, thanks, Maggie. I'll be out here." Sophia slipped the door shut, and Maggie Klein dropped her forehead to her desk. I saw her shoulder blades rise and fall with her deep breathing. After three breaths, she sat up and said, "Okay. Where were we? Todd, are you sleeping?"

I kicked Todd and he pretended to rouse from a deep slumber. "Oh, huh? I was so engrossed in my visualization I must have dozed off."

"You *are* a gross visualization," I muttered.

"Let's not start that again, Fiona."

Jeez, couldn't she tell I was kidding?

"Todd," she said, "why don't you describe what you visualized?"

"Well, Maggie, Fiona and I are on a white-sand beach on a tropical island," Todd said.

"And what are the two of you doing together?" Maggie Klein asked.

"Fiona has just handed me a piña colada."

"Nonalcoholic, I assume. Good."

"And now she's picking up an oyster shell."

"Okay. What's she doing with the shell?"

"She's using it to scrape the dead skin off my feet. But it's difficult, because she's on all fours so her ass can be a table for my coconut cup."

I swung out and smacked Todd in the shoulder. "All fours? Listen, if I had a shell that could cut skin, you'd better believe it wouldn't be your feet I'd slice."

"Fiona!" Maggie Klein snapped.

I ignored her. "Let's just say that your drink wouldn't be the only nut I'd hand you."

"*Fiona*," Maggie Klein bellowed. "Please!" It wasn't a request. She took a deep breath and let it out in little bursts. Then did it again. She took a third breath and closed her eyes. As she exhaled slowly, she made a downward motion with her hands as though pushing the bad vibes out of her body. She opened her eyes and fake-smiled. "Fiona, your hostility is severely impeding any hope of progress here."

"*My* hostility? I'm not the one who—"

"I'm afraid our time is up." She bolted to open the door before I could even finish. Totally unfair. She was so biased toward Todd. Plus, it was obvious now she blamed me for my mother's activism against this course, but whatever. As long as it got us out of counseling early, I didn't care. "Keep up the good work on your budget and journals," she said. As we left, Sophia Sheridan slid past us into the office.

"Catch you at practice, Princess," Todd said, and swaggered off.

"*Sí*, Señor. *Adios*," I called after him.

On my way to class, I turned a corner and found myself on a direct collision course with Johnny Mercer. (Impact in about T minus fifteen seconds.) I didn't want to have another awkward conversation. (Make that twelve seconds.) Why did seeing him agitate me so much? (Make that nine seconds.) He was just trying to be a nice person. (Six seconds.) So why did I want to avoid him? (Three seconds!) I couldn't take it. I ducked my head and veered into the bathroom. Bad choice.

Not only was Marcie in there, she was casually talking to Amanda. Naturally, they both turned to see who had opened the door. For one agonizing second, we stood frozen, staring at each other. Then, thankfully, millions of years of evolution came to my rescue. Fight-or-flight kicked in and I dove into one of the stalls.

Of course, I didn't actually have to pee. I'd only come in the bathroom to escape Johnny Mercer. So I felt ridiculous just standing there by the toilet. I couldn't help remembering Marcie's mantra: Dignity, Fiona. But what choice did I have? And by the way, were they freaking kidding? Marcie and Amanda were friends now? That seemed to fit with the way my life was going, so really, it shouldn't have been as much of a surprise as it was.

Mercifully, they didn't seem to want to continue their conversation while I was half an aluminum door away. They said, "See ya," and I heard the bathroom door creak open and shut. I peered under the stall and didn't see any feet, so I figured it was safe to come out.

Have I mentioned yet that I've never been lucky?

Amanda was still there. "A word of advice?" she said. As if I had any choice in whether or not I wanted to hear it. I braced myself for some bullshit tips on what to do if your best friend suddenly hates you, which Amanda no doubt had experience in. "You might want to consider getting contact lenses," she said. "In stunts and stuff, glasses can be . . . dangerous or whatever."

"Oh," I said, dumbfounded.

"It takes a while to get used to them, so you should get them soon." She stuck her boobs out, pulled the door open, and disappeared.

This time I was the one standing in the bathroom with my mental gears grinding together. My poor brain couldn't deal with Amanda not only being civil, but showing an apparent concern for another human being's welfare. Had Todd actually gotten her to be nice to me? And why was she suddenly all buddy-buddy with Marcie? My mind swirled in the absurdity of it all. I snapped back to reality when the bell rang. Crap, I was late. Typical bad luck. But at least that meant I was still me.

Wednesday, November 13

Not only should I get all the money collected from this marriage ed course, I should also get a freaking Congressional Medal of Honor. If part of marriage is sacrificing all of your dignity and self-respect for your partner, then I'm there. For over a week now, I've humiliated myself, brutalized my body, and strained my brain merely because my fake spouse asked me to. I must've gone loco for a second when I agreed to be a cheerleader. I forgot that I was supposed to hate Todd. All right, I guess I don't hate him anymore.

Amanda, on the other hand, is a different story. No matter how hard I try (which, let's be honest, isn't very hard), I just can't dredge up any love for her. Even when she was actually semidecent to me yesterday in the bathroom. (Another reason I should get the money from this course—to replace what I have to shell out for contact lenses.) The more I get to know Todd, the less I understand why those two are together. But I'll tell you one thing: if I was Todd's wife in real life, I'd have to kill myself. Because if being his "type" means being anything like Amanda, then I'd rather be dead.

Okay, maybe I'm being a bit dramatic. I wouldn't kill myself. But I'd definitely turn lesbian, at the very least.

THE DAYS LEADING UP TO THE PEP RALLY FLEW BY way too fast. I didn't get fitted for a uniform until the day before. I felt like a freak in that red-and-white polyester mini-skirt and V-neck sweater vest. Like a hooker clown. I should also mention that the fabric and knit of cheerleading uniforms prohibit the evaporation of any perspiration whatsoever. By the time I got to school Friday evening, I was dripping with sweat, even though it was only about forty degrees. Every time I thought about getting up in front of all those people, I felt all googly, and the sweat just poured out of me.

The pep rally was scheduled for six-thirty—just before the homecoming game against our archrivals, Lincoln. We were supposed to do a whole routine of cheers—ending with Catch the Fever—in front of a bonfire while everyone else got wasted so they could act like imbeciles during the game. At halftime, Hannah Fortis and Zack Braden were going to be crowned homecoming queen and king while the marching band played "Bohemian Rhapsody." So really, our big performance was at the bonfire.

Just after six, I got to the field where they were going to light the bonfire. Principal Miller and Mr. Evans were powwowing with the local fire marshal over by the giant pile of wood. Mrs. O'Toole was parked in a lawn chair beside the school. Todd, Amanda, and the rest of the squad were warming up. I wasn't sure whether I needed to warm up or not, because I was hot and shivering at the same time. My glasses kept slipping down, because even my nose was sweating. I'd gone to Zinnman's Ophthalmology at the Prairie View Mall the day before to get examined and fitted for contact lenses. Turned out I had some kind of freaky prescription, so the contacts weren't going to be ready for a couple of weeks.

"You're late, Princess," Todd said.

"Five minutes," I said. "What, are you going to make me do push-ups or run laps or something?"

"The squad's waiting," he said. "Line up."

We got into formation and ran through Steam, Success, and Eagle Pride, all of which had small partner stunts and a lot of tumbling. I pretty much just lunged and did jazz hands. Sparkle!

Then it was time to run through Catch the Fever. I was off a bit because my glasses slipped down during a turn, and I pushed them up just as I was supposed to be clapping. Then I clapped late and Amanda stopped us. "Fiona, I don't know if I've mentioned this before, but the idea of cheerleading is to do everything *at the same time.*"

I responded to her by hiking up one leg, reaching back, and pulling the giant wedgie out of my ass from the briefs-slash-diaper-pants we had to wear under the skirts.

Amanda scrunched up her nose. "Oh, very ladylike. You really represent the best in cheerleading."

I pretended to stick my finger up my nose and dig around. "Whassat you say?"

The robot turkeys said, "Ew!" Amanda said, "You're disgusting."

I snorted loudly through my nose and hawked up a fake loogie. The robot turkeys shrieked. I leaned over like I was about to spit, and Todd said, "Fiona!" I looked at him and pantomimed gulping. He said, "Let's just try it again."

We lined up again and this time we made it through the routine and even managed the pyramid stunt. My all-important job was to kneel on one knee while Simone stood with one foot on my other leg and one foot on Takisha's back as Takisha bent over. Other, more complicated stuff happened, but all I had to do was stay still and hold onto Simone's leg. But I got another wedgie, so I let go for a second to pull it out. When I reached behind me, I guess I kind of lost my balance, because my knee wobbled a bit. And Simone wobbled a bit. And everyone else wobbled a bit. I grabbed Simone's leg again. She gave a little cry and caught her balance. So did everyone else. So it was okay. But I made a note to self to ignore all wedgies. We dismounted and practiced the phony clapping and wooting and fist-pumps in the air. Gobble, gobble.

By then people were showing up for the bonfire. Before I headed into the gym with the squad to wait for our cue, I took a quick look for Gabe in the crowd. I didn't see him, but I did see Marcie walking toward me. If she thought she was going to chew me out just before I performed, she was off her nut. I pretended not to see her and turned around.

"Fiona!" she called.

I ignored her.

"Fiona, wait!"

Didn't hear that either.

"Fee!" I heard her jog up. She tapped me on the shoulder. I put on my best I-don't-give-a-crap face and turned around. "Yes?"

She stopped a second to catch her breath. "Hi. Listen. I just wanted to say that I think it's great that you're doing this for the cheer squad. Helping them out like this—it says a lot."

I half shrugged. Stared at the lightbulb above the steel door. "Thanks." I pulled the door open and walked into the gym. Mar followed me inside.

"I mean it," she said. I could tell from her expression that she did. She was my old Mar.

"Thanks," I said. And I meant it, too.

Mar smiled. "Wow, you look bizarre in that uniform."

"Tell me about it." I leaned in to whisper. "My only consolation is that maybe Gabe will think it's hot. Is he out there? Did you see him? Who's he with?"

Mar took a step back and crossed her arms, "Fiona, that's not why you joined the squad. Is it?"

As I thought about my answer, I picked a chip of yellow paint off the cinder-block wall with my thumbnail. "No. I mean, it wasn't my *first* thought when Todd asked me to join the squad. But it might have been my second. Maybe third. I mean, Mar? How could I *not* think about it? Cheerleading? Me? Especially with all the times Gabe stops by practice to talk to Amanda about some marriage ed thing or another."

"So you're doing all this to impress Gabe Webber?"

"No. Well, maybe. Not entirely. But I guess you could say it was a perk. A big perk. A huge perk. But seriously, can you blame me?"

Marcie turned a complete 360 degrees as she shot this little laugh up to the gym rafters. "I can not *believe* you, Fiona. You are something. What a piece of work. I can't believe you're masquerading as a decent human being just to fulfill your own personal agenda."

"*What*?" Where had my Mar gone? Hello? "What the hell are you talking about, Marcie?"

Someone opened the door and a rush of smoky air from the bonfire tumbled in. Marcie tossed her hair exactly like Amanda did. "I thought maybe you finally realized what a selfish jerk you've been, and you'd done something really generous and giving to make up for it. But no. You're just as self-serving as ever."

Right. This time the gloves were off. No way was I taking this lying down. I leaned into Mar and said, "Who the hell do you think you are? So high and mighty. Passing judgment on all the poor NOCDs. What difference does it make to you if I'm doing something to look good in front of Gabe Webber, huh? How the hell does it have any impact on your life?"

She blinked. "Impact on my life?"

"Yes. Your life. How is it any of your goddamn business?"

"My business?" she cried.

"Yes. How does what I feel about Gabe Webber have any bearing whatsoever on *you*?"

Her face went white. Tears pooled in her eyes. Every muscle in her face quivered. "It has bearing on me, Fiona," she said, "because I am Gabe Webber's girlfriend. *Me*. I'm the mystery girl you've been bitching about all semester. Gabe and I started going out at summer camp. He worked there too. I didn't have the heart to tell you before, because I knew it would kill you. But now, I just don't care. So there you go, Fiona. There it is." She wiped her tears with the back of her hand and smeared her mascara across her cheekbone. "And to be honest, I can't see how you missed it. It was obvious. Remember when Gabe said he liked a totally together woman? He meant me, not you. I'm the one he was winking and waving to at cheerleading tryouts, not you." She batted another tear away and stepped toward me. "In fact, we were making out under the stands while you were talking to Todd. How about that? And we also snuck off to be together at the dance. I'm the one you overheard him talking to there. Gabe loves *me*, Fiona, not you. In fact, he pretty much hates you after everything I've told him about the way you've been acting lately. So you may as well just give him up, because it's *never* going to happen. Now, if you'll excuse me, Gabe is waiting for me."

She spun on her shiny high-heeled boots and stormed away from me.

No way.

I had to be imagining this.

I was in bed, asleep, and this was not really happening. My best friend had not just turned every great moment we'd shared this year into lies. My sweet Mar was not some backstabbing traitor. She'd never be that selfish.

She wouldn't do that.

She hadn't done that.

But she had.

Now she was walking away. Out into the night and into the arms I wanted to be held by. The body I wanted to lean on. The face I wanted to touch. He was hers. She was going to him. I never would. And I'd never have her either. I'd lost Marcie. I'd lost Gabe. My best friend. My love. My hearts. Gone.

I felt a hand on the back of my shoulders propelling my body forward. My feet stumbled beneath me and I ran. The squad ran beside me. Our cue had come. It was time to perform.

Only I couldn't breathe. I couldn't see. I couldn't feel my hands or feet. The bonfire raged behind us. The crowd cheered and I was swept up into the routine. One cheer after another. I went through the motions like a machine. Wordlessly. With no smile. No. Not when my face was glazed with tears. Not when my glasses were speckled and streaked. When my legs were nothing but sponge for Simone to stand on. My arms channels of lead. Unable to hold her. Unable to keep her up as she tilted and fell. And everyone fell around her. Arms and legs crooked in all directions. The sound of screams building, like volume turning up. Then an elbow sharp in my cheek, sending my glasses flying. Me flying after them. And I was laid out on the hard ground along with the rest of the squad.

No one moved for a few seconds. Then everyone did. Two ink-black Doc Martens landed in the dirt in front of my face. Strong hands beneath my shoulders lifted me up. Gently wiped the muddle of tears and dust from my eyes. Eyes that could focus now and see the face of Johnny Mercer in front of me. With a worry-knit brow under his baseball cap, and quick hazel eyes that searched every inch of me for damage.

He asked in his deep voice, "Are you okay, Fiona?"

"I messed up," I said.

"Forget about it. Just be glad nothing's broken."

I tried to piece the scene together in my brain. "Is everybody else okay?" I didn't see any blood. I didn't see any bones. Everyone was moving. Getting up. Limping off.

Amanda charged up to me. "What the hell happened to you?"

I touched my cheek. Felt my missing glasses. "I'm sorry, Amanda. I couldn't hold her up."

"Couldn't hold her up? You totally collapsed underneath her! You didn't even *try*. Plus, you were late hitting every mark, your claps were off, your arms were bent, and I don't think you even tried to yell the cheers at all! I don't know why we ever thought you'd be any good at this. Letting you join the squad was a huge mistake!"

Amanda's yelling drew the attention of some students nearby. They clustered together to watch us in the frenzied light of the bonfire. I stared at Amanda, and all the emotions I had felt in the past half hour began spiraling inward. Turning in, and turning in on themselves until they formed a fine, highly pressurized point of focus on her.

Then they released.

"*Letting me join?*" I bellowed. "You think you *let* me join? Like being part of your goddamn freak show was something I wanted? Hell, *no*! *You* wanted *me.* The squad *asked* me to join. I didn't want to! I said no. I told Todd there was no way in hell I was joining. But he begged me. He begged! He needed me. *You* needed me. I never wanted to be here in the first place, so don't give me shit about bent arms and missed marks! I don't give a fuck about the stupid marks. You think the world is going to end because I didn't clap right? Get some fucking perspective, Amanda. Get your head out of your ass and look around you. The planet is not going to explode if your cheers aren't perfect. Or your makeup isn't perfect. Or your love life isn't perfect. The fate of the world does not hinge on every little thing you do! You're not the center of the goddamn universe!"

Amanda stood dead-still through my whole tirade. When I finally finished, I waited for her response. Her retort. Her return-fire.

There was none.

Instead, Amanda started to cry. Softly at first, then with big, heaving sobs and surging tears. Her hands flew to her face, and her shoulders shook with each trembling breath. Todd was beside her in a second, having heard the whole exchange from a few feet away. He pulled her sodden face into his chest, circled her with his arms, and held her. After a few moments, he whispered in her ear, and she slipped from his arms and ran through the crowd to the gym door. Then Todd turned to me. "What the hell was *that*?"

More people crowded around. I said, "She laid into me

first about what a crap cheerleader I am and how it was a mistake to have me on the squad!" A gust of wind drove the bonfire flames up and blew off a hail of embers.

Todd yelled, "Whatever she said, she didn't deserve to be screamed at in front of the whole school. Take it out on me—that's fine! Do it to me—I can take it! But leave her alone. She can't take it. She's extremely sensitive."

"Sensitive?" I cried. "Please, Amanda is about as sensitive as a toilet seat." A couple of guys in ECHS sweatshirts started snickering. Assholes.

"She's a hell of a lot more sensitive than you are!" Todd said. "You are totally insensitive."

I reared back. "What? I am *not* insensitive!"

"Oh, please, Fiona. You are the least sensitive person I know."

"How can you say that?" The wind shifted, and smoke blew into my face and stung my eyes. I squinted and blinked against it.

"Because it's true, Fiona. You slap on your I-don't-give-a-shit attitude, then sit back and pass judgment on everyone else."

Pass judgment on everyone. That was exactly what I'd said to Marcie. I hoped it had stung her as much as it did me.

Todd kept rolling. "You think you know everything about people, but you don't. If you stopped for one second—just for *one* second—and considered how things might be for someone other than yourself, you might not be such a snob."

"Snob? I'm insensitive *and* a snob? Why the hell are you being so mean? What the hell is wrong with you?"

Todd gave a sarcastic laugh. "See? There you go again. It has to be something wrong with *me*. It couldn't possibly be something wrong with you."

He might as well have slapped me across the face. "Fuck you, Harding," I cried. I spun and walked. After about ten paces, Johnny was on my tail. I swiveled around and said, "What do you want, Johnny?" I meant it as an insult, not a question.

"You forgot these," he huffed. He held out my glasses.

I'd been so angry and crying so hard, I hadn't even noticed I couldn't see right. I snatched them from his hand. "Thanks." I turned to leave.

"He's wrong, you know," Johnny said. I halted.

He said, "Todd? He's wrong."

I said over my shoulder, "Nice of you to say, Johnny. Thanks. See ya."

"Fiona!"

God, what did this guy want? I sighed and turned to face him for the last time. "*What*?"

He stepped closer to me. "You're not insensitive. I hope you know that. You're not a snob, either. Don't listen to him. You're . . ." He pulled on the corners of his black leather jacket and rolled them between his fingers. "Terrific. You're a terrific person, Fiona. And I just thought you might need to hear that, after what Todd said. You're not what he said. I think you're great. Really great. I like you a lot, Fiona. A lot."

Holy shit. Was he for real? Had Johnny Mercer seriously picked this choice moment to declare his affection for me? Could this night get any worse?

All I wanted to do was get home, get in bed, and crawl down under my covers as soon as possible. I was willing to employ any means to hasten that. I placed my palm in the air between us. "I appreciate it and all, Johnny, but you know what? I'm good. And really"—I shook my head so he wouldn't miss the message—"I'm not interested."

I walked away from him as fast as I could. Then I broke into a run. I had to get out of there. Away from Johnny Mercer. Away from the bonfire. Away from cheerleading. Todd and Amanda. Marcie and Gabe. Away from school. Screw school. Screw marriage ed. Screw graduating. Screw life. I just wanted to be home.

So I ran toward it through the cold night.

CHAPTER 19

I DIDN'T ROLL OUT OF BED UNTIL NEARLY ELEVEN the next morning. My eyes were crusty from crying and I had a wicked headache. I'd spent half the night thinking about Marcie, and how one, she'd been dating Gabe, and two, she had lied to me about it for months. The more I let those two things knock together in my brain, the more I realized that Marcie had chosen Gabe over me. Absolute betrayal.

I slumped downstairs and popped a couple of ibuprofen. I grabbed a cup of coffee and hunched over it at the table while Dad read a book across from me.

I heard the front door slam. Mom ran in waving a newspaper. "It's in here!" she chirped.

I groaned, and mumbled, "What's in where?"

Mom unfolded the paper in front of me, saying, "Cybil Hutton, the PTA president, called in a favor with someone she knows downtown at the *Tribune*, and they did a story on us. And look—front page!"

Not only was it front page, it was headline: SUBURBAN WOMAN PROTESTS MARRIAGE EDUCATION: PTA AND 300 AGREE. And this was no small-town paper, either. No lame-ass *Daily*

Ledger. This was the *Tribune.* The Chicago city paper. And there on the front page was my mother's face along with a two-column article describing her efforts to kill the course. This development either was terrific, because hey, maybe she'd succeed; or was terrible, because let's face it: my mother was on the front page of the *Trib.* Tongues were going to wag.

"You got three hundred names on your petition?" I asked. "But there aren't even that many seniors."

Mom gathered up the paper in her arms. "I didn't just target parents of seniors; I targeted all the parents in the school. First the petition. Then the letter-writing campaign, which has been a huge success so far. Now this." She gazed at the article again, and then held it up for Dad. "What do you think, Ethan?"

Dad closed his book and skimmed the paper. He got this goofy, sappy grin on his face like a wallflower who'd just been asked to dance. He leaned up and kissed Mom. "Elizabeth Cady Stanton would be proud."

Mom's eyes saucered. Then she bounced up and down. "Oh! What a great idea!" She kissed Dad hard on the mouth again and said, "Thanks, babe. I have to call Cybil. I'll go upstairs."

Thank God she left. If I'd had to watch them suck face any more, I would've suffered severe brain damage.

As bad as it was to hang out with my parents, I would've preferred it to going to school on Monday. When I got there, I kept my head down and avoided human contact as much as possible. Homeroom was a mess. I sat by myself in the back corner, keeping as much distance as I could from Marcie and Todd. I had one class with Johnny—calculus. It was easy enough to ignore him there. Of course, I bailed on cheer practice. Amanda had been pretty clear concerning how she felt about having me on the squad. And I figured I'd already clocked enough time to fulfill the marriage ed requirement. Each day, I just went to school and went home. On my freaking bike. In the icy November rain.

Then came calculus on Thursday. Now, normally, I find math fascinating. I love the universality of it. How mathematics transcends language and politics and religion. How the laws governing mathematics are absolute. I'm awed by how mathematicians must think. How they open their minds to possibilities within these rigid laws and ask, *What if?* And suddenly a whole new system of conjuring lays itself out before them like a labyrinth. And they puzzle their way toward some brand-new truth lying at the center of the maze. It's like magic.

But I couldn't concentrate on Thursday. So, as my calc teacher explained functions, I doodled on the cover of my notebook. I was just putting a set of voluminous boobs on my poorly rendered drawing of Mr. Tambor when I felt something slip under my arm. It was a note folded into a triangular football with my name on one side. I glanced around to see who'd passed it, but nobody owned up, so I unfolded it.

Dear Fiona,

I'm really sorry about what happened at the pep rally.

Forget everything I said to you. I didn't mean it. Pretend I never said anything. And whatever's going on with you and Marcie, I hope you work it out.

—Johnny Mercer

Well, aside from the fact that I'd just been passed my first note since seventh grade, I was pretty shocked. He hadn't meant what he said? So in other words, he thought I was an insensitive snob? Or wait—did he want me to forget that he'd said he liked me . . . *a lot?* I hoped that was what the note meant. That was the preferable choice, right? I didn't want him to "like me" like me. But I also didn't want him to think of me as an insensitive snob. Then again, the note did say to forget *everything* he said, so maybe it meant both. Maybe he thought I was an insensitive snob *and* he didn't like me. Wow. What a bummer note.

I crumpled it up and shoved it into my backpack. When the bell rang, I got out of there as fast as I could. The thought of having a conversation with Johnny Mercer right then made all these emotions flare up in me: anger, excitement, relief, fear—you name it. I figured I must have some raging PMS.

For whatever reason, I couldn't stop thinking about Johnny all week. What had that note meant? What did he think of me? And why did I care? At one point, I almost broke down and called him. Because I also wanted to know if Mar was upset. She'd better not have been feeling fine and dandy about stabbing me in the back after years of best-friendship. But then again, how could I ask Johnny about it? He had no idea about my lifelong crush on Gabe.

Or did he?

What if Marcie had told him? No, she wouldn't have done that. Would she? But, hell, she'd already done way worse. Could she possibly have told him?

The idea of Johnny Mercer knowing about my feelings for Gabe Webber set my chest on fire. But why? Why did I give a crap what Johnny Mercer thought about me? I had no idea. All I knew was that I felt like if he found out I'd been in love with Gabe Webber, I could never face Johnny again. Ever.

That made absolutely no sense.

It had to be PMS.

CHAPTER 20

LUCKILY, THE NEXT WEEK WAS A SHORT ONE FOR school, because of Thanksgiving. And I told Mom I had killer cramps, so I didn't even go on Wednesday. On Thursday, Uncle Tommy and Alan brought Nana down to our house for Thanksgiving dinner. We ate too much, drank too much (well, Dad did anyway), and listened to Dad's old records on the ancient turntable stereo system he insisted on keeping right in the living room. The house was cozy and smelled of roasted turkey, but the weather called for snow. Dad was stretched out on the couch singing along to "Ob-La-Di, Ob-La-Da" when Uncle Tommy announced that it was time to head home.

As he and Alan got their coats and said goodbye to Mom and Dad, Nana pulled me aside into the living room. "I have something for you," she whispered. She opened her paisley quilted purse and pulled out a small red leather box. She lifted the lid and held it out to me. "I want you to have these." Inside were a diamond solitaire ring and a gold band with diamonds encircling it. I knew them right away.

"Nana," I said, "I can't take those. They're your wedding rings."

"And you're my only grandchild."

I shook my head. "But they're yours. You still might want to wear them."

"No," she said. She reached up with her knobby hand to touch my hair. Then my cheek. Then the hollow of her own neck. "I'm not married anymore."

"But you and Grandpa didn't get a divorce."

Nana's eyes moistened and she blinked. "We parted at death."

I didn't get it. I'd always thought that even though Grandpa had died, Nana was still married to him in her heart. They'd been married almost fifty years. I always figured she didn't wear the rings because of her swollen knuckles. How could she just dismiss all that time together? Had she been unhappy? "Don't you want them?" I asked.

Nana swatted at her eyes. "I don't need these rings to remember your grandfather. He's with me every day." She closed her eyes and patted her heart. "Every day." She opened her eyes again. "To me, these are only tokens. I want you to have them so you'll think of us."

So they had been in love. For fifty years. Half a century. That was a span of time I couldn't wrap my mind around. "But I don't need them to remember you, either, Nana," I said.

We could hear Uncle Tommy and Alan out in the hallway, ready to leave. Nana pressed the box into my hand. "Take them. They're yours now."

I welled up. I didn't want to cry, but it felt like Nana was saying goodbye. I closed my hand around the box and gave Nana a soft hug. "Thank you," I said into her ear. She smelled like roses.

Just before bed that night, I tucked Nana's ring box into the back of my bedside-table drawer. I could still smell her perfume on me. I reached under my bed for my journal and wrote by the light of my bedside lamp. When I was done, I slid the journal back under my bed and switched off my lamp. Outside, snow had started to fall from the flannel clouds, so I lay on my bed and watched it in the dark. The downstairs window cast an upward light on the flakes, giving them a slanted beam to dance through. I opened my side-table drawer and took Nana's ring box back out. Even in the dimness, the diamonds caught a trace of light and sparkled. I lifted the rings out of the box and held them up to the window and the snow. I twirled them at the sky, then slipped them onto the ring finger of my right hand, and fell asleep with my glasses still on.

Thursday, November 28

Here's what I learned about marriage from this week:

1. You should marry someone who likes the qualities you possess, not someone who thinks those qualities suck.

2. You should marry someone who lets you be the kind of person you are inside, not someone who forces you to be a person you're not.

3. You should feel that same way about the person you marry.

4. If you find a person who fits 1, 2, and 3, then you're set for life. But be ready for when they die, because they're going to take part of you with them.

5. But they leave part of themselves behind for you, too. Which, I guess, is a good thing.

CHAPTER 21

IT SNOWED FOR TWO DAYS. THE WET, STICKY KIND. By Saturday night, everything was coated with a lumpy layer of white frosting. With the holiday weekend, plus the fact that I was pissed off at nearly everyone I knew, I had no plans that night. So I went to bed, listened to "Shelter of Your Arms" about a thousand times on my stereo (since I didn't have my iPod anymore), and had another good cry about Marcie. Then I wept again about the things Todd had said to me. I couldn't believe he'd been so mean. Truly mean, though, not just pretend-mean. It wasn't like him. When I faced this fact, the only conclusion I could come to was that maybe he'd been right.

Could I possibly be an insensitive snob?

Okay, maybe I had driven Marcie away because I wouldn't acknowledge her feelings for Gabe. And maybe I'd never even considered that Gabe simply might not find me attractive. Ever. Those things could be categorized as insensitive.

And I guess you could say that I was kind of a snob to Amanda. I did treat her like a dumb blonde. A person might say I acted superior around her. Like a snob. An insensitive, judgmental, bitchy snob. That was me. It snuck up and smacked me like a two-by-four to the back of the head, and my tears started up again.

After I was done crying, I watched the heavy flakes tumble down out of the blackness. It was only about ten o'clock, so I got up and crept down the back stairs to avoid my parents in the living room. I pulled on my coat and my dad's boots, and slipped out into the backyard.

The sky was quiet. Just the soft plopping sound of flakes padding the ground or the tree limbs or the roof of the shed. My glasses fogged up instantly, so I took them off. I inhaled the clean, snowy air and let it cool my runny nose and raw eyes. I closed my eyelids and let the flakes gather on my cheeks, slipping off like tears as they melted. I pictured myself sinking into the ground, growing roots like a tree. And reaching branchy arms up to the sky. I thought that if I could just stay there, perfectly still, the transformation would truly happen. I would become a solid, immovable, living part of nature. Not some wavering, loser organism. Part of absolutely nothing at all. I held my breath, and for one moment, I felt it. Then a noise from the shed ripped me back to my sucky reality.

I fumbled to wipe my glasses and put them back on. My first instinct was to run and get Dad, but then there'd be questions of why my face was so red and swollen as though I'd been crying. Which I had been.

Besides, as I looked closely at the ground, I saw a set of small footprints almost covered by snow, leading straight to the shed. Next to the footprints was a pink pen with a purple flower on top. I recognized it immediately. I picked it up, strode over to the shed, and threw open the door.

Samantha Pickler fell off the flowerpot she'd been standing on.

"Sam!" I said. "What are you doing?"

"Trying to hang this trowel back on the hook," she said. "I knocked it down."

"I mean what are you doing in our *shed*?"

"Oh, that." She hung up the trowel and sat on the flowerpot. "I ran away. But you can't tell anyone, Fiona. You won't, right? You're the only person I can depend on. Hey, my pen."

I considered the possibility that one or both of my parents might happen to glance out the window and see me talking to the shed, so I ducked inside and pulled the door shut. Luckily, Sam had a flashlight. I squatted in front of her. "Why did you run away?"

Sam sighed and doodled on her pant leg with the pen. Then she threw the pen down at her feet. "They're getting a divorce," she said. "Dad's moving out."

"Oh no." I put my hands on top of hers and squeezed. "Sam, I'm so sorry. But sweetie, how is running away going to help you?"

"It's not going to help me," she said. "It's going to help them. They don't want me. They don't want any kids. If I'm out of the picture, then they won't fight so much. Then maybe they'll stay together."

"What makes you think they don't want you?"

"I've heard them fight about me. Mom says raising a kid takes so much energy. And she doesn't have time for her own dreams, she says. Dad says that having a kid is a commitment. And they have an obligation to me. So the way I see it, all I am to them is an obligation. Who gets in the way. So I left."

"Sam, you are *not* an obligation. Your parents love you."

"No, they don't. Maybe they did when I was a cute baby, but not anymore. They hate me." Tears trickled down her cheeks. "And besides, I hate them too."

I wrapped my arms around Sam and she sobbed.

"Oh, Sister-witch," I said. "Please let me take you inside."

She shoved me away. "*No.* And if you try to make me or if you tell anyone I'm here, I'll just run away somewhere else."

She meant it, too. I'd never seen Sam so upset. And I sure didn't want her to go anywhere else in this snowstorm. So I said, "Okay, okay. I won't tell or try to make you go anywhere. But you're going to freeze out here." I half expected her to pull a blanket out from the duffel bag at her feet, or toss her head in her dramatic way and brace herself boldly for the cold. But she said, "I don't care." Dead serious.

"Then let me go inside and get you a blanket and some soup or something to eat. I pinky-swear I won't tell." I held up my right pinky.

She hooked her pinky into mine with half-effort. "Whatever. But I'm only staying here until the snow lets up a bit. Then I'm leaving."

Now, I wasn't a genius by any stretch, but I knew it was no accident Sam was in my backyard. It wasn't like she'd just been passing by when the snow got heavy and she ran to our shed for shelter. No, she'd set out to come here. She didn't have anywhere else to go. But that might not stop her from trying to find somewhere else. I didn't want to agitate her in any way, so I said okay. I crept out of the shed and snuck back into the house.

I'd managed to squirrel a little instant soup into a thermos when the phone rang. Mom answered it in the living room. I heard some muffled talking then she yelled my name up the front stairs. "I'm in the kitchen," I hollered. She hurried in with her hand over the mouthpiece of the phone.

"It's Victoria Pickler. Samantha's missing. They're frantic. You haven't heard from her, have you?"

Unfortunately, I was unprepared for this direct assault. I was, by far, an abominable liar when the stakes were high. I froze. My eyes widened. My mouth hung open. I managed to utter, "No," which was pretty obviously untrue. My mom growled, "Young lady, you tell me what's going on right *now*."

I caved.

I whispered, "I need to talk to you," and she told the Picklers I was in the bathroom and she'd call them right back.

"Mom, Sam's in the shed."

"What?" She picked up the phone and started dialing. I grabbed it from her.

"No, don't. She's really upset. She said that if I told, she'd run away. She's serious, Mom." She hesitated. I said, "Please just let me talk to her."

"Fiona, they've called the police. I have to tell them she's here."

I knew she was right. But I loved Sam more than pretty much anyone outside of my family. I couldn't stomach the thought of betraying her. "There's got to be a way to do this," I pleaded.

Mom sighed. "Okay. You take some blankets out and stay with her. Don't let her leave. I'll have her parents come over and we'll take it from there. Just pretend you don't know anything about us knowing. Maybe Dad can figure something out." She headed back to the living room, dialing the phone and saying to Dad, "Ethan, we have a problem. . . ."

It wasn't much of a plan, but the temperature was dropping. I grabbed the thermos, a package of cookies, and some blankets, and headed out back. Samantha sat shivering on the flowerpot. I folded one blanket for her to sit on and wrapped the other around her shoulders. Then I poured her a lidful of soup and sat on the ground in front of her. She breathed in the steam before taking a sip. "Chicken noodle, yum."

I needed to make some innocent conversation to keep her distracted from whatever plan my parents were hatching. "So, is Ginny's curse working yet?"

"Oh, we're friends again," she tossed off.

I blinked. "Really? How?"

"I dunno. She got sick of Olivia Purdy. Said she was always bragging about stuff. So we're friends again now."

"But what about that stuff Ginny said about you?"

Sam shrugged one shoulder. "Doesn't matter."

I didn't get it. Ginny had totally stabbed Sam in the back. And Sam could simply write it off? How was that possible?

"How can it not matter?" I asked, trying to tone down the sound of my doubt so I didn't get her riled up.

Sam looked at me like I was a moron. "Because we're friends!"

Because they were friends? It couldn't be that simple. Could it? I mean, they were only friends because Sam had forgiven Ginny. But Sam had only forgiven Ginny because they were friends. It was like one of those algebra problems where you needed to have A to find B. But to find A, you needed to have B. Those were so tough to figure out.

But Sam had.

She knew that if you just used one variable to assign a value to the other variable, then you could figure out both of them. Sam recognized that friendship contained forgiveness, then used forgiveness to resolve the friendship. She seemed to know far more about both those things than I ever had. Until then.

There was still no sign of anyone outside. I needed to stall for more time. "Whatever happened with that boy?" I asked. "What was his name? L-something?"

"Logan Clarke," she said. "We were kind of a couple."

"Were?"

"I broke up with him last week. He kept wanting to copy my homework. I let him at first, but after a while, I realized it was all he really wanted. He was truly tacky."

Sure, at eleven, Logan Clarke had been after homework. But give it a few years, and he'd be after something entirely different. I had a sudden feeling that if Logan Clarke had been in that shed, he might have suddenly found a trowel lodged between his ribs. "Well, I'm proud of you for not caving, Sam. Because believe me, you're better off without a guy like that."

"Speaking of. How's your marriage going?" she asked.

Sam didn't seem concerned that I was staying out there with her. Or maybe she'd expected it.

"Not so hot," I said. "We had our first fight. A biggie." Even as I said that, I recognized how absurd it was that with all the fighting Todd and I pretended to do, that the night at the bonfire had been our first real one.

"Over what?"

I had no idea why I was about to pour my soul out to a kid in a toolshed. But it was Sam, so I did. "He thinks I'm an insensitive snob. He says I judge everybody."

Sam huffed. "He's wrong. You are, too, sensitive. You always know when I'm sad about something. And everybody judges. They're a liar if they say they don't. But not everybody has the guts to say what they think out loud. You do. And you don't give a hoo-ha about what other people think. That's what I like about you best." She rummaged in the cookies and popped one in her mouth.

"It is? You think that's a good thing?"

She held up one finger while she chewed and swallowed. "Sure. You're a real person, Fiona. You don't let the fakes and phonies get away with their stuff—so what? If they don't like it, tough."

My legs were going dead from the cold. I shifted to a kneeling position. "Yeah, well, pretty much nobody likes it."

She chewed and swallowed another cookie and said, "I like it. And Marcie likes it."

"Marcie and I aren't friends anymore," I grumbled.

"*What*?" she said through a mouthful of half-chewed cookie. "What do you mean?"

"Remember Gabe? The guy I liked?"

"Uh-huh."

"She's been dating him since the summer."

Sam's eyes bugged. She swallowed her cookie. "She what?"

"And she totally lied to me about it."

"She told you she wasn't dating him, but she was?"

"Well, no. She just didn't tell me about him."

Sam twisted her mouth up and cocked her head sideways. "That's not lying, Fiona."

"Yes, it is."

"No, it's not. She never said she *wasn't* dating him. She just didn't tell you she was. Because she didn't want to hurt you, obviously!"

"If she didn't want to hurt me, she shouldn't have gone out with him in the first place!"

Sam slapped the cookie package. "Fiona, what if this is her *one* true love? What if she and Gabe were destined to be together? You'd have Marcie throw all that away? You wouldn't let her be happy like that? What kind of friend does that make you?"

What could I say to that? She was totally right. She'd nailed the truth. Again. I suddenly got the distinct impression that I was kneeling at the foot of a child Buddha. Some prophet of teenage wisdom who doled out morsels of insight while seated between a potting bench and a bag of old fertilizer.

"Sam," I said. I was about to tell her how great she was when we heard my dad's voice outside getting closer and closer.

"Sure, Jake," he yelled extra loud. "You can borrow the snow shovel. It's right here in the shed." The door flung open and there stood Dad and Mr. Pickler with phony looks of disbelief on their faces. But this time, I kept my mouth shut about the fakes and phonies. I played like I was as shocked as they were.

"Samantha!" Mr. Pickler cried. "Here you are! We've been looking everywhere for you!" He shoved me aside as he reached in to embrace his daughter. She fought him a little, but not with too much conviction.

"Oh yeah?' she said. "Well, if you were looking so hard, then why are you here to borrow a stupid shovel?"

Mr. Pickler stroked her hair and lied right to her. At least I figured it must be a lie. "Because your mother is so worried, she's pacing the sidewalk outside our house in her bare feet. She refuses to come in. I wanted to shovel the snow for her. Then I was going to go back out looking for you."

"You were? She is?" Sam seemed to buy it. Or maybe she just wanted to.

"Of course, Monkey-child." He hugged her tighter. "We couldn't live without you."

As the proclaimed queen of detecting fakes and phonies,

I could tell that this was not a lie. Sam knew it too, because she hugged her father back.

"Please come home," he said.

"Whose home?" she asked. "Mom's or yours?"

"You know what? Wherever *you* are is home. You make it home. Now will you come?"

Sam tossed her hair. Dramatics. A good sign. "Maybe just for tonight. Ape-man."

Of course we all knew—Sam probably, too—that it wasn't just for one night. But we let Sam have the last word. She needed to know that her message had been heard loud and clear.

We piled out of the shed. Sam headed off through the snow with her dad—his arm pulling her close. My dad did the same move on me and we walked toward the house. "You're a good person, Fiona," he said. I didn't fully buy it. But to my surprise, I didn't deny it, either.

Progress, I thought.

CHAPTER 22

MONDAY MORNING AT SCHOOL, JUST AFTER FIRST period, I heard this earsplitting screech of feedback from outside, then someone shouting through a bullhorn. There was no mistake; it was my mother's voice. I ran to the window. Outside, a group of people marched around in a circle. Carrying signs. Picket signs. The bullhorn screeched again and I heard my mother shout, "*Hey, ho! Hey, ho!*" and then the rest of the picketers—whom I hoped to hell were other parents—shouted, "*Marriage ed has got to go!*"

This, evidently, was her Elizabeth Cady Stanton–inspired "great idea." A full-on, strike-style, picketing protest in the snow. If it hadn't been my mother, I might have thought it was kind of cool. But . . .

"Is that your *mother*?" Callie Brooks was suddenly at my side with her upper lip curled in obvious disgust.

I was not about to expose my seething humiliation to her. "Yeah, it is! Where's yours? Why isn't she out there helping?"

Callie glanced sideways and smoothed the front of her argyle sweater. "She works," she mumbled. "But she signed the petition. Sent a letter."

"Oh," I said, because there was really nothing else to say, hostile or otherwise.

The picket line kept going the whole day. When Principal Miller tried to do afternoon announcements, they could hear her on the outdoor speakers. So the picketers cranked those bullhorns up to ten and drowned her out. After the last bell, Mom and PTA president Cybil Hutton stayed behind to relive the good times, so I rode my bike home. When I got there, there was a voice mail from Zinnman's Ophthalmology saying that my contacts were ready. Not that I needed them anymore for cheerleading. But I'd already paid for them, so I figured I might as well pick them up. Dad was home early from NIU, so I grabbed the car to run out to the mall.

I pulled into a parking spot and slushed through the grimy snow to the entrance. Inside the glass vestibule, I kicked the dirty dreck off my Chuck Taylors. When I looked up, I saw Marcie standing on the other side of the interior doors. Watching me.

Oh, crap. First Monday of the month. Nail appointment. I couldn't believe I'd forgotten.

There was no way to avoid her. I took a deep breath and pulled the door open. I got hit with the cinnamon-scented air from a pretzel shop nearby. "Hey Mar," I said. I'd meant to say "Marcie."

"Hey Fee. What's up?"

Even though I was inside the warm, gleaming mall and not outside in the freezing muck, I pulled my coat tighter around me. "Just picking up some contact lenses."

"Oh," she said. She hiked her purse higher on her shoulder. "I thought you liked your glasses."

I turned a palm up. "I ordered them a couple of weeks ago for cheerleading. I have to pick them up anyway."

"Yeah, Ga—" She stopped, and then started again. "I heard you weren't doing cheerleading anymore." She looked beside me, above me . . . anywhere but at me.

I huffed. "I don't think you could ever call what I did cheerleading."

Silence. The only sound between us was the instrumental Christmas music playing over the mall speakers. I could tell she didn't know whether to laugh or not. That tore me up. The old Marcie would either have laughed along with me or told me to shut up because I was great for just trying. Suddenly, all the fight drained out of me. I was done with it.

"Marcie, listen. About Gabe . . ."

She reached out and stepped toward me. "You don't know how sorry I am for going behind your back. And I'm so sorry for calling you selfish. I was just so frustrated because I couldn't tell you about Gabe."

I took a step toward her. "No, Mar. I'm the one who's sorry. I was being selfish. I was a total self-centered brat—you were right. I had no claim to him. It was all a fantasy. Just pretend. Gabe Webber never gave a crap about me and never would have, either. But he cares about you. I should have been happy for you. I know that you were only trying to protect me."

Tears filled Marcie's eyes and tumbled down her perfect peach cheeks. "I was, Fiona. I didn't want to hurt you. I'm sorry."

I said, "I'm sorry too!" Then I bawled, and we hugged.

Hurried shoppers eyed us as they tramped out the door. When Marcie and I were finally done blubbering, we decided to hang out for the rest of the afternoon. Her appointment wasn't for another half hour. So she sat with me while the doctor showed me how to put in and take out my contacts and told me how long to wear them each day.

Then we went over to the nail salon, where Marcie wanted to treat me to a French manicure as a peace offering. And as a peace offering to her, I agreed to get it. I had to admit, even though my nails had been torn and stubby, the technician magically made them look . . . well, girly, as my dad would say.

As our nails dried under a purple UV light, I told Marcie about Dad getting drunk and asking if I was gay. She laughed out loud like it was the funniest thing since stink bombs.

Mar was back. Damn, I'd missed her.

When we were done at the salon, we wandered over to the food court. She got a Diet Coke. I got a regular. We sat at the least filthy table we could find.

"I have to tell you something," she said between sips.

I mocked surprise. "You're dating Gabe Webber? How could you?"

She cocked her head and raised one eyebrow. "Ha, ha. *Too* funny. No, something else."

"What?" I couldn't take my eyes off my fancy fingernails. They looked so grown-up holding my plastic cup and straw. I pretended the cup was crystal—I lifted my pinkies and sipped my drink like the Queen of England to make Mar laugh.

But instead of laughing, she said, "Johnny Mercer wants to bang you, bad."

I froze mid–queen sip and gulped. Then choked and sputtered. Coke came out of my nose, which, if you've never had the pleasure, actually kills. The bubbles are like tiny razor blades slicing up your mucous membranes. I grabbed my nose and a couple of napkins at the same time. Marcie just sat there laughing at me.

I mopped up my face and the table. And my shirt. And the floor. "Omigod Mar, you are so NOCD."

"He's actually a very sweet guy. What do you think?"

"Think about what?"

"About going out with him."

I looked at Marcie like she'd just asked me to join her cult because the mother ship was returning for them soon. "You're not serious." It was more of a begging question than a statement, really. I thought about Johnny telling me he liked me at the bonfire. Then his note. And even though I found myself glad to hear he might not hate me . . . "I'm really not interested," I said.

"A phone call, then. Just give him one call. I'm telling you, Fee, he's a great guy. You know that prank you pulled that he took the blame for? The announcement one? Did you know he got in huge trouble for that?"

"What? No! He said everything was okay."

"Well of course he's not going to tell you he got in trouble. He likes you, Fiona."

He was the second person I'd treated like garbage after

they'd tried to protect me. First Mar, now Johnny. "How much trouble?" I asked.

"He's had to stay after school every day for a month, filing papers for Principal Miller to earn back your iPod and speakers. Actually, I think today was his last day."

I set my cup down. "*What*?"

"And that's not all. She's making him go to this interpersonal-skills-slash-anger-management workshop over winter break. And he has to pay for it. Can you believe that?"

I leaned my elbows on the table and held my forehead in my hands. "No, I can't. Oh, Mar, I feel horrible." I sat up. "I'm paying for that workshop. And he can have my iPod and speakers."

Mar waved me off. "He won't take them. I know he won't. He's that kind of guy, Fee. Now, Gabe? Gabe would take your money. But not Johnny. No way."

I picked up a napkin and started shredding it slowly. "How come I'm only hearing about this now? This has been going on for a month?"

"He made me *swear* not to tell anyone about it. And you and I weren't talking, so . . . Don't tell him I said anything, okay? He only told me because it ran into our ballroom dance lesson time. Otherwise I bet no one would know. He has never complained once, Fiona. I think he actually enjoys it because it's for you."

I got that same skin-full-of-bees sensation I'd had when Todd found out I'd had a crush on Gabe. Like every single nerve in my body was a strand of those fiber-optic light balls you get at the novelty store next to the lava lamps, and someone was running their hand over me. The closest thing to it I could think of was absolute, pure, life-threatening terror. Only, not scary.

I crumpled up the napkin shreds into one hard lump.

Marcie leaned toward me. "Come on, one phone conversation with him won't kill you. One call. You said yourself you think he's a riot. If it's his size that's bothering you," Marcie said, "then honestly, I'm surprised." She sipped her Diet Coke. I knew she was pausing to dare me to deny it.

I didn't.

She chopped at her ice with her straw. "You know, Fiona, sometimes the best-looking guys are the ones with the most bottom-feeder mentality toward girls. Looks only go so far. Trust me."

Hold on a tick. That was the second shady comment she'd made. Was there trouble in Gabe Webber paradise? Should I pursue this obvious invitation to investigate? Nah. I decided to leave it for another time. I'd filled my drama quota for the day.

"Yeah, but looks have to get you on the road first."

"Johnny's not bad-looking! He's just . . . husky. He has gorgeous eyes, you know. And you've got to admit his voice is sexy. But mainly he's just a good guy, Fee. He's thoughtful, sensitive. He's funny and super smart."

I swung for the obvious joke. "If you like him so much, then why don't you maaaarrrry him?"

"I am married to him—that's how I know," she zinged back.

"Seriously," I said, "would you go out with him? I mean, if you were available?" I was trying not to say Gabe's name out loud.

Marcie lifted her chin and declared, "Sure. Of course. In a heartbeat."

It almost seemed like she was sincere. Almost like she really would go out with Johnny Mercer. "But the fact is, he likes *you*, Fiona," she said. "Oh well. At least I got to learn to swing dance. You know, Johnny's actually pretty good." Her eyebrows danced up and down.

"*All right*," I said. "I get the message. Johnny Mercer is totally crushworthy. *Fine*. I feel like a fifth-grader. Maybe you should pass him a note for me. Do you know he actually *did* pass me a note in calc? Folded up like a football, no less. Have we accidentally slipped back in time to junior high or something? What are you grinning at?"

"The lady doth protest too much, methinks."

I chucked one of my Coke-and-snot-sogged napkins at her, missing on purpose, of course. "Screweth you, Suzy Shakespeare."

She giggled and slurped the last of her soda.

"You are totally enjoying torturing me, aren't you?" I said. "What, is this some kind of payback?"

She got quiet and set her cup down. "Nah. Never."

"How can you be such a decent person to me?" I asked.

"Because we're friends."

She said it exactly the same way Sam had in the shed. And that was how I knew we'd solved the problem correctly.

CHAPTER 23

THE NEXT MORNING, MAR PICKED ME UP FOR SCHOOL like always. But she spent the whole time before homeroom making out with Gabe. I saw them kissing, and frankly, it was disgusting. He was giving her the Roto-Rooter action with his tongue so deep that I thought he was going to burrow right inside her throat and pitch a tent in there. Talk about NOCD.

I escaped into homeroom and decided to take this opportunity to pull a twelve-step on Todd. What can I say? I was feeling humble. I spotted him sitting in the back over by the window. I zigzagged my way through the rows and thumped down in the chair next to him. I slid my backpack onto the desk and leaned on it with my elbow. "So, Marcie and Gabe are dating."

Todd doodled on the cover of his notebook and didn't look up. "I heard," he said.

"I found out about it just before the bonfire thing," I said.

"So?"

"So . . ." I drummed my fingers on the desk. I figured he could fill in the blanks. Apparently not.

He quit drawing but still didn't look at me. "What do you want, Fiona?"

He called me Fiona. I didn't like it at all.

"I'm trying to apologize," I said.

Todd huffed and started doodling again. "Oh yeah? Well, try a little harder. Usually apologies contain the words 'I'm sorry' in there somewhere."

I sat up, took a deep breath, and leaked it out slowly like Maggie Klein did. I breathed in again, glanced around to see who was about to hear this, and said, "I'm sorry. I'm sorry for yelling at you. I'm sorry for tearing into Amanda in front of everyone, and I'm going to tell her that when I see her." I closed my eyes and took another long breath. Opened my eyes. "I'm also sorry for how bad I did in the cheers. Especially for blowing the mount at the end. Marcie had just told me about Gabe the second before we went on, and I was . . . upset."

Todd stopped drawing and sat, bug-eyed and still as a stone.

"So that's it," I said. "I'm . . . really sorry."

Todd didn't move.

"Todd?" I said. "Nothing? No response at all?"

He shook himself. "Sorry, did you say something after 'blowing' and 'mount'? I got a mental picture of you having sex, and my brain shut itself down."

I smiled. That, I knew, meant apology accepted.

He said, "I guess I probably shouldn't have called you names either."

I held up my hand to stop any apology he might be headed toward. "No, I deserved them."

"Still . . ." (Subtext: He was sorry.)

"Whatever . . ." (Subtext: I accept.)

Time for a subject change. Sort of. "So, did you already know that Marcie and Gabe had been together?" I had to find out if he'd known about them all along.

"Nah, not until the pep rally. After you took off, he was all over her. Mauled her like a grizzly bear. I saw them and figured your lesbo lover had switched teams, and that must've been the reason for your Night of the Living Dead cheer performance."

"It was," I said.

"Still doesn't excuse you taking it out on Amanda."

"No, it doesn't. Not my best moment," I said. I ran my finger back and forth over the corner of my desk. "At least she must be having fun with this. Seeing me humiliated by my best friend. Who has she told? As if I even have to ask. The whole school. If loose lips really sank ships, that girl could be a weapon of mass destruction."

Todd leaned to the side and said, "Is this your idea of personal growth?"

I froze. Bit both lips for a few seconds. Then said, "Sorry. Old habits."

"Hmmm," he said, giving me a scrutinizing look. He went back to doodling. A couple of girls sashayed into the classroom. A few bleary-eyed guys lumbered in. He said, "Well, as it happens, Amanda doesn't know that you want to spread your hot creamy butter all over Gabe Webber's dry toast."

I leaned toward Todd and lowered my voice. "Okay, one,

want-*ed*, not want. Two, you're a pig. And three . . . what do you mean, she doesn't know? You never told her?"

Todd stuck out his tongue and blew a raspberry. "It never came up in conversation."

I straightened up. "Never came up in conversation?"

He shrugged and kept drawing. "I decided it wasn't interesting. It's not like it's breaking news." He tipped his head and looked at me. "I hate to shatter your dreams, but the whole school does not care about your lack of love life. You're not that popular." Back to doodling.

This time, my mental gears ground to a halt and burst into flames. Why would Todd pass up a perfect opportunity to humiliate me? Especially after I'd ripped Amanda a new one. But he had. That made no sense. Yet all the signs pointed to the absurd possibility that Todd had . . . what? Protected me, too? Was that insane?

The first bell rang. Mr. Tambor came in and started banging stuff around on his desk. One of Todd's buddies waved to him and sat a few rows up.

I spoke to the floor. "Thanks, Todd," I said, "for not telling her."

He swung around to face me. "Well, you can make it up to me. No! Not with a hand job, which I know is what you're thinking."

"I just threw up in my mouth," I said.

He poked me in the arm with the eraser of his pencil. "I want you to come back to the cheer squad."

I reared back. "I'd rather give the hand job."

He pantomimed thinking. "Hmm . . . tempting as that

isn't, I'll pass. Look, we have district competitions a week from Saturday, and we need twelve people."

"Find someone else."

"We tried to find someone else, but they all sucked. And now there's not enough time to train someone new."

"Judith Norton will be out of her cast by then."

"Nope. Not until the following week. Besides, Princess, to be honest, some of the girls like you. I don't get it myself, but there you go."

"Amanda doesn't like me. Amanda hates me."

He waved me off. "Amanda doesn't hate you."

"Well, she does a pretty good impression of it, then."

"Amanda doesn't hate you," he said. "She's jealous of you."

I drew upright and gaped at Todd. "*What*? Todd, listen. Drugs are bad, buddy. You shouldn't do them first thing in the morning. Wait until after lunch at least."

Todd unzipped his backpack and started putting his pencil and notebook away. "Think about it. Amanda's programmed to be perfect. She can never let herself show a single flaw. She always has to look perfect and act perfect. Can you imagine how stressful that's gotta be? I mean, I know for you it's a stretch, but give it a shot."

"You just get funnier and funnier," I said totally deadpan.

"But *you*, on the other hand . . ."

I pointed my finger in his face. "Watch where you're going here. . . ."

He zipped up his backpack and dropped it back on the floor. "You, on the other hand, don't worry about what people think of you. You don't give a crap if you look weird or act strange. And I don't mean those things as insults. I know! It shocks me too. But I don't. You say whatever you want. You do whatever you want. Amanda sees you and she can't process it. She can't understand how you can be so relaxed about stuff. Inside, I think it pisses her off that she can't be that way too. Be that free. So she takes it out on the source: you."

Talk about not being able to process it. Never in my wildest, weirdest, most twisted dreams would I have imagined Amanda Lowell was jealous of me. "If that's true," I said, "then I've wasted a lot of precious voodoo-doll-making time."

Todd snorted. "Something tells me you'll have no problem finding somebody else to use it on."

"Good point. Speaking of which . . ." I reached out and yanked a few blond hairs out of Todd's head.

"*Ow*!" he said.

"I'm gonna need these." I tucked them in my pocket.

Todd rubbed his scalp. "Look, I'll take care of Amanda. Come on, come back to the squad. You know you want to. Besides, you owe me."

"Owe you? For what?"

He grinned. "The marriage ed budget. I did it and turned it in last week. All by myself. With no help from you. Ergo, you owe me."

I had totally forgotten about the damn budget. How

bizarre that Señor Shitslacks had done it on his own. "You know, you're really coming dangerously close to being a nice person," I said.

"Thanks for the warning. I'll remedy that situation immediately," he said.

Marcie skirted into the classroom just as the final bell rang. Mr. Tambor yelled, "*Settle*? Take your *seats*?"

I stood up and swung my backpack onto my shoulder. "I'll think about the squad, and let you know after counseling," I said. "See you then." I started walking over to Marcie.

"Not if I smell you first," Todd called after me.

But I didn't really need time to think about it. Truth be told, he'd had me at "Princess."

CHAPTER 24

SINCE IT WAS TUESDAY, TODD AND I HAD OUR counseling session later that morning. We got to Maggie Klein's office at exactly the same time. I pride myself on courtesy, so I gestured for Todd to go through the open door first. But he smiled and made the same gesture to me. So I stepped forward to walk through, and so did Todd, shouldering me into the door frame.

"Terribly droll," I said, and elbowed him in the ribs. I pushed through the door and sat in a chair. He dropped into the other one.

"Welcome, Todd. Fiona." Maggie Klein droned. She looked a little worse for wear. Actually, a lot. Her skin sagged at the corners of her eyes. There was no luster in her complexion anymore—it was just drab. And her office smelled like ramen noodles. She'd slowly been slipping in the arenas of fashion and hygiene over the past few weeks. Normally, I'm in no position to criticize anyone's wardrobe, but even I thought today's selection of brown sweatpants and a sweatshirt from the Hoover Dam was pathetic. Stacks of those photocopied papers I'd seen before littered the office. I picked up a few at my feet, and just before Maggie Klein snatched them out of my hands, I saw what they were. Copies of the letter from my mom's campaign. Signed copies.

"I suppose you know all about these," Maggie Klein said.

"I . . . er."

Todd piped up and started rifling through a pile near him. "Did my parents send one? They said they were sending one. Actually, they said they were each sending one, so there should be two. . . ."

Maggie Klein slapped her hand down on the papers Todd was shuffling. "Yes. I got them. Principal Miller has *kindly* forwarded them all to me." She tried to straighten a pile, but it slid to the floor, and she just left it down there among the candy wrappers and balled-up tissues.

"Let's begin. First of all, I want to let you know that the total real-world cash collected so far is $4,846. With half to charity, right now, each winner would get . . ." She shuffled through the junk on her desk, found her calculator, and started punching in numbers.

"It's $1,211.50," Todd said.

Maggie Klein huffed and sneered at Todd. Until she hit the equals button. Then her face turned three shades of red. "That . . . that's, um . . . correct, Todd. . . . Well done."

I giggled and low-fived him.

Maggie Klein slid the calculator back under the mess and composed herself. She tried to do some deep breathing but ended up whistling like a deflating balloon. She slid our marriage ed file in front of her but didn't bother opening it. "Okay. I haven't had a chance yet to go over the budget you turned in last week. I've been a bit . . . busy. But anyway. I'm afraid I have a bit of bad news. As of today, Todd, you've been fired from your job. Luckily, you found part-time work in a women's shoe store. Your Income Factor has now dropped to 50."

Todd said, "Women's shoe store?" just as I said, "Dropped to fifty?"

"Interesting reaction," Maggie Klein said, like we were some kind of perverted science experiment. "You know, often in this situation it *is* the woman who cares about the drop in income. Whereas the man cares about the drop in status. Well done."

Well done? Maggie Klein was an idiot, I decided. Three months of counseling and she had come to the stunning conclusion that Todd was, in fact, male, and I was female. Eu-freakin'-reka. Call the Nobel Prize committee.

"Unfortunately, since you decided as a couple that Todd would be the sole wage-earner, you don't have Fiona's income to fall back on. If you had, half the cash you earned this month would retain the 150 Income Factor." She raised one furry eyebrow and bobbled her head several times before concluding with, "Something to think about, eh?"

All I could "think about" was whether or not I should seriously investigate eyebrow waxing, because Maggie Klein obviously never had. She looked like she had a pair of woolly bear caterpillars on her face trying desperately to kiss. How had I never noticed that?

Todd swiveled in his chair and put a hand on my shoulder. "Don't worry, honey. We'll figure out a way through this. No! No! I won't hear of you giving up your passion for carving soap elephants. I know how much it means to you."

What the hell?

Wait. I got it.

Playtime.

I glared at him and knocked his hand off of me. "Oh, really?" I said. "You do?"

"Didn't I let you go to that soap-carvers convention?" he said, feigning concern.

"Let me go? I practically had to get on my knees and beg you."

"Well, Lord knows you're not on your knees much. But you can't say I haven't been supportive."

Maggie Klein butted in. "Okay, Fiona and Todd. That's enough."

I didn't miss a beat. "Oh yeah? And what about Bobo? Six weeks I spent working on him. *Six weeks*. And you—you used him to wash your ass!" I buried my face in my hands and pretended to sob.

"*Fiona! Todd!*" Maggie Klein barked.

Todd threw his hands in the air. "One time! One time I make a mistake, and you *never let me forget it*."

I wheeled around to counter Todd, but he had this

hilarious look of exaggerated hostility on his face. It was too much. A guffaw gurgled up my throat. I pressed my lips together to stifle it, but it shot up through my nose and I did that backward-snort thing. That put Todd over the edge and he dissolved. We both cracked up uncontrollably.

Maggie Klein was not as amused. She pushed up her stretched-out sleeves and crossed her arms. "Very entertaining." We kept laughing. She settled back into her chair. "You two should audition for the school play." We laughed some more. "*All right.* That's *enough.*" We finally settled down. Maggie Klein pinched the bridge of her nose and sighed deeply.

Just then, we heard Mom on a bullhorn again outside. Apparently, this protest was going to be a daily thing. Mom shouted, "*Hey, ho! Hey, ho!*" followed by the rest of the parents: "*Marriage ed has got to go!*"

Maggie Klein flew to the window, pulled open her blinds, and snarled. She literally snarled like an angry dog. I'd never heard an adult do that before. Only a bratty, cranky toddler once. Her hands trembled. Then so did her voice. "Ou-ou-our time is up for today." She crossed her office in two steps and swung open the door. "Do your budget. Write in your journals. Goodbye." We'd barely gotten through the door when she slammed it.

"That was your mom outside, wasn't it?" Todd said. "I recognize her from the picture in the paper."

"Yup," I said, steeling myself for the impending volley of insults. But none came.

"Cool. So, did you decide about the squad and districts?"

I couldn't believe that one, he hadn't given me any crap about my mother, and two, I was about to forfeit my chance to escape global-size public shame. "Fine. I'll do it," I said. "Hell, I've got the contact lenses already anyway."

"As long as your motives are clear," he said. "See ya at practice, Princess."

"Not if I smell you first, Señor."

AFTER SCHOOL, THE BULLHORNS FINALLY DIED DOWN. I was walking to practice, enjoying the cavernous silence, when I heard my name called from the other end of the hallway. Johnny Mercer was walking toward me. I felt a warm little stir inside me, I guess because of what Mar had said at the mall. I mean, it's not every day you run into someone who wants to "bang you, bad." Even though I was pretty sure that wasn't true in Johnny's case. Especially after shooting him down at the bonfire.

The sound of his black boots echoed in the hallway with each step and got louder and louder the closer he came. As he strode up, he stared at me with his deep-set hazel eyes. His cheeks glowed with the pace he kept, and showed the faintest trace of rough, new facial hair.

"Hi Johnny," I said. "How's it going?"

In one smooth move, he swung his backpack off his shoulder and set it on the ground. He unzipped it and pulled out my iPod and speaker set. He stood up and flipped back the hank of tousled hair that had fallen over his eye. He handed me the equipment. "Here. I got these back for you."

He hoisted up his backpack, zipped it, and slung it over his shoulder. He lifted his chin at me. "Well, see ya."

"Wait!" I said. I touched the arm of his black leather jacket. I stood on tiptoe for a second to look up into his face. "Johnny. Wait. Listen, thanks for these. And I'm sorry for being such a bitch at the bonfire. I was just in a really bad mood."

He ran his fingers through his honey-colored hair and that same piece fell over his eye again. "No biggie. See ya."

"Johnny—"

"I gotta go, Fiona. 'Bye." He stalked away down the hall. I watched him the whole way until he turned the corner. The warm little stir inside me congealed into a cold ache. One thing was for sure: Johnny Mercer definitely did not want to bang me. Hell, he didn't even want to make small talk. Mar must've been wrong. Or maybe I'd just been so harsh at the bonfire that he couldn't get past it. Either way, it sucked.

I thought about Johnny the whole way down to the locker room. About everything he'd done for me. How often he'd stood up for me. How many times he'd been there to make sure I was okay. And I felt this overwhelming sense that I'd lost out on something. Or lost something. Of value.

And I wanted it back.

But for now, I faced a different sort of atonement. I popped in my contacts and slunk into the gym. I was not looking forward to apologizing to Amanda. I tried to hide behind the bleachers, but Simone Dawson spotted me and skipped over.

"Fiona! I'm so glad you're back." She gave me a hug, but I

just stood there like a moron, because I hadn't been expecting it. When I finally realized what she was doing, I went to hug her back but she'd already committed to detachment. So I ended up in one of those awkward half-hugging/half-patting maneuvers—the trademark move of sociopaths and germophobes.

"Thanks, Simone," I said.

"Oh! Your glasses are gone! Did you get contacts? They look great! Are they tinted ones?"

"Uh, yes, yes, thanks, and no, they're clear."

"That's your natural eye color? Oh, they're such a rich brown!"

"Thanks, Simone."

"You could really make those pop with the right shadow and mascara."

"Maybe," I said. "But it'd be kinda hard to see if I popped my eyeballs."

Simone giggled. "Fiona, you are *so* funny."

"Funny-looking," I said.

Simone giggled some more. "Oh, you are not." She grabbed my hand with both of hers and walked backward as she dragged me forward. "Come on—everyone's glad you're back."

Yeah, right. I was *so* sure Amanda would do a spontaneous backflip at my return. But when I got over to the group, she didn't yell or swear or storm off or anything. She actually acknowledged my existence in a nonhostile fashion.

I cleared my throat in an overexaggerated way and said, "Listen, I want to publicly apologize to Amanda, and to everyone, for my schizoid wig-out at the pep rally. I had temporarily left Planet Sanity, and some absolutely a-hole Fiona clone was in my place being a total jerk." I looked at Todd. He crossed his arms and didn't crack even the smallest smile. I sighed and said, "Okay, it wasn't a clone. It was me. I was the jerk. I said some really crappy things and I'm sorry. And I'm sorry about screwing the pooch on Catch the Fever, too. I hope nobody got hurt. Physically. Or otherwise. And . . . that's it."

Everyone watched Amanda for her reaction. She stood there for a second and then nodded once to me. She clapped her hands and said, "Okay, let's start with Eagle Pride," and the squad fell into formation for practice. I found my spot on the floor and we got to work.

As much as I hated to admit it, Amanda had been right about getting contacts. Not only did they not fall off my face like the glasses did, but I could actually see better. So I made it most of the way through the drills and routines without inflicting too much bodily harm. Okay, I accidentally elbowed Tessa Hathaway in the boob, head-butted Takisha King, and stepped on Simone's fingers. But that was all in one cheer. Other than that, I mostly just fell on my own ass.

At one point, they were trying to teach me this jump called a Russian, or toe-touch, wherein a human person, starting from a standing position, is theoretically supposed to jump straight up in the air, spread her legs out, flashing her coochie to all the world, reach for her toes in mid-air—with her legs still spread, mind you—and then land back on the ground, ostensibly on her feet. That last part was where I was having trouble.

I could jump up and spread 'em, fine. But by the time I got anywhere near my toes, my butt was already on the mat. I wasn't getting enough vertical lift, as they say. Whatever the hell that meant. Sounded a little too much like aerophysics to be cheerleader-speak.

"You need to tighten your abs, squat, and spring from here," Takisha said, slapping my thighs. "Not your chest. Here. Your hams and quads."

Hams and quads were two muscle groups with which I'd become painfully familiar since starting cheerleading. Also, my lats, delts, biceps, triceps, abs, glutes, and whatever malevolent muscles are responsible for shin splints. I think they're called Beelzebubiceps.

"I'm springing! I'm springing!" I insisted. Demonstrating that fact, I squatted like I was about to pee over a public toilet, clenched every muscle in my torso—and regrettably, also in my face—burst up into the air, splayed my legs out, slapped wildly at my shins, and then crumpled onto the floor in a crooked heap.

"I think that was actually better," Simone Dawson offered meekly.

"Look," Todd said as he strode over, "you need a spotter so you can get the feel of the jump." He offered a hand to pull me up. "You're not getting the rhythm of it."

I let him help yank me onto my feet, but I gave him the

stink-eye. "Rhythm?" I wheezed. "Not only do I have to defy gravity, I have to have rhythm while I do it?"

"The jump has a rhythm," he said. "Up and out and down. One and *two* and three. You're doing it like up and out and in and down. It's taking too long and you're hitting the ground. Here." He swiveled me around and wrapped his hands around my waist. "Let me spot you, and you'll feel it. Now squat," he said, and I did. "And *spring*." I bolted skyward again, but this time I felt Todd lifting and holding me up a millisecond longer than I could have myself. I touched my toes as he chanted, "*Two*." By, "and three," Todd had guided me down onto my feet.

"Did you feel it?" he asked.

"I think so," I said, actually a bit giddy. "Before, I was picturing going up, spreading out, coming back in, and going down. But this time it was like: Up, *flat*, down." When I said "flat," I stooped over and threw my hands out like I was an umpire calling safe. Or maybe I looked like a skinny pterodactyl, because everyone laughed a bit. But I didn't care. "Lemme try it by myself."

I squatted, leapt, yelled, "*Flat*," as I hit my toes, and came down, not on my feet, exactly, but into sort of a stumbling squat. Still, it was a far cry from my ass.

"All right, Princess!" Todd hooted.

The squad screeched and burst into applause. For me, partly, but also because now there was a chance we could do Maximum Spirit, a cheer that showcased the girls' gymnastics. The problem was, there was a Russian in the middle of the cheer that everyone had to do simultaneously. It was one of the squad's top cheers, and we didn't stand a chance without it.

"You'll get it now," Simone Dawson chirped.

Amanda wasn't quite bubbling over with optimism, but she did say, "Better. Keep working. You have a week and a half to get it perfect." She announced to the group, "That's practice, everyone," and together we chanted, "Go Eagles," and clapped once—the customary end-of-practice ritual. We splintered off into the waning afternoon.

I grabbed my water bottle and squirted a victory drink into my mouth. I hopped on my bike and pedaled home as fast as I could; I wanted to try the Russian again in my room. I recognized full well that I was a total dork. But I didn't care. Because I was now a total dork who could defy gravity. And that had to count for something.

When I got home, Mom handed me seven messages from Marcie. (My cell had been off at practice.) "She sounded desperate," Mom said.

I snatched the notes and the phone, ran up to my room, and dialed.

"Mar?" I asked when I heard a muffled hello.

"Oh, Fee. He broke up with me." I could hear her crying.

"I'm coming over," I said.

CHAPTER 26

TWELVE MINUTES LATER, WE WERE SITTING CROSS-legged on Marcie's canopy bed. An afternoon of weeping had turned her face into a war zone. Her mascara ran down her cheeks in dark trenches. Her usually dainty nose was engorged and dripping. Red blotches dolloped her skin like crimson camouflage. She hugged one of her lacy white pillows tight to herself.

"What happened?" I asked.

"Well, basically, I'm not pretty enough for him," she blurted.

"He said that?"

She smeared her nose across her sleeve. "No, what he said was that I'd become too high-maintenance. Too much hair and nails and makeup and crap. Said he'd always pictured himself with a . . ." Her breath shuddered as she tried to catch it. "A natural beauty." Marcie dissolved in tears. I wrapped my arms around her. *That sonofabitch*, I thought. Then I said it out loud.

"Marcie, you are a total natural beauty," I said. "You always have been and you always will be. Gabe is a blind horse's ass if he can't see that. And you know what? Even if he could see it? He's a shit-can for thinking looks are all that matter. You know that." I held her and stroked her hair exactly like Mr. Pickler had Sam's.

"I know," she sobbed. "Anyway, I think the real reason he broke up with me is because I wouldn't sleep with him."

"Well, who would?" I said, counting all the times I'd fantasized about it myself. "Gross," I added for extra believability.

"Lately, it seemed like that was all he wanted," Mar said. "He never shut up about it."

"He didn't like, force you into anything, did he?"

"No."

"Good," I said.

"Well, not quite."

I pushed her back from me to look her in the eye. "Not quite? What the hell does *that* mean?"

She fiddled with a lilac ribbon on the trim of the pillow. "Oh, nothing terrible. I mean nothing too terrible. He'd just get a little . . . aggressive sometimes. But nothing illegal or anything."

"It doesn't have to be illegal to be wrong, Mar. Don't defend him."

"I know. I'm not. It's just hard to pinpoint exactly what he did. He'd just get pushy sometimes. And mad when I didn't do what he wanted. But then afterward, he'd tell me he loved me, which I know now is complete bullshit, but when he said it, everything was perfect again. I really thought he loved me, Fee. And that I loved him."

I couldn't believe he'd broken her heart like that. Todd was right. Gabe Webber was toast. As in toasted. He was gonna burn. I would see to it.

She folded herself over the pillow and wailed, "When is it going to stop hurting?"

"It's gonna be okay," I said. I rubbed her back. "Forget him. You know what? Just pretend none of it ever happened."

She sat up and pleaded, "How can I?"

She wanted an answer. She sat there on her frilly, pure white bedspread waiting for me to give her the solution that would heal her heart and restore her dignity. Because that would be great right now, Fiona. Forgetting about it would be great. And you've led her to believe it can be done. So, how?

I thought about Nana surviving forty-three years of pain for Uncle Tommy. I thought about Principal Miller struggling through a speech about marriage, while hers had fallen apart. I thought about Maggie Klein's slow deterioration within a job that once fulfilled her. And that was when I knew the answer.

"You can't," I whispered. "You can't forget the bad stuff, and you can't pretend it never happened."

Marcie squeezed her eyes shut and pressed her lips together. "But I want to," she squeaked.

I hooked my forefinger under a tendril of her hair and moved it off her forehead. "No. You have to own it. You have to make it yours, Mar. Because once it's part of you, then you can build on it. It becomes a piece of the foundation of who you are. And who you'll become."

She opened her eyes and nodded faintly. "Not exactly a short-term solution," she said.

"I wish I had one for you." I truly did. Which gave me an idea. "But I bet I can cheer you up a bit."

She grimaced and shook her head. "Ha. Doubtful."

"Well, watch this." I crawled off the bed and stood in the middle of the floor in front of her. I put my hands on my hips, shouted, "READY? OKAY," and slapped my thighs. "WE'VE GOT THE SPIRIT, YEAH. WE'VE GOT THE MAXIMUM SPIRIT. YOU SHOULD WATCH YOURSELF, 'CAUSE WHEN WE CHEER YOU'RE GONNA HEAR IT. NOT A LITTLE," step and turn, "NOT A LOT," reach and hop, "IT'S THE," squat, "MAXIMUM SPIRIT," Russian, "AND YOU KNOW," kickety-kick, kickety-kick, "IT'S WHITE HOT!" lick-thumb-and-place-to-ass, "TSSSSSS."

"Oh. My. *God*." Marcie covered her face and rolled backward, laughing. "Omigodomigodomigod!" She sat up suddenly. "Fee! You were actually *good*."

"You're obviously delirious from crying."

"*No*, you were totally not bad. Although I admit that the sight of you cheering was one of the strangest things I've ever seen in my life."

"I need to work on the jump," I said.

"Whatever. I *loved* it." She beamed at me. "Thank you, Fee."

"Yeah, well. Only you get the private showing, Mar."

I called my parents to tell them I was staying for dinner. After dinner, I called to ask them if I could stay over. They said yes, so Mar and I stayed up late filling each other in on the details we'd missed out on during our "temporary discord" as we called it.

I told her about Samantha Pickler. She recatalogued all of Johnny Mercer's finer points. I told her about Uncle Tommy and showed her Nana's rings that I'd been wearing. She told me everything that had happened between Gabe and her. I listened, even though it was all about . . . Gabe.

It almost felt like the "temporary discord" had never happened. But we both knew it had.

It was just that now, we owned it.

CHAPTER 27

SO, I'D MADE UP WITH MAR. I'D MADE UP WITH SEÑOR Shitslacks. I'd even forged a shaky truce with Amanda. The only person I still needed to deal with was Johnny Mercer. Oh yeah, I had to kill Gabe Webber, too, but there was plenty of time for that. First, I had to make Johnny not hate me anymore. I tried to catch him in calc, but he always came in right before the bell and disappeared right after.

He got away from me again on Friday, and I couldn't bear to have it hanging over me all weekend, so I decided just to call him. I got his number from Mar, and after school, I snuck up to my room, did some deep breathing à la Maggie Klein, and dialed.

A woman answered. "Hello?"

"Yes, hello. May I please speak with Johnny?" I pride myself on my telephone etiquette.

"May I ask who's calling, please?"

"Fiona Sheehan," I said.

I could tell she put her hand over the mouthpiece to yell for Johnny. Then I could hear some muffled talking. Then louder muffled talking. And more. Then I finally heard Johnny's deep, chocolaty voice on the phone. "Hey Fiona."

I suddenly wanted even more privacy, so I hopped in my closet, pulled the door shut, and squatted in the pitch-black on a pile of dirty clothes. "Hi Johnny. Um, is everything okay?" I asked, referring to all the muffled talking, which I probably shouldn't have done, but whatev. "I didn't get you in trouble for calling, did I?"

"Nah," he said. "What's up?"

One more deep breath. I figured I might as well get it all out while I had the chance. "Okay, don't get mad at Mar and don't get mad at me, but she told me about all the crap Principal Miller is making you do because of that prank, and I wanted to say I'm sorry and thank you, and I hope you don't hate me because of it, or the bonfire, or because I crumpled up your note, which I only did because I thought you were saying I *was* an insensitive snob *and* that you didn't like me, and I hope you'll let me make it up to you by giving you my iPod and speakers, or at least letting me pay for your workshop or something, because I really can't stand you being mad at me, which I know you are, and I totally get, but I wish you weren't, so please tell me you'll forgive me."

Silence.

"Is that it?" Johnny said.

"I think so."

Silence.

I said, "Are you mad?"

"Nah."

"I really am sorry."

"Me too," he said.

"For what?"

"Avoiding you."

"I can't blame you," I said.

Silence.

"So we're cool then?" I asked.

"Yeah," he said. "Friends?"

"Um . . . yeah. Friends."

"See ya Monday," he said.

"Okay. 'Bye."

"Hey Fiona?"

"Yeah?"

"Thanks for calling."

"Thanks for listening."

"Okay. 'Bye."

"'Bye."

Click.

Silence.

I sat there in the dark.

Friends. He was cool with being friends. That should've made me happy to hear, right? It should've made me feel just fabulous that Johnny Mercer wanted to be my friend. That was what I wanted, right? To be friends?

So tell me why I felt like someone had just thumped me in the gut?

Saturday, December 7

I've done more apologizing in the past week than a politician with a crack pipe and a sex addiction. Everything was so harsh before I'd done it. And doing it was no freaking picnic. But having done it feels great.

I'm thinking about Mar, and I'm wondering . . . how do you know if it's really true love? You can't go by what's on TV, because everyone knows that's crap. But even a lie is based in some truth, right?

So is there really a true love for everyone? And how do you know when you've found it? Does it make you all blissed out to be in it? And totally destroy you when you're not? If the emotions of true love really were that extreme, then wouldn't true love be easy to identify? There'd never be a question of whether it was the real deal.

But it isn't easy to identify. So I wonder if true love is more subtle. If it sneaks up and just stands there next to you, and you don't recognize that it's true love until you turn and look at this thing that's been right there with you all along, and you realize that you never want to be without it.

Does that sound totally fruitcake?

Don't answer that.

CHAPTER 28

I SPENT THE WHOLE WEEKEND PRACTICING CHEERS and my Russian. Monday at school, Mom and her activist group, Parents Opposing Mandatory Marriage Education, or POMME, as they'd dubbed themselves, lined up to picket again. (I thought it ironic that their acronym was the French word for "apple," an actual symbol of education. But nerds like me notice these things.) The POMME chant for this week was: "*Marriage education class—can't decide which kids will pass!*" Only this week, they had about four more bullhorns, so the words were unmistakable and frankly kind of distracting.

But I made it through the day and headed down to the gym for practice. I slipped into the locker room to change into some sweats. Then I strolled casually into the gym. Only then—when I saw Mrs. O'Toole actually upright, talking, and pointing, and I saw the frantic looks on the cheerleaders' faces as they scuttled around—did I realize.

The district competition was this coming weekend.

We had five meager afternoons to pull our competition routine into some semblance of shape. But let's face it: it wasn't the routine that needed to be pulled into shape; it was me. I was the weak link by which the strength of the chain would be gauged. I knew it. The rest of the squad knew it. So I made a resolution then and there: no matter how much I needed to study for finals next week, no matter how badly I wanted to finish *Pride and Prejudice*, no matter who I pissed off and owed an apology to . . . this week, I was A Cheerleader.

Okay, a little over-the-top. But it's fun to pretend to be a martyr-hero. As much as I hated to admit it, though, it wasn't any noble sense of obligation that was motivating me; it was the prospect of public humiliation on an epic level. Epic, I tell you.

"Come on, Princess," Todd called. "You're late."

Was I? I checked my watch. I must have dawdled a few minutes too long in the locker room. "Sorry," I yelled and ran over to the group.

"Let's get started. Line up for Catch the Fever," Amanda commanded. Funny. I'd have to tell Mar that one. Commander Amanda. Amanda Demanda. Amanda the Pan—

"*Fiona*!" she barked.

Oops. Right. Focus. I jumped into line.

I threw myself into it, full-on. I dared anyone within a mile to resist catching Eagle fever. Because the Eagles were so hot, the fever couldn't be stopped. So if you couldn't take the heat, then you'd better just drop.

I belted the words from my diaphragm like I'd been taught. I smiled like a loony goofball. I hit all my marks, I didn't drop Simone, and I ended with a flourish. Ta-da!

So imagine my surprise when Mrs. O'Toole yelled, "That stunk! Miss Sheehan, you need to get with the program!"

"What?" I cried. I thought I'd nailed it.

"She's right," Todd said. "It blew chunks. You were way off, Fiona."

Todd must've been joking. But then again, he'd used my real name.

He said, "Your legs were bent. Your wrists were floppy. You were late on the jump and the clap *again*."

"I was trying my *best*," I bellowed. The dead silence that followed told me the obvious truth: my best was nowhere near good enough for this squad.

"We know," Simone Dawson mumbled.

Ouch.

Amanda sighed. "All right, look." She searched the ceiling like she was hoping to find some divine inspiration up between the basketball banners. "Fiona, come into the locker room. We'll work in front of the mirror. You guys keep going."

When I was in third grade, this kid had gotten pulled from math class because he couldn't grasp fractions. The teacher had sat him outside in the hall so he could work on the more remedial stuff. At the time, I'd thought he was lucky to be getting out of class. Now I realized how embarrassed he must have been.

I followed Amanda into the locker room like a naughty puppy. She stood me in front of the full-length mirror and told me to do the cheer. I did. And Todd had been right. I blew chunks. "I don't have a big mirror at home," I mumbled. Like that was the excuse. Truth be told, it had never dawned on me to use a mirror. What an idiot.

"Try it again," Amanda said. "I'll stand in front of you and we'll go through the moves in slow motion. Try to match me exactly."

We went through Catch the Fever at one-eighth speed. "Really feel the position," Amanda said again and again. "Cement it into your muscles." Whatever the hell that meant.

She explained that my muscles would remember where to go. Some sort of sense-memory thing. I was dubious, but I cemented as hard as I could.

After Catch the Fever, we did Steam. Then the next one. By the time we'd done each cheer at least a thousand times, practice was over. Once again, all Amanda said was, "Better."

I pride myself on gratitude, so I said, "Thanks."

I'd meant thanks for the—albeit minuscule—compliment. Amanda must have thought I meant thanks for the one-on-one help. Because she said, "No problem." And added, "That's how I learned, too. I had the same trouble as you." She didn't even cast a backward glance at me as she sailed back into the gym to find Todd.

I felt strangely quasi-honored. Amanda Lowell had just passed on secrets of the cheerleader sisterhood to me. And thrown a little secret about herself into the mix. Plus, I noted, she hadn't even insulted me once. Surely I had slipped into a parallel universe.

I grabbed my stuff and headed out the door to go home. I pedaled home through the cold, flinty dusk thinking that maybe if I was lucky, my parallel-universe parents would be decent ones.

But I mean, really, who was I kidding?

CHAPTER 29

WHEN TODD AND I GOT TO MAGGIE KLEIN'S OFFICE the next morning for counseling, we stopped dead in the doorway. Her office resembled a violent crime scene. Trash littered the floor. One of the fluorescent lights had blown. Mom's campaign letters were stacked on every surface. And Maggie Klein seemed to . . . well, to be honest . . . smell. We crept in cautiously and sat down. She did not say, "Welcome." She didn't even say our names. All she said was, "It's about that last budget you turned in."

I cast a sideways glance at Todd. He'd filled out the budget on his own, and it had never occurred to me to ask what he'd done. Maggie Klein lifted three sheets of paper from her lap like each weighed ten pounds. "Let me get this straight. In September, your budget allowed you to save twenty dollars." She slapped one sheet down. "In October, you earned well above your costs, so you bought a fancy TV, and saved $807.50 to carry over to November . . ." She slapped the second sheet down. She held up the third. "Which is the budget I have here. Am I correct?"

I said, "Yeah," checking Todd again for some indication

of what was going on. He sat rock-still with his lips pressed together to keep from smiling.

Oh, crap. What had he done?

"Now, in the month of November, you earned"—she flapped the page in front of her face—"*zero* dollars of real-world money." She looked at us over the top of the paper. "But instead of scaling down your expenses to meet the eight-hundred . . . and-whatever dollars from your savings, you spent the whole amount on"—she peered at the paper again—"an all-inclusive, five-day vacation in Jamaica." Maggie Klein dropped her arm like it was made of stone. "And then you declared bankruptcy."

Todd buried his mouth in his fist and tried unsuccessfully not to laugh.

"How do you explain this?" she asked.

I didn't budge. Todd was going to have to field this one on his own.

He reached over and grasped my hand. "My wife and I never had a honeymoon," he said. "All that talk about white sandy beaches and tropical islands put us in the mood for one, so we finally went. But by the time we got back, we didn't have enough cash to pay the bills. So we decided the best thing for us would be to declare bankruptcy and start fresh." Todd squeezed my hand and gazed lovingly at me. "Debt-free."

Maggie Klein clenched her jaw. And then her eyes. She ground her palms into the sockets with both hands. Outside, the bullhorns' chant of "*Marriage education class—can't decide which kids will pass!*" crept through the concrete-block walls.

Maggie Klein raked her fingernails back and forth over her scalp, and then dragged her hands down over her face, pulling her skin along. "Why?" she demanded. It wasn't a question; it was an accusation. "Do you think this is fun for me? Do you think I enjoy sitting here while you little shits turn my job into a joke?" Todd's face fell. "For three months, I've tried to give you kids a heads-up about the goddamn combat zone you're about to face in the future. You think it's easy to find someone? You think they'll just show up at your door and love you, and everything will be perfect and turn out like a fairy tale? Ha! Like that ever happens! It's awful out there! It'll eat away your soul! And here I am, trying to help you out so you don't have to go through this, but all I get back is sarcasm and practical jokes. Well, you know what? To hell with you. Figure it out yourself." She stood up and walked to the door. "Get out. Take your little smartasses down to the principal's office. Let her deal with you." She opened the door and stood there. "I'm done."

Todd didn't move. I followed his lead.

"*Get out!*" Maggie Klein bellowed.

We both jumped up and bolted out the door. She slammed it shut behind us, and the sound echoed down the empty hallway.

"Okay, then," Todd said.

"Did she just kick us out of marriage ed?" I asked.

"Looks that way. There goes all that sweet cash."

"Screw the cash. Doesn't it also mean we don't graduate?"

Todd slugged me playfully in the arm. "Look, Maggie

Klein can't stop us from graduating. She's only a guidance counselor. And we didn't do anything wrong, anyway. We filled out the budget. We went to the counseling. We did the shared activity. You did your stupid journal, right?"

I nodded yes.

Todd said, "Then she can't touch us." He grabbed my sleeve and pulled. "Come on." He led me down the hall toward the administration offices.

The receptionist, Mrs. DelNero, a sixty-something woman with a passion for appliquéd sweater-vests and Jean Nate body wash, pecked at her keyboard. Todd leaned on the counter and crooned, "Hi there. We're here to see Principal Miller."

"Is there something you need, hon?" One of the bullhorns outside squealed with feedback. Mrs. DelNero jumped and tipped over her mug of multicolored pens.

"Not really," he said with absolutely no urgency in his voice. "Maggie Klein just suggested we come see her."

She picked up the phone receiver and said, "I'll see if she's got a minute for ya." She punched three buttons with her pudgy finger and said into the phone, "Principal Miller? Two of the senior class are here to see you." She paused and then hung up the phone. "Go on in, hon." She winked at Todd. Apparently, I had become invisible. Todd had that effect.

We weaved our way through the reception area and into Principal Miller's office. She sat hunched over a mess of paperwork spread over her desktop. Picket signs and chanting POMME marchers passed in front of her window at regular intervals, but she gave no indication that she noticed.

"Ms. Sheehan, Mr. Harding. Good morning. Take a seat." We sank down into the two sagging orange chairs facing her. "I just received a call from Ms. Klein." She let that statement hang in the air for a few seconds. Typical principal maneuver. "You two seem to have upset her quite a bit. Explain."

I let Todd do the talking. Charming older women was clearly his department. His God-given talent and forte, even. Might as well use it.

"It was a huge misunderstanding, Principal Miller, believe me," he purred. She showed no signs of weakening. Todd leaned forward. "All we did was push the envelope a little bit, in terms of the marriage ed budget. We didn't break any rules. But it seems like Mag—uh, Ms. Klein didn't care for our choices. I hope you can see it from our point of view."

Principal Miller leaned back in her chair and crossed her arms. She wasn't buying any of it. She sent laser eye daggers at us over the red rims of her glasses. "From what I've seen over the past few months, your 'point of view' has been nothing less than hostile and disruptive. But I stood back and let you two try to work it out."

"And we have," I blurted. "Look at us. We're sitting here together presenting a united front."

"I see that. However, Ms. Klein feels that you've made a mockery of this whole course, and her work in it as well. Don't congratulate yourselves, though, because you're not the only ones. Several of your classmates have exhibited the same lack of seriousness as you two."

"But we took it seriously!" I argued. "We did everything you asked. We kept up our assignments. We went to the counseling. It's not fair to keep us from graduating because of what someone else did."

She leaned forward on her desk and laced her fingers together. She scrutinized one of us and then the other. Back and forth, like a lioness scanning the savannah for prey. "No, it's not fair. Is it?" she growled. "It's not fair to spend so much time working toward something, only to have someone else's lapse in judgment, poor choice, one mistake, destroy it all."

Todd and I recoiled deeper into our seats. I tried to puzzle out what specifically, Principal Miller was talking about. Was it Todd and me and the other students in the course? Was it the betrayal and disillusionment she felt in her own marriage? Was it Maggie Klein's unraveling counseling career?

"Principal Miller," Todd said in a dead-serious voice completely devoid of syrup, "this isn't Fiona's fault. She didn't know about the last budget. I did it by myself. She had nothing to do with it. She should graduate."

Principal Miller took aim at him and fired. "I'll decide who graduates and who doesn't." I couldn't believe this was the same woman who could dirty-dance with Mr. Evans and break down in front of the whole student body. The woman in front of Todd and me was hard as stone. Impenetrable. Invulnerable.

"Please," Todd said. "If I don't graduate, fine. But let Fiona."

She sighed and sat back in her chair again. Her face softened slightly. I hoped that Todd had made a hairline crack in her exoskeleton. But I was worried that she was about to agree to his bargain, and I couldn't let that happen. "Wait," I said. "This isn't Todd's fault. I'm the one who started everything. I threw a hot dog at him. I kept provoking him. I made it difficult for Maggie Klein. Todd deserves to graduate more than I do."

Principal Miller inhaled and her face lit up slowly, like a sunrise. In fact, by the time she finally spoke, I could have told Principal Miller that I was going to become a nun and devote my life to prayer and celibacy, and her expression wouldn't have approximated the look of surprise she'd developed. "Hot damn," she whispered. "It worked."

"Excuse me?" Todd stammered.

She waved the question away. "Nevermind. All right, kids, here's what's going to happen. Your behavior, although negative and destructive, has not, in fact, violated the parameters set forth in the marriage ed course. Therefore, you are still enrolled in the program and eligible for graduation, and you remain in the running to win the cash prize. On one condition: the two of you must write a letter of apology for your behavior to Ms. Klein." She leaned toward us. Her eyes narrowed to dark slits behind her bifocal lenses. "Otherwise, you fail."

Todd and I squirmed and groaned in objection.

"And you must turn it in first thing Monday morning," she said.

Now we had some complaints to sink our teeth into. "But we have midterm exams next week," I cried.

"And districts this weekend," Todd added.

"Yeah, districts!" I echoed. "Did you know we're doing districts on Saturday?"

"Yes, Ms. Sheehan. I am aware of the cheerleading squad's competition this weekend. What that has to do with our situation is beyond me."

Todd and I both gaped at her. Then at each other. Then back at her. Like two comic-strip characters. The text bubbles above our heads would've read: *How could she say that? Is she blind? Deaf? Has she not seen us working together all semester? Are we not literally working together as a freaking team? Is she a total dictator, emphasis on the "dick"? Is there a question?*

"Now, Ms. Sheehan, Mr. Harding. You may return to class."

The flared bell of a bullhorn appeared at the window. "*Marriage education class—can't decide which kids will pass.*" Todd and I craned our necks to see who was out there. Principal Miller reached behind her and snapped the blinds shut. "*Back to class.*"

We didn't wait around to hear it again. Todd and I clawed our way out of the orange chairs and boogied out of the office.

"This is ridiculous," Todd said.

I said, "Let's just focus on districts. We'll figure this out after."

CHAPTER 30

DESPITE THE DISTRACTION OF PRINCIPAL MILLER'S verbal spanking, cheer practice the rest of the week actually went okay. It was no coincidence that this "okay" week ended on Friday the thirteenth. Ask anyone who's unlucky what the one day is when they *are* lucky, and I bet they'll say Friday the thirteenth. And this Friday the thirteenth proved it. I found myself one, best friends with Mar again; two, not in hand-to-hand combat with either Todd or Amanda; and *three*, one day away from the end of my cheerleader prison sentence. And if that doesn't convince you that Friday the thirteenth is lucky, then you're nuts. It's solid science.

The squad all wore our uniforms to school Friday to gear everybody up for the competition on Saturday. Callie Brooks saw my candy-cane-colored polyester disaster, and got this expression on her face like she was passing a pinecone backward through her intestines. I gave her the finger as I walked by.

For practice after school, we ran a kind of dress rehearsal. I have to say, when we did the whole competition routine in perfect synchrony, it was cool. We all moved together. And I was part of it. Part of a team. I'd never felt that before. I had a hard time putting my finger on the precise name for the sensation. But I finally figured it out. Pride. Oh God. I actually had Eagle pride. Ain't irony a pisser?

Finally, we broke off and agreed to meet outside the gym at eight in the morning to get onto the bus that would take us to Stonemount High, the school hosting the competition.

At home, I nibbled at dinner. Tried to force some carbs down my gullet for energy the following day. Talked on the phone to Mar for a few minutes. Begged her not to show up for the competition. Took out my contacts and stared out the window at the fuzzy night sky for about a hundred hours. Finally fell asleep and dreamed about cheering. Not exactly what you'd call a restful night.

My alarm went off at 7 a.m. I showered, popped my contacts back in, pulled my hair into a ponytail, and slipped on my uniform. Dad drove me to school so I wouldn't have to bike in bare legs.

Mrs. O'Toole was remarkably animated as she inspected our uniforms and checked our names off on a clipboard. By eight-twelve, we were all on the bus, inhaling the engine fumes that leaked in through the heating system and trying to forget that in three hours we'd either be on our way to regionals or on our way home as losers. Well, I wouldn't be going to regionals—Judith Norton would. I'd be there with the orange water cooler. That is, unless Mom actually succeeded in killing the marriage ed course. I'd probably go anyway, though. Just to watch.

"Whatcha thinking about, Princess?" Todd had swiveled

around in his seat to bug me. Amanda sat next to him but didn't acknowledge my existence. I was fine with that.

"I'm relishing the fact that this is the very last day of my cheerleading career."

"Say whatever you like, but I know you're going to miss that little skirt," he said.

"Don't worry," I said, "you'll get it back today. I hope it still fits you."

"At least I know you didn't stretch out the sweater."

"Unlike the poor sweater you're wearing. Your man-boobs are much bigger than mine."

"You have man-boobs?"

Amanda sighed in our general direction. Todd turned to the front again and leaned over to nuzzle her ivory neck. I turned on my iPod, slipped in the earphones, and tuned out everything else.

When we got to Stonemount an hour later, I was half-asleep. The music, the rocking of the bus, and the lack of sleep the night before had zoned me out. In fact, we all seemed to be in zombie mode as we lumbered off the bus and filed into the school gym. Then everything changed.

Einstein's theory of relativity put forth the idea that mass and energy are interchangeable. Poor Albert spent years analyzing and refining his equations to come to that conclusion. Years spent hunched over a ledger or scratching at a chalkboard. All he'd ever needed to do was go to a cheer competition.

The energy in the gym was palpable. I could actually

feel it thick and prickly around me. Cheerleader-shaped atoms streaked across the space at blinding speeds, leaving the fabric of reality shuddering in their wakes. Everywhere, ponytails swung, skirts twirled, fists pumped, legs splayed, and color-coated bodies flipped, flew, and fell in a kinetic frenzy. Tearing through the chaos were sounds of cheering, clapping, stomping, and screeching. The noise bounced and rebounded off every surface without ever losing a decibel.

Each squad clustered together in a spot on the floor to practice. We snaked our way through them toward the registration table. As we did, our competition eyeballed us like rival street gangs. We did the same to them. Amanda was particularly adept at this. She never looked away first. I swear she could have stared down a bull in Pamplona without dropping an eyelash. She gave an especially frigid glare to the captain of the Lincoln squad. The rivalry between East Columbus and Lincoln went back as long as any of us knew. It didn't help that their football team was the one that had injured Todd, either. And last year, Lincoln had beaten East Columbus by a hair at these competitions. So Amanda and the rest of the squad were ripe for revenge. I gave them the best evil eye I could muster, but I think it probably looked like I was impersonating a pirate.

Mrs. O'Toole got us registered and we staked out a spot on the floor. We warmed up and plowed through our whole routine at double time and half-effort. The purpose of this strategy was twofold. One, we didn't want to waste energy, and two, we didn't want to tip our hand. If the squad next to us knew we were doing a certain complicated stunt, they might change one of theirs to up the ante.

As soon as we finished, my guts started churning. I realized that the next time I did the routine, I would be out in the middle of the floor, in front of a crowd that was presently growing at an exponential rate. Simone Dawson must have known I was freaking out inside, because she pulled me over to the bleachers and sat me down. "Nervous?" she asked.

"Nah," I lied.

"I am," she said. "Hey, could you do me a favor?"

"Depends," I said.

Simone's face sparkled. "Would you let me give you a makeover?"

"A what?" I asked, although I knew exactly what she meant.

"You know. Do your makeup. It takes my mind off stuff. Calms me down."

Well, far be it from me to let poor Simone vex away beside me. "I guess," I said. So there I sat as Simone opened something that looked like a purple fishing-tackle box full of makeup and proceeded to paint my face. It made me think of Sam's makeovers. I really wanted to see Sam again. Find out how she was doing. I wished she was here to see me, because she'd understand the ridiculous hilarity of this situation like no one else. Except maybe Marcie. Even so, I prayed Mar wouldn't show up.

"Relax your face," Simone cooed.

I closed my eyes and let the brushstrokes on my cheeks

sweep away the tension. I tried a little meditation. Zen and the art of makeup application.

I heard a voice say, “Good luck, Fee!” and I opened one eye. Then my stomach clenched again. There was Mar. And standing next to her was Johnny Mercer.

I tried to talk as Simone coated my lips with opalescent pink goo. “Oh God, why did you guys come to submit yourselves to this torture?”

“If you think I’d miss it, you’re crazy,” Mar said. “Johnny and I did our marriage ed job this morning, so I asked if he wanted to come with me to the competition after. Right?”

“Yup,” Johnny said. He ran his fingers through his hair and then shoved his hands into the pockets of his black leather jacket. He bounced his knees in and out one at a time. But when I caught his eye, he stopped and winked at me. I grinned, and Simone poked me in the tooth with the lip gloss wand.

Mar tapped me on the elbow. “Johnny even brought his video camera. We’re going to post the whole thing online.”

I tensed up like someone had just given me a surprise rectal exam.

“She’s kidding!” Johnny blurted.

“Just do me one favor?” I pleaded. “Sit where I can’t see you.”

Mar guffawed in the most undignified manner. “Fat chance,” she said. I tried to kick at her sideways.

“How many schools are here?” Johnny asked. “When do you guys go on?”

"I'm not sure," I said. I looked at Simone for an answer. "Do you know?"

"There are ten squads," she said, "and each does a five minute routine featuring their best cheers. The first slots are rough, because the judges keep scores low, in case better squads come next. The middle slots are best because the crowd is enthused and the energy is good. The worst slot is the last one, because everyone is tired, and usually the squad has been psyched out by the competition."

"Which are we?" I whispered haltingly.

"Mrs. O'Toole drew us as last."

My stomach rose up at least halfway into my esophagus. I gagged and tried to swallow, but ended up semiconvulsing. Marcie and Johnny backed away.

"Uh, we're going to get some seats," Mar said way too nicely. "You just . . . try to relax and . . . have fun. Come on, hubby."

"Good luck," Johnny said. The two of them slunk away.

Good luck? Have fun? Wasn't that what the freaking marriage ed packet had said? Goddamn marriage ed. If it hadn't been for that stupid-ass course, I wouldn't have been here poised on the brink of eternal disgrace. And why did Johnny Mercer have to come? Why did Mar have to bring him? I knew she wanted me to "get to know" Johnny better, but why here? I needed to focus on the cheers, but all I could think about was Johnny Mercer out there somewhere, about to watch me make a frenzied monkey's ass out of myself. I couldn't bear the thought of looking idiotic in front of him. I wrapped my arms tight around my aching belly, tipped over, and laid my head in Simone's lap. She started petting my hair. "It's okay, Fiona. You'll do fine."

I didn't think even sunny-faced Simone herself believed it.

CHAPTER 31

AN HOUR AND A HALF LATER, WE WERE ON DECK. The second-to-last squad—the one from Stonemount, actually—was racing out onto the floor. And I was crapping my briefs. Almost literally. I'd been to the bathroom three times so far. Apparently, my body was involved in a last-ditch effort to relieve me of my doom. As well as the entire contents of my lower GI tract.

But now we were five minutes out. The competition had been stiffer than the muscles in my neck. The squad from Lincoln had clearly set the bar. They'd gotten the prime fifth slot, of course. They'd nailed all their jumps and tumbling sequences and done this stunt that looked like a flower blooming, or fireworks exploding, or something. Even so, I figured we stood a chance. If it had been Judith instead of me, I was sure ECHS would run away with the title. I glanced over at Todd. He was looking at me. He came over and whispered, "Something looks different."

The squad from Stonemount was halfway through their second routine.

"Simone put makeup on me," I whispered back.

He pursed his lips. Turned his head back and forth to get a look from every angle. "It looks good."

I sighed. "Spare me."

"What's that? Oh, I thought you said, 'Spear me.'"

What the hell was he talking about? "Spear me?"

Todd stretched his arms up, laced his fingers behind his head, and got this shit-eating grin on his face. "Yeah. I figured you wanted me to bone you."

My mouth fell open. I could not believe he was saying this, minutes before we had to go out. "You are a disgusting, depraved caveman, Señor Shitslacks, and I would rather get beaten to death with a stick full of nails than get"—I did the quote thingy with my chewed-nail fingers—"'boned' by you."

"See?" he said with a smirk on his face.

"*What*?"

"Stick? Nail? Beat? Come on, you want it bad."

I gave Todd my best I'm-trying-to-swallow-back-my-own-puke look.

"Not that I'd give it to you," he continued, "'cause I know you like the ladies. I wouldn't want to spoil that for you."

Well, that was it.

I put on my best sex-kitten demeanor and stood up. I brought my face within inches of his and purred, "You know, in a way you're right. Because I would sooner sleep with Amanda than sleep with you."

Todd faked a pained expression and brought his hand up to his heart. "Oh! Ouch."

"That's right," I said, straightening up again and smoothing over my body with my hands, pretending I actually was sexy. The squad from Stonemount finished up. "As much as I'd *love* to continue this revolting conversation, I've gotta go kick some cheerleader ass." I lined up behind Simone and the rest of the squad.

Todd lined up behind me. "Hey Princess," he whispered. "You and Amanda—would I get to watch?"

I snorted and pranced out onto the floor with everyone. Typical Todd. Any normal person would've given me a pep talk or some other phony thing. I hit my mark on the floor and struck ready position. Todd was far from normal, that was for sure. Then again, he'd taken my mind off the competition for a minute. Amanda called out, "Ready?" I yelled, "Okay!" and realized that Todd had done it on purpose. He'd distracted me on purpose. So I wouldn't stress.

The squad and I launched into Steam. I kept my arms as straight as I could and clapped and smiled like a lunatic. Then we rolled into Catch the Fever. In the huge, gravity-defying pyramid at the end, all I had to do was go down on one knee at the side, hold up Simone, and flare one hand. Done. We dismounted and positioned ourselves for the final cheer, Maximum Spirit. Only, I must have been off my mark by a foot or two.

I started the cheer fine. Then the Russian came. I hit the jump, nailed it, even, but somehow, I landed even further to the right. Now, the next part was where Amanda, Takisha, and Tessa Hathaway do double back handsprings into back tucks. Todd and Jamar Douglass do round-off Russians. Kendall

Armstrong, Hillary Larchmont, Ainsley Finn, and Marissa Yee do round-off back handspring layouts. Simone does three back tucks front and center. And Christine Loving and I just do kicks on the sides. Christine only does them to balance me out. She actually can tumble pretty well.

But like I said, I was off my mark.

So when Amanda came toward me, mid–back handspring, and my leg was on its way up for the first of a series of forgettable kicks, somehow—and I cannot to this day account for it with anything besides pure coincidence and poor spatial comprehension—but somehow, my foot connected with the back of Amanda's head.

Hard.

Her left arm also bore a good part of the blow, but there was no mistaking the feeling of my foot bones cracking against her skull. My knee crooked with the halted motion, and the inertia threw me forward. Amanda managed to plant her hands on the floor, but the next instant, the pain must have hit, because she collapsed like an accordion, clutching her head. I lunged for her, easing the rest of her body to the wood floor as best as I could with my balance off-kilter.

I'd screwed everything up. I knew that. All I could do now was damage control. I looked into Amanda's face for some clue of what to do. She grunted, "Up," and I obeyed. I hooked my arms in her armpits and hoisted her to her feet as the rest of the tumblers finished. We struck the final pose with everyone else in the squad at the same exact moment. "TSSSSSS."

The crowd exploded. Whistles and hoots echoed through the gym. I guess the only thing more impressive than a perfect routine is a resurrected one. The applause seemed to buoy up the squad. Nevertheless, I was sure I'd lost the competition for us. Lincoln had been flawless, and we had definitely been flawed.

We pranced back over to the bleachers to wait for the judges. As we sat, Amanda held her head in her hands. Todd sat with his arm around her and whispered in her ear. Some guy from first-aid brought over an ice pack.

I prayed that there was such a thing as a sympathy vote.

Finally, the head judge strode to the middle of the gym.

Nobody moved.

He tapped the mic.

Announced the results.

Lincoln took the title.

We got second. Again.

I sat alone on the bus home. I'd expected as much. I deserved it. But when we pulled into the school parking lot, I stood at the front and said, "I'm really sorry, everyone. I'm sorry I messed up." What could I say? I'd become the queen of contrition lately.

As people filed past me off the bus, some smiled, some patted my shoulder, and some kept their eyes on the floor. Takisha gave me a half-smile and a wink. Simone gave me a hug. I can't prove it, but I'm pretty sure Mrs. O'Toole farted at me.

Finally, Amanda and Todd were the only ones still there.

Amanda got up from her seat and walked toward me. She still held the ice pack on her head. She stood in front of me and gave me her coldest running-of-the-bulls stare. I inhaled and prepared for the verbal lashing of a lifetime.

"We took second," she said. That was it. She shouldered past me and climbed down off the bus.

I stood there dumbfounded by her cryptic statement. She meant that second place sucked, right? That she was disappointed, right? Or did she mean it as a good thing—that second place was okay and I'd helped them get there? Or did she mean that I'd sucked, but even so, they'd managed second place? I couldn't figure it out.

Todd sauntered up the aisle. I looked to him for some kind of clarification, or absolution; I wasn't sure which. "Is she mad?" I asked.

"She wanted to win," Todd said. "And you kicked her in the head."

"I didn't mean—"

"Let me finish. She wanted to win, but she knew we wouldn't. To be honest, she didn't think we'd even place. But you kicked her in the head, and we still got second. She's not mad, Fiona."

I couldn't help it; I suddenly welled up. Why the hell I would cry over whether or not I disappointed Amanda Lowell was a concept I simply didn't have the energy to explore. But there I was. "I tried my best," I whispered.

"Everyone knows that," Todd said. "She knows it. You did great, Princess."

Then Todd Harding, Señor Shitslacks, the no-necked

Neanderthal wrapped his arms around me and hugged me.

It was too much.

"Your neck smells like cheese," I said.

"Oh," he said, "that's my cheese cologne. I have a whole selection. Cheddar, American, Swiss."

"Fromunda."

He laughed. We broke apart. I looked at him. He looked at me. And I felt . . .

Nada.

Todd Harding was hilarious, smart, brave, compassionate, and my friend. That was all. It would never be more. But I honestly hoped it was for Amanda and him. That was how cuckoo for Cocoa Puffs my life had become. I actually wanted something to happen to Amanda that didn't involve her going bald, breaking out in boils, or getting a tapeworm. Remarkable.

Todd and I stepped down from the bus, and he splintered off to find Amanda. I looked around for Dad, but he wasn't there yet. One by one, everyone got into their cars and drove off. I stood there in the middle of the parking lot. With no ride home. All alone.

Then the bus pulled away.

Johnny Mercer was on the other side of it. Leaning on his car. Smiling at me.

My skin filled with bees again. I smiled back.

"Need a ride?" he said.

CHAPTER 32

I HITCHED MY COAT UP AROUND MY NECK AND TRIED to look as cute as possible while walking through the frigid parking lot toward Johnny. "What are you doing here?" I asked.

"I saw the bus. I thought maybe you'd be up for some pizza." The sound of his voice warmed the cold December afternoon air.

"Sounds great. Where's Mar?"

"She had to get home. Had a thing."

"Oh. Okay." I wasn't sure what kind of "thing" Mar could have had that I wouldn't have known about, but I didn't give it much thought. I was starving and pizza sounded fantastic. I pulled out my cell and called Dad to tell him not to bother rushing over to get me, since he'd obviously forgotten.

Johnny opened the car door for me, and I got in. His car smelled like . . . cinnamon. And what—peaches? But not real peaches: that fake, flavored-candy-type smell. And was that cloves? Weird. Maybe Johnny Mercer liked to bake. In his car.

"Sorry, it smells a little . . . fruity," he said when he got in, as if he'd read my thoughts. Maybe I'd sniffed loudly without realizing it.

"It's not bad," I said. "Kind of yummy."

"My mom sells candles," he said. He hitched his thumb toward the back. Eight or nine white cases sat stacked on the seat. "It's her car."

"That's a lot of candles," I said.

"That's nothing. Those are just her samples. You should see the guest room. It's packed. The whole upstairs reeks like a card store."

Silence while we buckled our seat belts and Johnny started the car. The radio blasted, and his hand shot out to crank the volume down. He must've been listening to an oldies station, because the song "Come Sail Away" by Styx was playing. I knew this only because Styx is my dad's all-time favorite band. He plays their vinyls all the time. So I knew "Come Sail Away" pretty well. It starts out as a ballad about throwing off the mantle of everyday responsibility for a life of freedom and adventure, but somehow ends up in an alien abduction. Whaaaatever.

Johnny twitched his head and slipped in a Radiohead CD. He drummed his fingers on the steering wheel. I wondered if he was nervous because we were alone. But you know the weird thing? I felt kind of nervous myself. Which was strange. I mean, it wasn't like a date or anything. We were just taking a ride in his car.

"It could be worse than candles," I said.

"I guess." We pulled out of the school parking lot. Once we

were off school grounds, off our main social turf, away from the comfort of our familiar, shared environment, the whole mood changed. We were out. Out in the world. Together.

After a couple minutes, I said, "For example, your mom could sell bat guano for fertilizer. That would be worse than candles."

Johnny huffed. "Yeah." We stopped at a light. Johnny stayed quiet.

Oh, crap. I'd tried to lighten the mood a bit, but I might as well have burped out loud. I was such an idiot. Why did I always have to turn every awkward situation into a joke? Couldn't I just leave it alone?

Just to make things more uneasy, "Creep" started playing. Perfect. That song pretty much summed me up. What the hell *was* I doing here, anyway? Wearing a cheerleading uniform. And makeup. In a car with a guy. Alone. Who did I think I was? I was nothing more than a weirdo, and I didn't belong here.

Then Johnny said, "You know what would be worse?"

I inhaled uncertainly and said, "What?"

"She could sell slop to pig farms."

I laughed, relieved. He was playing along. Making sure I was okay. And it dawned on me that maybe Johnny had been thinking the same thing about himself when that song played. Well, not the uniform and makeup part, but the rest. And it might be bananas, but I found the idea that we were just two weirdos together strangely comforting.

"You know what would be worse?" I said. "She could sell

owl pellets." I warmed my hands over the heat coming out of the dashboard.

"Owl pellets?"

"Lumps of owl puke. Full of bird and mouse bones. Schools use them for science classes."

"They do not."

"They do."

"That's disgusting."

I snuck sideways glances at him. His straw-colored hair had that kind of long, messy look and hung just over the tops of his sideburns. I was watching his long eyelashes blink when he turned and looked straight at me. I quickly spun toward the front so he wouldn't catch me staring, but it was too late. I knew he'd seen me.

A block later, he said, "You know what would be worse? She could sell dead frogs."

I laughed a bit too loud and nodded. "Eww, yes. For dissection, of course."

"Of course."

We smiled and spent the rest of the ride trying to one-up each other on the most revolting things his mother could sell. I thought I'd had him with "buckets of chum" but he pulled out "raw pork skin" just as we got to Gino's East.

As we got out of the car, I tried to tug my coat down over my miniskirted butt. "I wish I had something else to wear. I feel like a dork in my uniform."

Johnny held open the door to the restaurant for me. "Are you kidding? You look hot. Besides, do you know the odds of a guy like me being seen with a cheerleader? You're lucky I'm letting you wear the coat."

I laughed and said, "Letting me? As if." But what I was really thinking was, he thinks I look hot? And what did he mean by "seen with?" Did he mean that this was a date? Were Johnny Mercer and I on a date? And tell me this, would it have been totally bizarre-o, crazy, insane for me to want it to be? Not that I did. I just meant *would* it? In a philosophical sense. That's all I'm saying. Hypothetically! Whatever.

We sat in a booth by the window and ordered a pepperoni pizza and two Cokes. Johnny said, "I was totally impressed by you today."

"What?" I said, thinking I should keep things light, just in case it wasn't a date. Which it probably wasn't. I mean, I knew it wasn't. "You mean by my sparkly jazz hands?" I treated him to his own personal showing of my jazz hands.

He took my hands and lowered them to the table. His touch made my throat feel tight and furry. The waitress brought the Cokes and I pulled my hands out of his. I picked up my straw and started slowly peeling the end off its paper wrapper.

"Seriously, Fiona," he said. "You should be proud of yourself. You stepped way out of the box, and lived."

"Unfortunately, as I stepped out of the box, my foot landed on Amanda's skull. I'm pretty sure that means I royally failed."

"No, you didn't. I mean, yes, you booted Amanda in the head. But it wasn't a failure, because you didn't back down. You were out there. Not everyone could do what you did.

That takes some courage."

As Johnny finished talking, I put the opened straw end in my mouth and blew. The paper shot off the straw and pinged Johnny in the forehead. I tried not to laugh, but I didn't try too hard.

Johnny touched his head where the paper had hit. I giggled. He frowned, knit his brows, leaned forward, and said, "Why can't you take a compliment, Fiona? I'm trying to be serious, here. Why do you always have to turn everything into a joke?"

Same question I'd asked myself in the car.

I stopped giggling. I hung my head and examined my straw. I turned it end over end in my hands. "Sorry," I said. "It's just what I'm comfortable with. I dunno. I guess it's a defense mecha—"

Ping.

Johnny's straw paper had thwacked me in the head. I looked up, and he sat there grinning, with the straw sticking out of his mouth. I couldn't believe it.

He'd pranked me.

Johnny had gotten me all serious just so he could get back at me with his straw. Brilliant. I reached out to snatch his straw from his perfect teeth, and at that exact moment, right there, the precise instant I grabbed that straw . . . that was the moment I wanted this to be a date. It was the moment that, from that point in time onward, I would see, and think about, and feel about Johnny Mercer differently.

Even though he'd been right there with me, all along.

Or maybe because of it.

And there were the bees again. More of them. Big ones. The size of small cars. Buzzing in my ears. Buzzing in my cheeks. Buzzing in my chest. Buzzing in my fingers.

I handed Johnny his straw back and concentrated very hard on folding the paper wrapper into an accordion. Fold and fold. Back and forth. Fold and fold. *Do not think. About the fact. THAT YOU LIKE. JOHNNY MERCER. JUST KEEP FOLDING. KEEP ON FOLDING.*

"Embalming fluid," Johnny said.

My fingers froze midfold. "Huh?" It sounded like I had an air leak.

"That would be worse. If she sold embalming fluid."

And, like a magic trick, the bees vanished. Flew away to buzz up some other girl. I scrunched the paper between my fingers and pointed in the air. "Fish guts. For shrimp farms."

"Nice," he said. His hazel eyes flashed as he smiled. "Well played."

The pizza came and we split it. I ate as much as Johnny, which impressed him for some reason. I guess he thought girls were supposed to be dainty eaters or something.

The waitress walked by with a basket of fries, and Johnny said, "Did you know that if you strain old fryer grease, you can use it in a diesel engine instead of diesel fuel?"

Not exactly what you'd call sweet talk. Not exactly an appetizing subject for a restaurant. But totally and utterly cool. "No way!" I said.

"Yeah. I saw it on this science show. These guys got a vat

of fryer grease from some restaurant, strained the chunks out, and poured it into the tank of a diesel car. It ran as well as on diesel fuel. Too bad it doesn't work in cars that run on gasoline, though."

"Yeah, otherwise your mom could sell vats of used fryer grease out of the guest room. That would be worse."

Johnny laughed. I loved making him laugh. And it seemed so easy to do. Talking to him was different than talking to Todd. It was all of the fun without the effort of maintaining it. Just totally organic. Johnny made me feel like I was clever without trying to be. And pretty. And valued. He made everything about me seem more special.

Like, say I was a song. Well, Johnny made me feel as though I'd been remixed. The melody didn't change, but it wasn't just the same one-dimensional sequence of notes anymore. Instead, he brought out all these harmonies—these low and high notes—that made the music fuller. No more discord or dissonance. Around Johnny, I was the best possible rendition of myself.

When the check came, he paid for the pizza, even though I offered to cover my half. Normally, I'd have felt bad not paying, but the fact that he paid provided further evidence that this might be a date, so I was okay with it.

We played "What would be worse?" all the way back to my house. Johnny pulled into our driveway but left the engine idling.

"Thanks for the pizza," I said. "And the ride."

"No problem," he said. "Anytime."

Now, if this had been a date in a romantic movie, then that would've been the point where we leaned into each other and kissed. But this wasn't a romantic movie. And apparently this wasn't even a date. Because here's what happened: I sat there for a few seconds and he made absolutely no move toward me. So I got out of his car. He watched me walk to the door and waved goodbye. I let myself in and slammed the door behind me. Not a date. Not a romantic movie. Just my own lousy, unlucky life.

CHAPTER 33

I SPENT THE REST OF THE AFTERNOON READING. I finished *Pride and Prejudice* and decided Elizabeth Bennett was a moron. She'd fallen in love with Darcy just because he did a few nice things on the sly. Did that make up for the fact that he'd been a prick to her all along?

She should've married the guy who was taking over her father's estate. Okay, so he was her cousin. That was a little gross. But he was a nice guy. Probably not too bad-looking. Polite. And, in the end, good enough for Elizabeth's friend. It seemed to me that Elizabeth Bennett was a bit of a snob herself. She and Darcy were both a bit jerky.

But maybe that was the point. That they realized the error of their jerky snob ways just in time. And Darcy fixing everything for Elizabeth's sister without anyone knowing was pretty cool. All right, so maybe it was a bit romantic after all. I couldn't exactly blame Jane Austen for being a romantic. What the hell else was there to do back then for fun?

On Sunday, I put off calling Todd about our apology letter as long as I could. When I finally got around to it, Mom was just finishing up on the phone in the kitchen as she stirred a bubbling pot of meatballs and sauce for dinner.

Spaghetti and meatballs was my favorite. It would be a nice concession for having had to do this stupid letter. Mom said, "Great, Cybil. Everything's all set. See you tomorrow," and hung up. I asked her for the phone and took it up to my room for privacy. I hadn't told my parents about getting in trouble at school, and I didn't plan to.

I dialed Todd's number. He answered. "Yo, hello?"

"*Hola*, Señor."

"Hey there, Princess. Calling about the letter?"

"Yup."

"Hey, I heard you were with Mercer yesterday," he said.

"How did you know?"

"I've got spies everywhere," he said. "Are you two going out?"

My stomach shriveled up into a nut when I realized I couldn't say yes. "I dunno. I mean . . . no. I dunno. I guess not. No."

"You should," Todd said. "Mercer's a good guy. Much better than that tool Webber."

"No kidding," I said.

"I tried to warn you. Amanda can't stand him. She says he's a selfish bastard."

"So I've heard," I said.

"Listen, what are we going to write for this letter?"

"I don't know. Every time I think of apologizing, I get pissed. We didn't do anything wrong. Technically."

"So let's not write it," he said.

"What? Just blow it off?"

"Yeah. Screw the letter. How can they keep us from

graduating? Our parents would raise even more hell. God, your mom would probably get Principal Miller fired and she knows it. I don't give a damn if I fail marriage ed. I'm not sorry for anything that happened. They're the ones who forced us into this."

"And I think we did a pretty good goddamn job of it considering how much we hate each other," I added. "I'm not sorry for anything either."

Todd laughed. "I'm really not sorry for that blow-up doll."

"And I'm not sorry for the hot dog. Or your shitslacks. I'm a little sorry for the fake announcement, but only because Johnny got in trouble."

"Yeah, but that was a good one. You definitely should not be sorry for that."

"Okay, then, I'm not."

"And I'm not sorry that you had to fill in on the squad."

"And I'm not sorry that you had to take so much time to teach me to cheer."

We just sat there together for a few seconds. Not sorry at all.

"All right, so we don't do the letter?" Todd said.

"Nope. But I think we should let them know why. Stand our ground, and all."

"Sounds like a plan," Todd said. "See you tomorrow."

"Not if I smell you first."

Click.

I didn't get much sleep that night, trying to think about what we were going to say to Principal Miller and Maggie

Klein. Even spaghetti and meatballs didn't make me feel better. But whenever I thought about caving and writing the damn letter, I felt even worse. So I knew Todd and I were doing the right thing.

I hoped so, anyway.

First thing the next morning, Todd and I marched into Principal Miller's office. Todd slapped the counter, and Mrs. DelNero jumped and clutched her chest so violently that the light-up red-nosed reindeer on her sweater stopped blinking. "All right, hons. Take a breath, now." Her fat fingers trembled on the phone keypad. "Principal Miller, the kids are here to see you," she said all breathily into the phone. She hung it up. "Go right in."

Maggie Klein was in the office already, standing behind Principal Miller's desk.

Principal Miller sat in the chair next to her. "Hello, Ms. Sheehan and Mr. Harding. I assume you're here to turn in your letter of apology this morning."

Maggie Klein sneered. She extended her hand open-palmed to us to take the letter.

"Not exactly," I said.

Todd said, "There is no letter."

Maggie Klein curled her fingers into a fist and slowly withdrew her hand. Principal Miller drew herself upright. "Explain yourselves," she said. Outside, the POMME bull-horns started to blare their chant-o'-the-week: "*Marriage is a choice! Give our kids a voice!*"

"We haven't done anything to apologize for," I said. Maggie Klein huffed her disagreement in the most undignified manner. I ignored her. "We played along with this course. Followed the rules. Did everything you asked because you dangled our diplomas above our heads. And yeah, we made fun of it. But come on, did you really think you were going to spare us some future heartbreak by making us fake it first?" Principal Miller broke my gaze and looked above my head. "Because, from what I've seen of marriages and relationships, there aren't any rules. You deal with what comes, like anything else in life. There's no template. No freaking outline. And that's what makes relationships interesting, right? The element of surprise."

Todd added, "Like finding love in the janitor's closet."

My stomach dropped. I couldn't believe he'd said that, but I didn't flinch. Whatever Todd said, I'd back up. I looked at Principal Miller, expecting her to steam with rage. But her face wasn't angry. It was something else. Something softer.

Not Maggie Klein, though. She shook. Her jaw clenched, her eye twitched. Then she blew. "How *dare* you voice such accusations? You two have been nothing but insolent and juvenile!"

Principal Miller raised one hand and closed her eyes. "Maggie, that's enough."

"Enough? What do you mean, 'that's enough'? Why isn't anyone on *my* side? When do my feelings start to matter? What about *me*? Why does everyone hate me?"

Principal Miller whispered, "Maggie! *Enough*. Go to your office and compose yourself!"

Maggie Klein clearly did not want to be stifled. She had some serious pressure that needed release. She huffed and squeaked and finally stormed out. It dawned on me that what she probably needed was to get laid.

Principal Miller opened her eyes, and then her mouth to speak, but suddenly, a booming electric drumbeat shattered the droning bullhorn chant. The principal wheeled around and flicked open the shade.

I stopped breathing.

A huge group of rainbow-T-shirt-clad POMME picketers, led by Mom, Mrs. Beaufort, and PTA president Cybil Hutton, were marching—well, dancing, really—and waving rainbow flags and rainbow banners. Just behind Mom, Dad was pulling a rainbow-painted wagon holding his stereo equipment on a long extension cord: a techno remix of "It's Raining Men" blasted from the speakers.

See you tomorrow, Mom had said yesterday. *Everything's all set.*

I'd had no idea.

As much as I had to admit that it was brave of my mother and father to do this—as altruistic as it was—there was simply no way I could ever live this down. How do you socially survive your parents leading a gay pride parade in front of your high school?

Todd put his hand on my shoulder and said, "Well, at least now I know where you get it from."

Principal Miller reached up and drew the blind shut again. "Fiona and Todd, you are excused. Please return to your classroom. The homeroom bell is about to ring."

Todd and I walked like zombies out of the office, through the reception area, and down the hall. In every room we passed, the students and teachers were plastered to the windows like sticker decals.

We made it to homeroom just as the bell rang and Mr. Tambor started hollering for everyone to get away from the window and sit. I dropped next to Mar. Todd sat with his buddies. I steeled myself for the whispers and stares about my freak-show family. When it didn't happen, I realized . . . pretty much everyone's parents were out there. I think even Callie Brooks's mom was.

Maybe I'd live through this after all.

After attendance, Principal Miller's voice came over the PA system.

"Good morning, students. First, a reminder that Friday night is the senior winter formal, and I hope to see all seniors and guests in attendance." She paused, and the PA clicked and squealed as she turned it off and on. "In a related matter, I have decided to cancel the program on marriage education. It has come to my attention that the course is somewhat . . . redundant in its skill development and narrow in its scope. Therefore, I hereby declare the senior class marriages annulled. All the money collected for the prize pool will be returned in full."

A cheer rose through the school that could've blown the roof off. We were death-row prisoners just paroled. POW camp detainees finally freed. Wriggling fish let off the hook and tossed back into the churning sea. And, because the PA also transmitted outside, the protesters cheered too.

We were free. I looked at Todd. He winked at me. I winked back, smiled, and gave him the finger. He laughed.

CHAPTER 34

LIKE I SAID, AROUND HERE, NEWS TRAVELS FASTER than mono, and by the end of the day, the whole school had heard about Todd's and my standoff with Principal Miller and Maggie Klein. By the time the story circulated and came back around to me, I had apparently bitch-slapped Maggie Klein and then tongued Todd in front of Principal Miller.

Oh, and Mom was a former showgirl in an all-gay revue.

Everything became a legend. A made-up one, sure, but most legends are.

Mar told me that Johnny got excused from his interpersonal-skills-slash-anger-management workshop. I hoped he'd tell me about it himself. I also hoped he'd ask me to the winter formal, too. But neither one of those things happened. Once again, luck was not on my side.

So Mar and I decided to go to the formal together. I decided that if Johnny happened to be at the dance, and I happened to look hot, well, that was a coincidence that couldn't be avoided.

The problem was, the night of the formal, I was having a hard time putting "hot" together. It was seven-thirty. The dance started in half an hour. And I was buck-naked. Which probably would have made for an interesting night, but the last time I'd checked I was neither a porn star nor a prostitute. So I had to dress. In something. Aye, there was the freaking rub.

I'd already tried on every half-decent outfit, every quarter-decent outfit, even every limit-of-f-as-decent-approaches-zero-is-infinity outfit.

$$\lim_{\text{decent} \to 0} f(\text{decent}) = \infty$$

Nothing said, *Clothes to Wear When You Want to Impress a Guy You Initially Shot Down, But Now You Realize You Like Him and Want to Get Him Back.* Where was the outfit for that? I'd called Marcie to ask her to bring over everything she had, but she was taking too long.

Finally, I heard the doorbell ring, and her footsteps click-clacking quickly up the stairs. Marcie flew through the door, wearing a black spaghetti-strap dress and high heels. She looked straight off a New York runway. Totally chic. And not in a modest way. Her mother must've gone ballistic.

She carried a shopping bag full of clothes. "You're not wearing anything!" she cried.

"Brilliant observation, Einstein," I said back. "Besides, that's not true. I'm wearing my contacts. And some makeup. I know—don't faint or anything."

"Fiona, you could have put on panties and a bra." She pulled a few fancy outfits out of the bag and laid them on my bed.

"I did," I said in the same patronizing tone she'd used. "Big ol' granny ones. But then I thought, what if whatever you brought over required low-rise panties? Or, God forbid, a thong? I only own one, you know."

"Yes, Fiona, I know."

"And what if I needed a strapless bra? Or a halter?"

"Okay, okay, I get it. Jeez, Fee. It's just a dance."

"Well, I want to look . . . nice." If Mar knew I was dressing up to impress Johnny, she'd never shut up about it. I flipped through her clothes. "What about this?" I held up a green dress with a tiny floral pattern and a crocheted sweater over it.

Marcie stuck out her tongue. "Nah."

I tossed the dress and picked up a blue blouse and a—what was this? "A miniskirt?" I cried. "Are you freaking kidding?"

"Look, I grabbed what I could and ran! Relax!"

She was right. I was totally out of control. "I'm sorry," I said and threw myself down on the clothes and buried my face in my arms.

Marcie tossed a blanket over me. "Why don't you admit that you like him?"

I didn't lift my head, so she couldn't read my face. I just mumbled, "What do you mean?"

"Johnny Mercer. You know you suck at hiding stuff."

I lied terribly. "I don't know what you're talking about."

"Give me some credit, Fee."

I sighed and looked up at her. "I just want to give him every incentive to like me."

She grinned. "He likes you."

"Did he say that?"

"Well, not in those words, exactly. But I can tell these things. Now, here, put this on." She handed me a deep red not-too-mini halter-dress. "But you'll need to break out the thong."

"More like break in. It still has the tag." I fished it out of the deep recesses of my underwear drawer and waved it like a stringy flag.

Marcie scrunched up her face. "You didn't wash it yet?"

I froze midwave. "No. Do I need to?" A level of panic rose in me far disproportionate to what I should have felt about wearing an unwashed thong. Marcie must have read it on my face.

"Nope. Nevermind," she piped, snatching the thong and ripping off the tag in one movement. "It's fine." She smiled and thrust it at me. I knew she was full of crap, but I pulled the thong on anyway. I didn't have time to indulge Marcie's germophobia right then, at any rate. I twisted myself into a padded halter-bra and stepped into the dress. I wound my hair into a bun and held it in place with a pair of enameled chopsticks.

Marcie rifled through my closet and pulled out my one pair of black heels, which Mom insisted I own.

"Heels? You want me to wear heels?" I cried.

"What are you going to wear, your sneakers? Now put these on and shut your mouth. Put on some earrings and lip gloss, and then we'll go."

I stood stock-still for two seconds, and then did exactly as I was told.

We got to the dance at about eight-fifteen. I was bummed that Johnny hadn't asked me to the formal. But I knew that if he showed up, then there was still a chance he had feelings for me. So my heart thumped and my breath got all jiggly when I spotted him sitting over on the bleachers. Not only that, but a song by The Connells was playing, and I was pretty sure he'd picked it for me.

Mar gave me a shove from behind, and I walked toward Johnny. I tried to ignore the thong riding up my butt, because I knew it was making my ass look great. Not that he could see; he was staring off at the people dancing in the middle of the gym floor. I tried to think of something clever and sexy to say to him if he didn't notice me, but everything sounded moronic in my head. I got right up next to him and he still hadn't seen me. Then I thought of the perfect thing to say.

"Rectal-probe lube."

"Wha? Rectal wha—?" Johnny blinked several times and jumped to his feet. "Holy . . . yeow. Wow, Fiona. You look great."

"Thanks," I said. "You too." And, truth be told, he did. He'd scrunched his honey-colored hair with some kind of product. Putty, I think is what Mar calls it. It gave his hair the coolest messy look with his adorable little cowlick above his right eye. The cut of his dress jacket across his broad shoulders made him look strong. He was wearing a tie, but he also had on black jeans and his black Doc Martens. All in all, he looked kind of . . . dangerous. Like he could kick somebody's ass, big-time, but with style. Like a suave, tough-guy super spy.

I liked it.

"Rectal-probe lube," he said. "Good one. That would definitely be worse. I'll have to get back to you on mine, though. I'm having a hard time thinking of anything disgusting right now."

I suddenly didn't know what to do with my hands. "Um . . . thanks for the Connells song," I said. "Was that for me?"

He nodded.

I tried to inhale without looking like I was trying to inhale. "So are you and Mar going to show off your new ballroom dance moves?"

Johnny snapped his fingers. "Damn," he said sarcastically, "I forgot to put a waltz or foxtrot on the playlist tonight."

"Well, tough. I want to see it. I think it's cool that you guys learned how to fancy-dance."

"Yeah, sure."

"I do!"

"Oh, that's right," Johnny said. "I forgot about your secret yearning for balls."

I smirked and punched him in the arm. He grabbed my hand and held it as "What a Good Boy" by Barenaked Ladies started playing. He pulled me to him and circled my waist with his right arm, placing his hand on the bare skin of my lower back. He held my right hand out with his left, and nestled his index finger below my grandmother's rings. I looked up at him and watched his soft lips move as he spoke.

"This is called dance position," he said. "Now, you follow. I'll lead." He stepped forward and steered me around an invisible circle. I couldn't have objected if I wanted to, because the fact that he was holding me against him scared away my command of the English language. But being shocked into submission also allowed me to move in total fluidity with him.

He led me backward into a quick turn. His mouth was right next to my ear, so when he spoke quietly, his velvet voice was even deeper. "Remember the last dance?" he asked, referring to the diaper prank on Todd, I thought.

I said softly, "Remember it? I have every moment burned in my memory."

"I wanted to dance with you so badly then," he said.

We took a few more steps and I said, "Why didn't you ask me?"

He spun me out in a circle and gently reeled me back in. "'Cause I couldn't dance."

We took a couple more steps. I pressed myself lightly against him and lifted up my face. "But now you can?"

He stopped our dancing and looked down at me. "Yeah," he said. "I think I just realized that now I can." And I knew he wasn't talking about dancing at all. He was talking about his feelings for me. And my feelings for him. And what he was going to do about them.

"I'm glad you finally figured it out," I said.

Then Johnny slid his right hand up my bare back and skimmed his warm fingertips over the hair at the nape of my neck. He lingered there for a second, then cupped his other hand behind my head, too, and pulled my face to his.

We kissed.

It was, without a doubt, the sexiest moment I'd ever experienced.

When we separated, I stared into his deep, hazel eyes shining with gold flecks. I felt him breathe against me and sensed the warmth of his hands on my body.

He said, "If anyone had told me a year ago that I'd be kissing a cheerleader at a formal dance, I'd have . . . oh, I don't know. Punched them in the face and run away."

I took what seemed like my first breath in an hour. "Punched them in the face?"

He looked at me and we both started giggling.

"Jonathan Mercer, you crack me up."

We caught each other's eyes and held them. "Life's weird, huh?" he said.

I nodded. "Uh-huh."

"Hey," he added lightly. "I like you calling me Jonathan. It sounds sexy when you say it."

I smiled. "Oh yeah? Then it suits you . . . Jonathan."

"Say it again," he said smoothly, leaning toward me.

"Jonathan," I purred, leaning toward him.

We met in the middle.

Afterward, I saw Callie Brooks out of the corner of my eye staring at us like she'd just watched us shed our skins, revealing our true identities as lizard-people. I gave her the finger behind Johnny's back. Callie checked left and right to see if anyone was watching, and then gave me the finger back. I laughed, and gave her a thumbs-up. I said to Johnny, "We should probably go find Marcie. She's my date."

Johnny took my hand and said, "She *was* your date."

We found Mar standing against the wall near the refreshment table. She said, "You know, if you two had just listened to me in the first place, we could have avoided all this difficulty."

Johnny and I both said, "Yeah, yeah," at the same time. Then we both said, "Jinx. You owe me a beer," together. And then, "Anytime." Then we laughed together, too.

Mar said, "Doesn't Fee look hot?"

Johnny blushed, but I came to his rescue. I said, "I should. It's your dress."

Mar smiled. "Yeah, but it's your ass underneath it."

Johnny rotated away from us saying, "And that's my cue to get drinks." He wandered down to the end of the table.

I said to Mar, "Maybe if you're lucky, I'll even let you dance with your ex-husband."

Mar laughed and said, "You're too kind." She glanced behind me and her smile dissolved. Her face paled. I turned to see why.

Gabe Webber swaggered toward us, listing to the side with his arms flailing like he couldn't get his balance. His eyelids were half-closed and his mouth hung open. His white dress shirt was untucked and stained down the front.

"Hey Marshie," he slurred. He leaned past me, reeking of beer. "You look hot." He turned to me. "F'yona. I hear yerrin love with me."

I recoiled at the stench of his breath. Apparently, some of the beer had made a repeat appearance, because his breath also stank of puke. "Piss off, Gabe. You're disgusting." I grabbed Marcie's hand and tried to pull her away, but he positioned himself right between us.

"Come on, Marshie. Yannow you wanna get back with me." His head teetered from side to side. Marcie froze. I tried to elbow Gabe away, but he turned and shoved me hard and then made a grab for Marcie.

Johnny was at my side in an instant and caught me before I fell. He straightened me up, then in one motion, wheeled Gabe around and pinned him up against the concrete-block wall. "Back off, Webber."

"Whaddrya gonna do about it, tonsofun?"

Johnny's face hardened. He inhaled and leaned into Gabe. "Wanna find out?"

I reached up and held Johnny's arm. "Just let him go. He's wasted. He's a waste." I felt Johnny's arm relax beneath my touch. He slowly eased back from the wall.

Gabe stumbled out from under Johnny's arm and muttered, "Pussy."

Johnny grabbed Gabe's shoulder, spun him around,

and hauled back with a huge, clenched fist. I grabbed his wrist and hung on. I did not want to get kicked out of this dance. I hadn't worn heels for nothing. "*Don't*," I said. "Please just leave it. He's not worth it." I could feel the muscles in Johnny's arm, rock-hard and trembling. But he didn't swing. He shoved Gabe away, but Gabe staggered back toward us saying, "Ya wanna know whass not worth it?" He hitched his thumb at Marcie. "Tryin' to get anywhere with that tight-ass fuckin' prude." He closed his eyes and laughed.

And then something welled up inside me. I lost complete control over my body. It was as if I was standing outside myself, watching. I saw myself ball my fingers into a fist, draw my right hand back, step forward with my left foot, and crack Gabe across the cheek with all my strength. Gabe's head flew sideways and backward; his body followed, and a second later, he was laid out on the gym floor.

Pain like a knife blade shot through my knuckles, especially in my ring finger. I shook my hand to try to get it to stop throbbing. Only then did I notice that I was the only person moving in the whole place.

Until Principal Miller pushed through the crowd and called for the music to stop. "What happened?" she cried. "Who did this?" Mr. Evans was with her. He crouched down over Gabe, who was coming around. Blood seeped from a scrape in Gabe's cheek where Nana's diamond had caught his skin. Mr. Evans leaned in for a closer look, but when he got a whiff of Gabe's breath, he jerked his head back and said, "Phew. He's drunk, Barbara."

Principal Miller's hands fluttered to her hair. "Um,

thank you, Jero—uh . . . Mr. Evans. Did he pass out, then?" She looked around for an answer.

"Yup," Johnny said. "Just passed out cold."

"That's what I saw," Marcie said.

Principal Miller scanned the crowd. "Can anyone else confirm this?" Her eyes darted from face to face.

"I saw him fall," a voice called out. The crowd separated and Amanda stepped forward with Todd beside her. She lifted her chin toward Gabe. "He was just standing there. Then he fell," she said.

"That's what happened," Takisha King called from the other side of the circled crowd.

"Yup," Simone Dawson chirped. "Just fell over. Cracked his face on the floor." She smiled at me and winked. I couldn't help but smile back at her.

Mr. Evans shouldered Gabe to his feet. Gabe staggered forward a few steps and vomited all over Principal Miller's suede pumps. She gasped and shuddered and turned her head away, but she didn't move her feet an inch. "Jerome, would you please see that this boy's parents are called, and stay with him until they arrive?"

"I'll do *it*?" Mr. Tambor boomed. He marched forward, took Gabe by the back of the neck, and steered him through the crowd and out the door. Mr. Evans went to Principal Miller and said, "Come on. Let's get you cleaned up." He took her hand gingerly in both of his and led her into the locker room. A few minutes later, he returned with a mop and bucket and cleaned up the puke. We didn't see Principal Miller again.

The music came back on. I asked Johnny to dance with Marcie to cheer her up, and I walked over to Todd and Amanda.

"Thanks," I said. "You didn't have to do that. I mean, I'm glad you did, but I know you didn't have to. So thanks." I smiled.

Amanda rolled her eyes and tossed her hair. "Gabe Webber is a dick, anyway."

"Hey," I said, "you know what's hilarious? And kinda disgusting now, but still funny? I swore that I'd touch Gabe Webber by the end of the year. I guess technically I did."

"Sure as hell, you did," Todd said. "Hauling that water cooler must've built up some muscles." His face beamed. If I hadn't known better, I'd have said he looked proud. Just a tiny bit.

Callie Brooks poked me in the back. "Look at that," she said, pointing to the dance floor. Johnny and Marcie stepped and twirled and dipped and swirled as a crowd of people stood watching.

"Check out Mercer," Todd said.

Callie sighed. "I can't believe you're with a guy who can dance like that. You're so lucky."

I laughed. I was lucky?

Now that was a shocker.

But really, when you think about it . . .

By then I should have known.